PRAISE FOR *H*

"What a ride! This modern-day, gender-flipped Indiana Jones-style adventure led me straight into the depths of hell, and I loved every minute. Rory and Gram are the perfect demon-hunting duo and *Hellfinder* is the ideal mix of mystery, metal, media, and romance—all wrapped up in a love letter to Iceland. The only question I have left is, what adventure are Rory and Gram going on next?"

– Marcy Beller Paul, author of *Underneath Everything*

"A teenager's coming-of-age tale...with demons? Yes, please! *Hellfinder* is a gripping exploration of demons, both personal and literal, set amidst the beautiful yet treacherous Icelandic landscape. A powerful take on the notion of good versus evil."

– Kristi Helvig, author of *Burn Out* and *The Wing Collector*

"*Hellfinder* is a captivating tale of action, romance, and magic unfolding across an epic setting. Stokes captures Iceland from all angles—the charming, the majestic, the desolate, and the deadly."

– Victoria Scott, author of *Fire & Flood* and founder of Scribbler

"A fast-paced and fun adventure through a gorgeous and dangerous Icelandic setting, with cute boys, fluffy sled dogs, and maybe a couple of hostile demons along the way. I couldn't stop reading it!"

– Tina Connolly, Nebula-nominated author of *Seriously Wicked*

"World-building at its best, *Hellfinder* is a wild ride of a YA novel brought forth in fresh, vivid prose. At seventeen, Rory and her grandmother, Ingrid, team up with Gunnar, son of a family friend, to track his twin brother. Ingrid reveals bit-by-bit a surprising and at times horrifying family history, and somewhere beneath a treacherous glacier and above a simmering molten volcano, Rory discovers that answers come in complicated layers. Power can be terrifying, especially when it's our own; discovering it and defining ourselves by how we use it might be the ultimate coming-of-age adventure."

– Laura Scalzo, author of *American Arcadia*

"*Hellfinder* is like the ultimate Netflix series. It's *The Amazing Race* meets *Supernatural*, and I enjoyed every twist and turn."

– Jude Atwood, author of *Maybe there are Witches*

"*Hellfinder* is a whirlwind of twists and turns that will leave you breathless. Fans of *Shadowhunters* and *The Chilling Adventures of Sabrina* will find a kindred spirit in Rory as she battles evil while also trying to navigate complex and unfamiliar emotions for the new guy in her life."

– Philip Siegel, author of *The Break-Up Artist*

"An author gifted with the ability to jump genres and stick the landing every time."

– *Paste Magazine*

HELLFINDER

Paula Stokes

Fitzroy Books

Published by Fitzroy Books
An imprint of
Regal House Publishing, LLC
Raleigh, NC 27605
All rights reserved

https://fitzroybooks.com
Printed in the United States of America

ISBN -13 (paperback): 9781646033584
ISBN -13 (epub): 9781646033591
Library of Congress Control Number: 2022943700

Cover images and design by © C. B. Royal

Regal House Publishing, LLC
https://regalhousepublishing.com

Printed in the United States of America

For my mother,
who has supported all of my wild adventures

1

I know almost immediately that the phone call is going to ruin everything. As I stand in the kitchen doorway, I tell myself that maybe someone is calling to wish us happy holidays. It's not necessarily urgent. It doesn't mean our Christmas in Paris is going to be wrecked.

But when Gram answers the phone, her smile quickly fades. Her eyes scan the room and I can tell she's looking for a pen and paper to take notes. Gram knows people who work in government surveillance, so she never puts anything onto an electronic device that she wants to keep secret.

"Rory, do you have—?"

I've already dusted off my flour-coated hands and retrieved a mini-notebook and pen from the kitchen counter. "Here."

Thank you, Gram mouths. She turns away, toward the hallway that leads to our bedrooms. This call isn't just important. It's also private.

Sighing, I lean my forearms on the table, where two trays of freshly baked sugar cookies are waiting to be decorated. My eyes are drawn to the large kitchen window. Outside, the perfect winter day is reflected in the partially frozen water of the Seine. People hurry along the Quai de Montebello with tote bags full of brightly wrapped packages. Ice glistens from the façade of Notre Dame. The snow is coming down in soft flakes, veins of white gathering in the cracks of the concrete walkway. I pull out my phone and snap a picture of the scene. The condensation fogging up the window panes gives the image a hazy, dreamlike appearance.

Slipping my phone back into my pocket, I tiptoe across the hardwood floor and linger outside of Gram's bedroom as she talks quietly. My grandmother is a freelance location and recovery specialist, what a lot of people would call a "treasure hunter." Her last job was here in Paris, finding a cache of misplaced family jewels for a trio of siblings after their mother, an eccentric recluse, passed away in her sleep. Both sisters and their brother seemed positive that one of the others had stolen the jewels until Gram located them buried beneath an elm tree in the woman's backyard. Apparently, she'd become paranoid in her final weeks of life, suspecting her servants and groundskeepers of conspiring to rob her.

Gram usually lets me come along on jobs so I don't have to stay in Seattle by myself. She said we could sightsee in Paris through the end of the year. This is the first time I've been to France, and to say I made plans would be a bit of an understatement. We've already hit the big stuff—the Louvre, the Eiffel Tower, Notre Dame, L'Arc de Triomphe—but I wanted to tour some lesser-known chapels, check out Christmas lights across the city, sip coffee at sidewalk cafes. I wanted time to experience the real Paris, whatever that is.

The smell of smoke snaps me out of my reverie. Swearing under my breath, I race back to the kitchen, but it's too late. I remove a tray full of charred cookies from the oven just as Gram turns the corner.

"I think in certain cultures blackened snowmen are a portent of oncoming doom," she teases. "Did you get distracted by that perfect winter snow?"

"Just thinking," I say. "So what's the word? New job?"

"Can't fool you, can I?" She tucks a wayward strand of silvery hair behind her left ear. "Do you know what's even better than Christmas in Paris?"

My shoulders slump. Pretty sure the answer to that is nothing. I dump the tray of burned cookies into the trash can. "Christmas in Bangladesh?" I suggest. "Mongolia? Topeka, Kansas?"

Gram chuckles. "Silly girl. I was going to say *New Year's Eve* in Paris. Imagine a rainbow of fireworks exploding above the Eiffel Tower at the stroke of midnight."

"That does sound nice, but it doesn't explain where we'll be for Christmas." I struggle to keep my expression neutral. I can't believe Gram took a job after the two of us made special plans.

"I was thinking you might like to spend Christmas with Elaine and Mark," she says.

Elaine and Mark are my paternal grandparents. They're nice people and I see them occasionally when Gram and I are in Seattle, but I always feel weird around them. Probably because I don't have any kind of relationship with my father.

"Feels a little last minute to impose, doesn't it?" I ask. "Can't I just come with you?"

"To Iceland?" Gram asks. "It's a pretty dreary place in the winter. I don't think you'd enjoy it much."

"You took a job in Iceland?" Hurt bleeds into my voice. "I thought you hated it there." Gram grew up in Reykjavík but left the country shortly after I was born.

"Well, I haven't been so fond of going back ever since your mother died," she says. "But the client is a dear friend of mine. I went to school with him when we were children and he desperately needs my help." She pauses. "What about staying in Paris? I can call Alannah and see if she'd be willing to fly here to keep you company."

Alannah is my homeschool tutor. She's twenty-six and has an advanced degree in art history. Spending a few days in Paris with her would be cool, but I haven't been away from Gram for more than a day since I was little. Being separated for a major holiday feels unbearable. And what if she went to Iceland and didn't miss me? What if her work went more smoothly without me? She might not invite me along on her next job. It's sad, but my grandmother is one of my only friends.

She scrolls through her phone contacts, looking for Alannah's number.

"No, wait," I say. "I want to go with you."

"I really don't think it's a good—"

"Come on, Gram," I plead. "I promise I won't cause any trouble." *At least I'll try not to.*

"All right," she concedes. "But you'll have to stay in Reykjavík with our client, Henning, while I'm on the road. He has limited mobility so he doesn't get out much, but you could explore the city on your own."

"Is there any way I can actually help out for once?" My voice rises in pitch. I widen my eyes and give Gram my best innocent-granddaughter look. "You told me you'd consider letting me work with you once I turned eighteen and I'm seventeen and a half. Close enough."

Unfortunately, she's grown immune to my innocent looks. "Rory, I'm going to be traveling in highly remote areas. It could be dangerous."

"All the more reason for you to bring me along so I can help out if needed."

Gram starts to say something and then stops. She looks past me, out the window at the falling snow. For a few moments, she's silent. Then she clears her throat. "I suppose it could be nice for you to see some of what Iceland has to offer. Much of the country is quite beautiful."

My grandmother has never called Iceland beautiful before. She usually describes it as cold, windy, rainy, and gray. "And we've spent a lot of time in cities lately," I point out. "Time away from all the noise and pollution could be…therapeutic for me." Gram is a huge fan of the outdoors. She thinks nature has "healing properties."

She sighs. "All right, fine. You can assist me on this job, as long as you promise to be very careful. But this doesn't mean I'm officially hiring you, okay? When we get back, you need to focus on graduating high school. And then…we'll see."

"Sure, whatever," I say, surprised by how easily I wore her down. "Can we leave our stuff here?"

Gram and I have been living in this apartment for two weeks, and the belongings I brought from home, plus the items I've purchased since we arrived, have gradually taken over my room, the bathroom, and half of the living room.

"Absolutely," Gram says. "Henning needs us on the next available plane, which leaves in three hours. So pack a bag of warm and weather-resistant clothing and the best hiking footwear you've got. Everything else will be provided."

"Three hours?" I gesture toward the trays of sugar cookies waiting to be decorated. "I hope he's paying extra for the expedited service."

"We can freeze the cookies and finish when we get back," Gram says. Christmas cookies for New Year's will be a little strange, but life with my grandmother hasn't really ever been what you'd call normal.

One thing you should know is that Gram isn't a criminal. You tell someone your grandmother is a treasure hunter and they start going on about *Lara Croft: Tomb Raider* or that guy who stole the Declaration of Independence.

"Those are movies," I've told at least a half-dozen people. Gram doesn't steal, though she has been known to borrow things without asking from time to time, if I'm being completely truthful. But she always returns them to their rightful owners. And real treasure hunting is a lot more about doing research and interviewing people than it is about excavating ruins or diving for pirate gold. Before Gram can even make a plan to go after a treasure, she first has to figure out who might have legal claims to it and what sort of permits she might need from the country where the cache is rumored to be. Sometimes her jobs involve reaching out to families for permission to hunt for things on private property.

And then, like today, sometimes people come to her for help.

❧

Two hours later, Gram and I are in the security line at Charles
de Gaulle airport. We inch forward and I show a uniformed
security agent my passport and boarding pass. I slide off
my boots and jacket, my tablet computer and Ziploc bag of
toiletries already out of my carry-on.

"Don't forget your jewelry," a lady in blue says, gesturing
at the small silver MedicAlert ID bracelet I wear on my right
arm.

"That's a medical device," Gram pipes up, showing her
own matching bracelet. "Airline regulations say that medical devices don't have to be removed unless they trigger an
alarm."

Gram and I both have a condition where if a paramed-
ic or doctor uses the wrong drug to sedate us, we develop
something called malignant hyperthermia, an illness where
our internal body temperature can rise to over 110 degrees.
This is how my mom died and it's why Gram never—and I
mean never—lets me take off my MedicAlert bracelet.

I give the security agent an apologetic look. I've witnessed
this conversation more times than I can count. When I was
younger, I used to ask Gram why I couldn't just take off
the bracelet. I mean, it's not like I was going to collapse in
the sixty or so seconds it took me to step through the metal
detector. And if I did, Gram would be there to tell the para-
medics about my condition and what they can or can't use
to treat me.

Gram said it was about the principle of the matter, that
the security agents needed to know what was and wasn't ap-
propriate to ask passengers to remove. She also reminded me
that she wouldn't always be there, and if I got in the habit of
removing the bracelet, I might very well take it off at some
point and not be wearing it when I needed it.

I try not to notice the line growing longer behind us, passengers fidgeting and muttering to each other as the agent skims over the paperwork Gram hands her, printed straight from the French airline security website.

"Very well." The agent ushers Gram and me through the metal detector one at a time and as always, it doesn't beep.

We pull over to the side to collect our belongings. "I hope you enjoy this assignment," Gram says, as we both slip back into our shoes. "It'll probably involve some hiking and cave exploring. Good for your...vibrant personality."

"Vibrant" is a nice way of putting it. I'm probably more impulsive—okay fine, reckless. When I was younger, I went to international schools in Thailand, Vietnam, and Australia because my grandfather was a diplomat stationed in those places. I managed to get expelled from academies in Sydney and Ho Chi Minh City, and in Bangkok they simply asked us nicely if I could try school somewhere else. Gram gave up and got me a homeschool tutor.

Next semester I'll receive an official diploma from an ac-credited international online high school and after that I'm hoping Gram'll make me an official partner in her business. Lately she's started pushing me to apply to college instead of work for her, which is weird because since my grandfather died, I'm pretty sure I'm one of her only friends too. But maybe she's just trying to make sure I consider all my options.

So far I'm not inclined to pursue college, at least not one where I'd go to class on campus. Traveling the world with my grandmother seems like way more fun than sitting in a lecture hall listening to an instructor drone on and on while I struggle to stay awake. Maybe when Gram gets a little older, she'll retire from treasure hunting, and then I can think about doing something different.

Right now, her lifestyle appeals to my free-spirited soul.

2

Gram and I are seated in the back of the plane, which means we're two of the first people to board Iceland Air 747. We buckle ourselves into our seats—aisle for her, window for me—and thankfully no one comes to sit between us. The flight attendants are all business in their navy-blue power suits and jaunty little pillbox caps. They march down the narrow aisle, tapping passengers and telling them to stow their electronic devices for takeoff.

I send a quick text to my best friend, Macy, and then put my phone on airplane mode. I watch the safety video intently, taking time to identify the two closest exits and to reach under both Gram's seat and my own to make sure that the pouches with our lifejackets are where they're supposed to be. We fly a lot, but I always pay attention to the safety briefing and do my own checks, especially when we're crossing a body of water. I don't swim very well because I don't like to put my face underwater, and the thought of ending up alone in the ocean is one of the most terrifying things I can imagine.

Next, I listen as the flight crew does all of their announcements in Icelandic, English, and German, including informing the passengers that the plane we're flying on is named after one of Iceland's most famous volcanoes, *Eyjafjallajökull*. Say that three times fast, I dare you, or even one time for that matter.

Gram falls asleep soon after the plane lifts off. It's going to be a short trip—just three hours from Paris to Keflavík Airport, which my phone says is about forty minutes outside of Reykjavík. I was hoping she'd give me more information about what we're going to be doing, but she told me it'd be best if we both got the full story from the client at the same time. All I know is we're going to be searching for a missing family heirloom.

I spend the flight alternating between peeking out the window and looking up basic information about Iceland on my phone. We fly over England and Scotland and I see Big Ben, the London Eye, and then the English Channel. After Scotland, it's all ocean down there. I pull the little plastic shade down and use a language app to teach myself a list of Icelandic phrases.

When we land at Keflavík Airport, Gram and I quickly pass through customs and head to baggage claim. I check my phone while we wait. Macy has replied to my text.

> **Macy:** Iceland? What happened? I thought you were spending the holidays in Paris.
> **Me:** Gram took a last-minute job. And she's actually going to let me help her this time.
> **Macy:** Nice. I know how much you want to be her official partner.
> **Me:** Fingers crossed! How's Okinawa?

Macy's dad is an officer in the Marines. She lives with him during the year and spends summers with her mom in Seattle.

> **Macy:** Okinawa is probably great if I can ever convince my dad to let me explore. He doesn't think I'm old enough to go off base by myself.
> **Me:** Ugh.
> **Macy:** Double ugh. Take pictures of whatever is in Iceland for me. Ice? Land?
> **Me:** Ha. Will do.

Gram nudges me. "I think I see our bags coming around."

I heave my suitcase off the silver carousel and then turn to help Gram but she's already retrieved her bag. We take the escalator to the lower level, which is mostly meeting areas, transport options, and a coffee shop called Joe Muggs. My mouth waters at the thought of a latte, but the line is about twenty-five people long. Behind the counter, two male baristas move fluidly between the cash register, espresso grinder, and a case full of pastries and fresh fruit. One of them has shoulder-length hair with his sides pulled back in a high topknot. It's a hairstyle I've never seen on a guy before.

Beyond the coffee shop there's a hallway leading to a set of sliding glass doors. A guy about my age is holding a sign with INGRID ÓLAFSDÓTTIR on it. Ólafsdóttir is Gram's surname, which literally means "daughter of Ólafur." I have my dad's last name, Quinn.

This boy also has long hair, but it's hanging loose down to his shoulders. He shifts his weight from one foot to the other as we approach, shaking his hair back from his face to expose flawless skin and a pair of cheekbones that would make supermodels weep with envy.

"There's Gunnar." Gram quickens her stride. She waves a hand and calls out his name.

The boy strolls over to us and reaches out for the handle to Gram's suitcase. She shakes him off and they have a mini-argument in Icelandic before he eventually gives up.

I smile to myself. I'm the only one who ever wins an argument with Gram.

"This is Rory," Gram tells Gunnar.

"Pleased to meet you," he says in softly accented English. His eyes flick to me just long enough for me to notice how blue they are—light blue, almost turquoise, like the water off the coast of Thailand's Ko Phi Phi.

I swallow hard and the handle of my suitcase slips out of my grasp. My bag falls to the tile floor with an awkward thud. Gunnar bends down to grab it.

"I got it," I say, probably a bit sharper than needed. I scoop the handle up and grip it tightly, focusing my eyes on the floor ahead of me. Growing up with Gram means I'm sophisticated beyond my years when it comes to business practices and interacting with adults, but I'm a little lacking in social skills when it comes to people my own age. Even before I was being homeschooled, I always felt awkward around other kids.

I sneak another peek at Gunnar as we head for the exit. I'm trying not to stare, but it's hard. I mean, whose skin is that perfect? He looks like he escaped from a pedestal in the Louvre.

We follow him through the sliding glass doors, where outside the sky is heavy with clouds. Raindrops splash against the dark pavement. I exhale a foggy breath.

"We'll wait here." Gunnar fiddles with the zipper of his quilted winter jacket. It looks expensive, like something made by Patagonia or The North Face, but I can't quite read the label.

Gram and I huddle under a covered awning. Other travelers push past us in twos and threes, rolling their bags down a wide sidewalk toward a big silver bus that says *Reykjavík Excursions*. A red-haired girl with a backpack that looks like it weighs more than she does squeezes between Gunnar and me, murmuring a quiet "Afsakið," which I learned on the plane was Icelandic for "excuse me." She gets in line for the bus with everyone else.

"Where are they going?" I ask.

"To the city, mostly," Gunnar says. "And some go to a nearby spa."

My eyes roll back in my head a little. A spa sounds heavenly right about now, and according to what I researched on the plane, there are natural hot springs here that people can bathe in. I might not like putting my face in water, but that doesn't mean I don't enjoy putting my body in it, especially if it's hot and bubbly. Maybe Gram and I can spend a little time relaxing here before heading back to Paris.

Down at the end of the covered awning there's a large pile of black rocks with a metal sculpture of an egg on the top of it. A long silver tail is protruding from a hole in the shell.

Gunnar follows my gaze. "That is the Jet Nest."

"Oh, I get it. Like where planes are hatched."

He starts to reply, but then his phone buzzes. Pointing at a long black limousine approaching, he says, "Our car is here."

"Whoa, fancy," I say.

The limo slows to a stop and the driver exits the vehicle. He takes our luggage and stows it in the back. My eyes are drawn to the license plate. Three letters and two numbers.

The driver opens the passenger door for us. Gunnar waits as Gram and I step into the limo. It's dark and plush and smells a little like medicine. There's an elderly gray-haired man back here, covered in blankets. I assume it's our client, Gram's childhood friend. He appears to be asleep.

Gunnar climbs in after us and the driver shuts the door. My eyes take in the supple leather seats, the minibar, the TV screens. Gram and I aren't hurting for money, but this is one-percenter territory.

"Aurora," the old man says suddenly.

I flinch as I turn back to him. It weirds me out when strangers know my name. Also no one ever calls me Aurora unless I'm in trouble. The man is looking at me with a softness that's usually reserved for relatives.

"Hi," I say. "You can call me Rory."

"I'm Henning." He speaks to me as if Gunnar and Gram aren't with us. He leans toward me, but I can't make out much of his face in the dim lighting—just the deep crevasses in his forehead and the loose skin around his mouth and neck.

"It's nice to meet you," I say, tacking on a *sir* at the end because he seems like the kind of man who might appreciate it.

"I can hardly believe it's you—you've grown up so much since I last saw you." Henning pauses. "I'm sure you don't remember me, but I knew your parents quite well when they were young. Do you ever see your father?"

"It's been a while," I say stiffly.

My father lost his mind with grief after my mom died, and that's how I ended up being raised by my maternal grandparents. After Dad's breakdown, Gram and Gramps brought him back to the US, where his parents live. He's currently in a long-term mental health facility outside of Seattle. Gram took me to see him a couple of times when I was young, but it didn't go so well, so I don't visit anymore.

"Such a tragedy for everyone involved," Henning says, perhaps reading the truth from my facial expression. "He's a good man who loved your mother very much."

I force a smile, because I have no idea if that's true or if Henning is simply being kind. He greets Gram in Icelandic, and I turn toward the window and watch the scenery fly by. It's mostly just a barren landscape of dark lava fields overlaid in places with patches of green moss.

"Henning, you didn't need to come all this way to receive us," says Gram.

He clears his throat. "As time is of the essence, I thought I'd use the drive to brief you so you can get on the road as soon as possible." He reaches down by his seat and extracts a leather portfolio. Opening it, he pulls out a glossy picture which he hands to Gram. It's an image of a dark, five-sided rock, with a smear of red across the middle.

I lean in for a closer look. "Did someone in your family squeeze blood from a stone or something?"

"It's a pentacompass," Henning explains. When I still look confused, he adds, "A Hellfinder. Legend says it will lead whoever is in possession of it to the nearest doorway to hell."

I glance from Gunnar to Henning. "So you're missing a rock that people believe is magic?"

"More or less," Henning says. "I suspect my other grandson, Einar, took it from my vault at home. As of late, he's befriended a local music group. Perhaps you've heard of them—Black as Death?"

Gram and I both shake our heads.

Henning exhales deeply. "They claim to be Satanists, but some of the younger people here adopt that moniker just to be…controversial. They're releasing their next album on Christmas, and they've announced online that just before it goes on sale, they're going to open the doorway to hell and let evil spill out into the Icelandic wilderness."

"Wait. So people think there's a doorway to hell and it's in *Iceland*?" I scoff. "That'd be a little ironic, wouldn't it?"

"Some people believe that each of the seven continents has doorways that lead to heaven and hell," Henning says. "One such doorway is rumored to be located at the base of Huldulogafell, a dormant volcano on the southern part of the island that is covered by a glacier. Einar and the four members of Black as Death are heading there as we speak."

I point at the photo now sitting on Gram's lap. "And you think they're going to use this rock to find the alleged doorway?" This is more than I usually talk at these meetings, but Gram is being extra-quiet, like maybe she and Henning discussed a lot of this on the phone.

"What I do or don't think isn't critical at the moment. What matters is that where Einar and the others are traveling is dangerous, especially in the winter. Einar is not a skilled outdoorsman and I'm quite certain none of his friends are either. I wish to have the pentacompass returned to me and my grandson back home safe. That is why I reached out to Ingrid and contracted her services."

I turn to Gram. "Did you know all this? You're not a bounty hunter, Gram. Don't you think this job would be better left to the police?"

"Einar is eighteen," Henning says. "The Icelandic police aren't going to chase him across the country because he removed something from the house that has no specific monetary value."

"But what makes you think we can find him, and if we do that he'll even come with us?"

"Finding the group shouldn't be too difficult." Henning absentmindedly strokes a silver chain he's wearing around his neck. "At least not if you get on the road quickly. They've been posting their location on social media for the past few hours. I imagine they'll continue to do so as long as they have Wi-Fi or cellular service. And there's really only one way to get to the eastern section of the glacier Vatnajökull, which is the icecap that covers the volcano."

"And then what?" I tap one foot repeatedly against the floor of the limo. "Are we supposed to take Einar back to Reykjavík by force?"

"Then I take over," Gunnar replies. He's been so quiet for the ride that I almost forgot he was with us. As I look at him, something outside the car catches his attention and he turns toward the window. The neon lights of a gas station illuminate his long nose and pronounced cheekbones. He turns back to me, a fierceness in his pale blue eyes. His voice takes on a sharp edge. "I'm Einar's twin—he'll listen to me. It's my job to talk sense into him, but first it's your job to find him."

3

After his mini-outburst, Gunnar relaxes back into his seat, his long legs crossed at the ankles. We reach the outskirts of Reykjavík and I peer out the window as the limousine navigates a highway that cuts through the middle of the city. Unfortunately, the sun has set and even with the streetlights and neon signs I can't see much in the dark. We turn onto a smaller road and start making our way up a large hill. The limo turns onto an even smaller road and eventually pulls through a set of wrought-iron gates.

The house that comes into view is one of the largest I've seen since we landed. It's two stories tall and all white brick with blue trim around the windows. The roof is steeply pitched and made of what looks like corrugated iron.

The limo slows to a stop in a circular driveway. "Here we are then," Henning says gruffly. "Gunnar, if you'll assist me with my chair."

"Of course, Grandfather." Gunnar climbs out of the limousine and heads around to the trunk where our suitcases are stashed.

I exit the car behind him, turning back to see if Gram needs a hand, but as usual she shoos away my help. Gunnar and the driver have lifted both of our suitcases out of the trunk and are now wrestling with something that I realize is a wheelchair.

As Gunnar and the driver assist Henning from the limo, I pull Gram off to the side, far enough away where the men can't hear. "Gram," I start, unable to keep concern from leaching into my voice. "Why would you take this job? Are we going bankrupt or something?"

She laughs. "No, my dear. Our financial situation is fine."

"Well then, surely your friend could have found more suitable people to chase his grandson across the country."

"Perhaps," she replies, "but there are only three days until Christmas and Einar already has a head start. Henning couldn't very well waste a lot of time researching his options and negotiating fees. Though, to be frank, I believe the two of us are very well suited to this task. Our training in hiking and climbing will serve us well."

What Gram is saying makes sense. She's been an avid mountain climber since she was my age, and before my grandfather died the two of them summitted major peaks in several countries. I haven't climbed any mountains, but I've done plenty of strenuous hiking with her. Still, for some reason I feel like she isn't telling me the whole story.

"And you've excelled at following trails since our very first hunt, remember?" she adds.

After my grandfather died, Gram and I stayed in Australia for a while. We had to move out of our Embassy housing, but we got a place nearby. When you lose someone, it can be tempting to stay close, keep everything the same, as if by doing that you can hang on to the last little bits of them forever.

But that isn't how it works, as we discovered during our first summer alone. Gram found an online article about an eccentric millionaire named Devin Blackrock who had hidden a chest full of gold coins in the Four Corners area of the Southwestern United States. She convinced me that we should go on vacation there, do our best to try to locate the treasure. I thought she was having some sort of three-quarter-life crisis, but we were both miserable at the time, and I knew Colorado and Arizona were beautiful, so I agreed.

The treasure had been hidden years earlier, so we didn't have to compete with a lot of other people. We started out at Mesa Verde State Park, where I noticed a carving in a remote cave that felt more modern than the rest.

The two of us used internet sources to decode this carving, which led us to New Mexico, where additional clues took us to Northern Arizona before leading us deep into the wilds of Grand Staircase-Escalante National Monument in Utah. There I noticed a cairn made entirely of black rocks propped next to a cactus. Gram and I fanned out and I eventually found a second cairn. We followed the trail of cairns until we found the chest, locked securely and hidden in a slot canyon, miles away from the nearest trail.

We were mini-celebrities for a couple of months, invited on talk shows and interviewed in major magazines. That success led to people contacting Gram to offer her money to help them recover family treasure or lost items. At first she said no—she wanted to focus on me and spend time healing from the loss of her husband. But gradually we both realized that our trip to the Southwest had healed us more than hiding away in Australia. We relocated to Seattle, where Gram slapped up a website and started accepting jobs. The rest, as they say, is history.

"You're right," I say. "Something just feels off to me."

Gram exhales a frosty breath. She tightens her scarf around her neck. "Maybe what we both need is a nice cup of tea to settle our nerves before we get on the road again."

Tea is Gram's go-to for any sort of worry or stress. She drinks at least two cups every day. I like it, but it's not a magical elixir for me the way it seems to be for her.

"We're leaving tonight?" My eyes skim the darkened yard. "What time is it?"

She smiles. "It's actually not even dinnertime yet. It just feels late because of how early the sun sets here in the winter. But don't worry. Gunnar will be driving, and Henning assures me he's an excellent night driver."

"I'm not worried," I say, and I mean it. But I still feel a little on edge.

Gram steps inside the house to see about getting us some

tea. Gunnar waves an arm to get my attention. He's standing behind a black SUV with the back open. "Take a look at the gear we bought for you." He pulls a large green backpack out from behind a metal tub and sets it on the ground. "Let me know if you think something won't fit. You'll also want to pack the warmest clothes you brought and a pair of sturdy, waterproof boots, if you've got some." He peers down at my slip-on clogs. "If not, we can make a quick stop in town."

"These are my comfy shoes for plane rides," I say. "I have hiking boots with me."

"Good. We might be doing quite a bit of hiking. You'll want something you can attach crampons to." Gunnar fusses with the equipment in the back of the SUV, arranging and rearranging the items in a way that reminds me of how my grandfather used to pack the freezer after a major grocery delivery.

I kneel down to go through the backpack. There are two pairs of gloves, two pairs of wool socks, a pair of crampons, a pair of waterproof ski pants, a hat, a neck gaiter, and a fleece hoodie—most of which have a tiny label on them that reads *66° North*. It's the same label as on Gunnar's coat.

"Sixty-six north?" I ask. "Is that the big brand here?"

Gunnar nods. "Iceland is at sixty-six degrees north latitude. 66° North makes most of our performance outerwear."

"How very…literal." The only other thing in the backpack is a thick gray and red pullover that looks like something straight out of an ugly sweater contest. "Seriously?" I hold the knitted monstrosity up against me, which doesn't help matters any. It's really soft, but the design is hideous. "Have you never gone shopping for a girl before?"

Gunnar coughs. "That sweater cost twenty-five thousand kronur."

"I don't know how much that is, but I think you might have—"

"About two hundred American dollars." He cuts me off.

"It's wool. It will keep you warm." He unzips his coat to show me that he's wearing the same one in slightly different colors.

My initial thought is one of relief, which is weird, but that sweater doesn't look good even on *him*. And that's actually helpful, because it makes Gunnar feel a little less "museum specimen" and a little more "guy my age who happens to be beautiful but dresses like an elderly fisherman."

"Are they all the same pattern?" I ask.

"Most of them are similar. It's a traditional Icelandic sweater. Women knit them for their families. It's a point of cultural pride, but if you like we can exchange it for a different *pattern*."

"No, no," I say. "I'm sorry. It's really soft. I didn't mean to be disrespectful."

He shrugs. "You're American, right? You probably can't help it."

"I'm part Icelandic," I say staunchly.

"Sad then that you don't even recognize a traditional sweater."

Sculpture Boy: 1. Rory: 0.

"We moved away when I was little and my gram never told me much about the country. My mom died here and I think it makes Gram sad." I clear my throat. "But FYI, not all Americans are the same."

"No? You're not all loudmouthed narcissists who want to take over the world and act like you're doing it a favor?" His accent makes everything he says sound pleasant—almost musical—so I can't tell if he's being serious or just messing with me.

I jam my hands in my pockets. "Nope. In fact I got kicked out of school in Vietnam for helping organize a protest against US foreign policy."

"Kicked out of school?" Gunnar arches a thin blond eyebrow. "A hardened criminal, eh?"

"I've actually been expelled twice. The second time I was arrested, but that wasn't about a protest. Well, I guess you could say I was protesting the school's underage drinking policy."

"I see." A smile plays at his lips. "I'll be right back. Try not to cause an international incident while I'm gone." I open my mouth to reply, but he's already disappeared inside the house. He returns with an armload of nylon bags that I recognize as a tent and sleeping bags.

"Are we going camping?" I ask.

My face is literally freezing right now and I'm sure the temperature plummets overnight. I can't imagine getting any sleep in a tent in this weather, no matter how warm those sleeping bags are.

"Not necessarily," Gunnar says. "There are places to stay along the Ring Road, but if we go all the way to the glacier, we'll need equipment in case we end up sleeping in the ice caves."

"Oh…cool. Literally." Man, this Henning guy better have been Gram's long-lost love or something. I can't believe a cozy Christmas watching snow fall along the Seine has turned into some fresh hell where I have to hunt down a bunch of pseudo-Satanists and camp in an ice cave.

I lay my suitcase flat on the cold ground and unzip it, trying to discreetly transfer some bras and underwear into the backpack without Gunnar noticing. I also add my hiking boots, a pair of running tights, a Polarfleece hoodie, and a pink plastic lunch box that Gram and I refer to as our worst-case-scenario kit.

"What's in that?" Gunnar asks, and I realize he's been watching me.

"Spare phone, flares, matches, water-purification tablets, hand warmers, hunting knife, bleeding kit, emergency blankets. Gram takes it on all of her jobs."

"We have emergency supplies packed already."

"You can never be too prepared."

Gunnar lines the sleeping bags up next to the rest of our

gear. "Just keep in mind that you might be carrying that pack for several kilometers. The lighter the better."

"I'll be fine," I say, adding a couple of extra items just to make a point. When I'm done, I zip my suitcase closed and leave it sitting next to the back of the SUV. I cinch the drawstring to the backpack and fold the top flap over it, clipping the buckles to secure all of my gear. It is pretty heavy. I hope he was kidding about the several kilometers part.

Gunnar takes the pack and tosses it into the back of the vehicle like it's made of feathers. Of course he would be some sort of skinny Adonis who also has superhuman strength.

"Just one more thing I need to grab." He turns back toward the house.

This time when he returns it's with a long quilted bag in his arms. Gram and I didn't bring weapons to Iceland because the handguns she owns are illegal here, but I know enough about guns to know Gunnar is now packing a rifle in the back of the SUV, or perhaps a shotgun.

"What is that for?" I ask.

"Protection," he says tersely.

"Here? Are we going to get attacked by sheep? Or one of those cute horses with the long bangs?"

Gunnar ignores my questions. "Can you handle a rifle?"

"Yes. I took a weapons certification class last year."

"Good. There's no time for training."

Gram pokes her head out of the front door. "Tea is ready, Rory." She gestures at my zipped suitcase. "Are you all packed up? If so, bring anything you don't want to take with us inside." She disappears back into the house.

"Better go get your tea." Gunnar smirks slightly, as if drinking warm beverages somehow makes me a weakling.

"Whatever." I carry my suitcase up the porch steps. Ducking inside the front door, I swallow back a gasp. I don't know what I was expecting—dusty furniture covered with sheets and the smell of mothballs, maybe—but the inside of Henning's home is like a combination zoo exhibit and high-end hotel.

The small foyer opens up into a great room with a high vaulted ceiling. Streaks of moonlight filter down through a hexagonal skylight, illuminating three massive wire cages set against the far wall of the room. The other side is decorated more conventionally, with a sofa, a recliner, and a coffee table. Gram sits on the sofa, skimming through something on her phone with one finger. A TV hangs on the wall across from her, a news program playing on mute.

My shoes thud softly against the hardwood floor as I cross the room to one of the wire cages. A medium-sized bird sits on a perch, studying me with piercing black eyes. It stretches out its brown-and-white speckled wings for a moment before folding them neatly again.

"What's with the animals?" I ask.

"Henning has been known to collect the occasional stray," Gram says.

The second cage contains what looks like a common house cat. It's beautiful—with long gray fur and wide orange eyes. "Why is this guy locked up?"

Henning wheels through a doorway that appears to lead to a dining room, his chair gliding easily across the wooden floor. "That is Dóni," he says. "He's feral."

"If he's wild, then why did you bring him inside?"

"He was injured when I found him in the yard. Leaving him outside would have been a death sentence."

"So instead he gets a prison sentence?" I regret the words as soon as they're out of my mouth. This cage is decent-sized and filled with toys and bedding. Even if it weren't, it's not my place to criticize the way Gram's clients treat their pets. "Sorry, I didn't mean—"

Henning waves off the apology. "I hope once he adjusts more to being around people that he can have the run of the house."

"And what about this one?" The third cage is empty, but from the looks of it, it once housed another bird.

"That one was…released back into the wild."

Henning looks as if he's going to say more, but then a servant arrives, carrying a silver tray with three cups of tea. I follow the two of them across the room to where Gram is sitting. I wait for Gram and Henning to select cups and take the remaining one. I sip the warm beverage quietly as Henning gives us a quick rundown of how the next couple of days will go.

"Black as Death made a stop about an hour ago, where they posed for photos in front of the waterfall Seljalandsfoss. The good news is it's currently raining in that area, so their progress will be slowed. They'll probably stop for the night somewhere between Vík and Kálfafell, which is just a few hours away. You might be able to catch up with them tonight or early tomorrow. If not, you'll proceed onward to the Hoffell area where you can rent snowmobiles to take you across the eastern portion of Vatnajökull."

"Why are we bringing weapons?" I ask. "I saw Gunnar loading a rifle in the back."

Henning drums his fingertips together. "Because, Aurora, you can never be too prepared."

"Are there wild animals here I'm not aware of? I thought you mostly had sheep and horses. Surely you don't think your own grandson or his friends are dangerous."

"The weapons aren't for wildlife, or for people. They're for anything else you might encounter on your trip." Henning strokes the chain around his neck again. It's got some sort of amulet or medallion for a pendant, but I'm not close enough to see the insignia.

"Like what?" I ask.

"Like demons."

"You seriously believe in demons?" I try to keep my voice polite.

Henning gestures at the television set. Even without sound, the images give a clear picture of what's going on. It's a report about a car bombing in Turkey from earlier today. There are bodies covered with tarps, bloody people being loaded into ambulances. "Look around you," he says. "At the way hate and darkness have managed to bleed into the very fabric of our world. The fool is not he who believes in demons. The fool is he who doesn't."

4

I want to ask Henning more, especially about what kind of gun supposedly works against actual demons, but Gunnar bursts through the front door, his cheeks red from the cold. "Weather report shows a storm heading in. Probably just rain, but it could turn to ice and snow as the temperature drops overnight. We should get started as soon as possible."

Gram sets her half-empty cup on the silver tray in front of us. "We're ready."

I chug the rest of my tea quickly. The liquid sends a rush of warmth through my extremities.

Henning folds his hands in his lap. "It's raining along much of the south coast right now. If Einar and his friends don't know they're being tracked, then hopefully they'll make their way at a leisurely pace. It is my sincere hope that you catch up to them by midday tomorrow, before Jökulsárlón." He turns to me. "It's the most beautiful lagoon. You must stop for a few moments if at all possible."

"We'll see if there's time, Grandfather." Gunnar gathers his blond hair back into a ponytail with one hand, giving me another view of his chiseled cheekbones. He catches me staring and lets the hair fall loose around his face. "If we leave now, I might be able to stay between the storms."

I hop off the sofa and head for the door, with Gram and Gunnar right behind me. "Thank you for the tea," I call to Henning as we're stepping outside into what is now near-total darkness.

The SUV's engine is already going, a cloud of exhaust hovering above the ground. Gunnar slides into the driver's seat and Gram takes shotgun. I climb into the second seat.

The back seat has been laid flat to accommodate all of our gear. Gunnar circles around the driveway and through the iron gates. We descend the hill and turn onto the dark streets of Reykjavík.

Gram points out a few places of note as we head toward the outskirts of the city. "There's Hallgrímskirkja, the town's most famous church. You can see the top of the spire from almost anywhere in the city," she says. "Oh, and coming up on the left is Perlan. It's a science museum with a restaurant at the top."

I squint. The building looks like a glass dome balanced on top of six giant concrete cylinders. "What kind of architecture is that?"

"Those are hot water tanks," Gram says. "I believe they're still in use."

"They are," Gunnar says. "Grandfather's water comes from them."

He asks my grandmother something in Icelandic. The two of them have a mini-conversation without me, which is vaguely annoying, but I don't say anything because I can't imagine what it would be like to go years without speaking my native language the way Gram has done.

I focus on the scenery, wondering what my life might have been like if I had grown up here. The outskirts of Reykjavík don't look much different from the suburbs of Sydney or Seattle, aside from the lava fields. The city lights fade into darkness as we turn onto a highway that leads into the countryside. Gunnar has lapsed into silence. He's concentrating on the road now, his hands at ten and two like a model driver.

The rain catches up to us about twenty minutes after we leave, pounding the front windshield. I watch the drops for a few minutes, marveling at the ferocity with which they batter the glass. Gunnar has the wipers on high speed, but the visibility is still limited and I'm glad no one else seems to be on this road.

Gram tries to point out a couple of volcanic steam vents as we drive through an area with geothermal activity, but the combination of the darkness and rain makes it impossible to see much. The road splits and we veer left to stay on Route 1, the Ring Road, which runs along the entire perimeter of the island. A few minutes later we drive under a bridge and I get the briefest moment of silence and clarity, but still all I see is darkness, shadows of hills and mountains stretching out in all directions. As the pattering resumes, I settle back into my seat and close my eyes. I shouldn't be tired already, but I am.

"Going to sleep at nineteen hundred?" Gunnar asks. I catch a glimpse of his blue eyes in the rearview mirror. Once again, I can't tell if he's making fun of me or not.

"I'm just resting," I mumble. "But it feels so much later here than it is."

"The dark does that to people. And then in summer we have the opposite—university students wandering the streets of the city all night long because it's still light out."

"How many hours of daylight will we have tomorrow?"

"About seven, depending on your definition of daylight. I hope we find my brother before he and the others head out onto the glacier. There's a real risk of hypothermia for people who venture into the wilderness here without proper gear."

"Does your brother have a traditional Icelandic sweater too?" I can't resist asking.

"Indeed he does." Gunnar clears his throat. "And you're going to be thanking me for that sweater by the end of this journey."

I bite back a smile. "We'll see about that."

❧

The rain continues to slow our progress. We make a quick stop at Seljalandsfoss, the site of the last Black as Death Instagram post, just to make sure they're not hanging out in the area for any reason. There are a few other cars in the parking area, at least two of which seem to be occupied.

"Why are people just sitting in their cars?" I ask.

Gunnar shuts off the engine. "They might be students here on dates, or people hoping to catch a glimpse of the Northern Lights." He opens his door and peers up at the sky. "I don't see that happening tonight, though."

"I was named for the Northern Lights, but I've never seen them," I say.

"It's true," Gram tells Gunnar. "Her mother loved the aurora."

"Interesting," Gunnar says blandly, like it's the least interesting thing he's ever heard. I can't tell if he hates me or just doesn't care one way or the other about me. "I imagine the lights might make an appearance at some point in our journey," he continues, sliding out of the vehicle without waiting for a response.

"I'll ask around the lot while you two go check out the falls," Gram says.

"Great." I pull my hat down over my ears and flip up the hood of my jacket before leaving the SUV. The rain has tapered off to a drizzle, but the wet air chills me to the bone.

Gunnar is already heading down a wide concrete path. I have to run to catch up with him. *He hates you*, my brain informs me. *Everyone hates you, remember?*

That's a bit of an exaggeration. Macy doesn't hate me, though she does get frustrated with me from time to time. My tutor, Alannah, doesn't hate me. Of course, my grandmother pays her so that could be why. And then there's Gram. I used to worry she might hate me—that she might blame me for my mom's death—but my therapist told me that no one would blame an innocent baby, and I decided to believe her. Still, I shouldn't have made that snide remark about the sweater Gunnar packed for me. My mouth works faster than my brain sometimes. It's not one of my better qualities.

The path fades into gravel. The two of us are walking side by side now. I skid to a stop as we come upon the waterfall. It's tall—like skyscraper-tall—and lit up with bright yellow floodlamps that make the spray gleam gold against the blackness of the night.

"Whoa." I blink away the raindrops collecting on my eyelashes as I crane my neck to look up at the top of the falls.

"Nice, eh?" Gunnar says. "Believe it or not, we have others that are far more impressive."

There's an older couple here, snapping pictures with their phones. Gunnar jogs over and speaks to them. When he returns to me, he's got a damp tendril of hair glued across his forehead. "They've been here only for fifteen minutes, but they haven't seen anyone else."

"Well, it was worth a try, I guess," I say.

The two of us head back to where Gram is waiting for us. She says no one in the parking lot has seen Einar or the band either, so Gunnar and I pile back into the SUV. I text the picture to Macy with the words *How about some liquid ice?* She doesn't reply right away and I realize it's late in Japan—she's probably asleep.

The next town we come to is called Hella, which sounds like the kind of place the band might stop for a photo op, but there's nothing new posted to their Instagram.

"Foreigners often stay here if they plan to go hiking on the volcano Hekla," Gunnar says. "This town was settled by Irish monks. Hundreds of years ago, they believed Hekla was a portal to hell."

"Lots of hell portals in this country, huh?" I say.

"Well, they thought that due to how active Hekla can be. It's been known to erupt for years at a time."

I shudder. "I'm glad we're not hiking there."

I swallow back a yawn as we pass through the outskirts of the town. I could get away with sleeping, but I should use this trip to show Gram how valuable I can be. Then she'll *want* to hire me. I pull out my tablet so I can do some research into Black as Death. The SUV has its own Wi-Fi and I have no trouble getting onto the internet.

The group consists of three guys from the Reykjavík area and a female lead guitarist from Sweden. Their web page is full of what you'd expect from a death metal band—anarchy signs, pentagrams, a lot of 666s.

I click on the *History* tab and start reading. All of the members are in their mid-twenties, except for guitarist Annika Lee who is nineteen. The guys formed a band while they were undergraduates at Reykjavík University. It was mostly just for fun, but they wrote their own music and played live shows around the city where they gained enough of a following to be invited to a Swedish metal band festival, and that's where they found Annika.

Or, I should say, Annika found them. At just sixteen she tracked down Lars, the lead singer, after their set and told him she thought his vocal work was being overshadowed by his guitar playing, that the band needed to find a separate guitarist. And then she offered to audition. The guys were blown away by her, so Annika moved to Iceland and officially joined the band. The next year they returned to that same festival and were signed by an Icelandic label. And now they're getting ready to release their second album.

I click over to the photo gallery. Again, no major surprises. Annika Lee has a nose ring, an eyebrow ring, and stick-straight black hair with dyed blue tips. Her trademark style seems to include combat boots, ripped tights, and baby-doll dresses. The guys are a mess of flannel shirts, skull tattoos, and facial hair in serious need of trimming. Lars's beard is long enough that he's actually woven it into two thin black braids that look like horns.

"What are you concentrating on so intently?" Gunnar asks.

"Just reading up on Black as Death," I say. "A computer

programmer, two grad students, and a girl from Sweden? They definitely don't sound like hardcore devil worshippers."

Gunnar scoffs. "They worship whiskey, tattoos, and hot women. The devil thing is just some PR angle they adopted when they were recording their first album." He pauses. "Of course, if you study satanism, you'll find there are different schools of practice, one of which is more like a mix of hedonism and anarchism than actual devil worship. It's possible they subscribe to *that* version. But they're definitely not performing blood sacrifices like their songs would have you believe."

"I see you're well-versed in the dark arts," I joke. "Should I be worried?"

He peeks over his shoulder at me, his expression unreadable. "Not unless you're hiding something."

Gram points out the front windshield. "The town of Vík is coming up."

Gunnar drums his fingertips on the steering wheel. "Rory. Check the Black as Death feed. See if they've updated it."

I open Instagram and find the band's account—@BADband666. Sure enough, there's a new story. They've hashtagged it #Vík. "They're here," I say excitedly. "Or at least they were. They're standing in front of a church."

"That church?" Gunnar points at a white building with a red-tiled roof that's perched at the top of a small hill.

"Yes!" I'm fidgeting in my seat now. If we can find Einar and the others tonight, Gram and I could be back in Paris in time for Christmas.

"How old is the posting?"

"It's from about forty-five minutes ago." I scroll back through the last couple of posts—one of the band posing next to what looks like a waffle stand, one at Hallgrímskirkja, and one at the waterfall we stopped at. "Are you sure your brother is with them? He's not in any of these pictures."

"He's basically their roadie. He's probably the one taking

the photos." Gunnar turns off Ring Road and heads for the center of town. "The church won't be open this late, but we can check out the area and ask around whether anyone has seen them."

It's a solid plan, but when we get to the blacktop parking lot for the little red-and-white church, it's completely empty. There's no one on the street either, probably because of the rain that's pounding the pavement. The three of us flip up our hoods and walk a full lap around the building, pausing at the far side to look out toward the dark ocean.

"Now what?" I ask. "Should we check out the local hotels?"

Gunnar sighs. "Believe it or not, there are more than twenty of them within a few kilometers of here, and I don't know what kind of car my brother and the others are driving. You didn't happen to see it in any of the posts, did you?"

I check the @BADband666 feed again. "No cars," I confirm.

"Well, the hotel owners aren't going to give out information about guests, especially not celebrities, so I guess we're stuck until they post again. Unless we want to just head toward the glacier and give up on finding them tonight."

I do a quick search for "Black as Death" and "Vík" on all the major social media platforms just to see if maybe someone in town saw them and recognized them, but there are no hits. "If they're here, no one is posting about it."

"We could take the opportunity to grab some dinner," Gram says. "We're going to have to eat at some point."

"Good idea." Gunnar turns back to the SUV. Gram and I follow him. We drive down the street and park in front of a long white building he says is one of Vík's best restaurants. The three of us exit the car and hurry across the gravel parking lot.

Inside the restaurant, an older woman leads us to a table in the far corner of the room and sets a menu in front of each of us. It's translated into English, but it's about eight pages long and the sheer volume of choices is exhausting.

Gram points at a picture of a sandwich. "This one is made of traditional Icelandic bread and lamb fillet."

"Works for me," I say. "I like to try new things."

When our server comes to take our order, I'm surprised that Gunnar orders a pizza. "What?" he says, when he hears me snicker. "Grandfather would keel over in his wheelchair if I asked to order a pizza for dinner. I have to take advantage of the opportunity."

"Are Icelandic pizzas good?" I ask.

He shrugs. "Some are better than others."

Gram orders a bottle of Icelandic beer to drink and Gunnar and I have water. Our food arrives quickly and we all dig in. My sandwich is on crisp dark rye bread with tender meat, lettuce, tomatoes, onions, and a delicious sauce that I can't identify. One thing I've learned about eating in foreign countries is that if something is delicious, it's best to just enjoy it. Asking too many questions about what's in a certain meal or how it's made doesn't always end well. *Don't ask unless you really want to know,* Gram likes to say.

Tonight, all I want to do is enjoy my first real meal of the day. Unfortunately, with Gunnar sitting across from me, I'm overly conscious of the occasional onion string or lettuce chunk dangling from my lips. I take small bites and blot my mouth frequently.

Clearly less concerned with table manners, Gunnar holds a slice of pizza in one hand and swipes at his phone with the other. I'm pretty sure I could shove my whole sandwich in my mouth and wash it down with his glass of water and he might not even notice. *So then why do you care what he thinks?*

Good question. It's not like Gunnar is the first boy my age I've ever seen or anything. I grew up going to schools with other diplomats' children. Some of the classes were segregated by gender but most weren't.

He slides his phone into his pocket. "No new posts yet."

"Do you think they're still here?" Gram asks.

He tosses his hair back over his shoulders. "No way to know for sure. They might have continued on."

"Should we do the same?" I blot my mouth with my napkin again.

Gunnar peers out the closest window. "The rain is predicted to clear up later. I think we can make quicker time tomorrow if we stay here tonight and let the storm pass."

"Sounds good." In between bites of her sandwich, Gram tells me about the town of Vík. Apparently only a few hundred people live here, with a couple hundred more in the surrounding countryside. The church is the most famous building in the town. It was erected in the 1930s, during a financial depression. Vík used to be a merchant post and many of the townspeople were either shop owners or slaughterhouse employees, but now the markets and slaughterhouses have gone away and the main industry is tourism.

Gunnar slams another slice of pizza while Gram is talking. I start on the second half of my sandwich.

Gram takes a sip of her beer. "It's tricky when tourism takes over a place. No one likes to exploit their culture and resources for cash, but the more tourists who arrive, the more built up and commercial cities become. What's good for a town can be bad for the individual families living there."

She starts to say more, but falls silent as an elderly woman shuffles up to our table. She's dressed all in black, with silvery hair pinned up in a bun. Sniffing the air sharply, the woman mutters something in Icelandic. She claws at the front of her dress until her knobby fingers latch onto the beaded necklace she's wearing around her neck—it's a crucifix. She holds it out toward Gram, who is sitting closest to her. Grabbing the salt shaker with her free hand, the old woman begins to sprinkle salt on the table, pausing midway to toss some over her shoulder. Gunnar and I both stare at the woman. Gram speaks to her in Icelandic, her voice gentle and soothing.

A middle-aged man hurries over. "I am terribly sorry," he says, wrapping one hand around the old woman's wrist. "My mother is not well." He bends down so he's at eye level with her and speaks quietly. The woman pulls free from his grasp. She flings the salt shaker to the floor where it shatters, spilling white crystals across the polished wood.

Other people in the restaurant have noticed the disruption. Some are peeking over discreetly to see what the commotion is about, while a couple are unabashedly recording the whole scene on their cell phones. I lean forward and angle my head so my hair blocks my face from view.

The woman locks eyes with me for a moment, and perhaps realizing I'm an outsider, switches to English. "Evil," she says, her withered voice growing in volume and fullness. "Evil, evil. Black evil. Must go. Must fight." She reaches out toward Gunnar.

He leans away, one hand lifting to his chest. His fingers brush against a small silver medallion. It's similar to the one Henning was wearing.

"Mother," the man says firmly. "These people aren't evil. They're just a nice family out enjoying a hot meal together. Let's leave them in peace."

The woman reaches toward Gram this time. Her gnarled hand closes around Gram's fingers. She whispers something in Icelandic. Across from me, Gunnar goes pale.

"Perhaps we should go," he says smoothly. "We were just about finished anyway."

"No, please," the man says. "You should stay. We can go. Come on, Mother. Let's get you into your coat."

"It's all right." Gram takes one last bite of her sandwich. She slips back into her jacket.

Gunnar dons his jacket as well and drops a handful of bills on the table. Gram is already heading for the exit. I hurriedly wrap the rest of my sandwich in a napkin and follow them through the dining room, feeling a little lost because I couldn't understand the Icelandic spoken.

Gram is first through the door. As it swings shut behind her, I grab Gunnar's arm. "What did she say?" I ask. "What did that woman say to my grandmother that made everyone decide we needed to leave?"

"She asked us to go," Gunnar says. "Before the evil could kill everyone in the room."

5

What does that even mean?" I ask Gunnar as we head back outside.

"It means she thought one of us was evil. Her son said she was sick, didn't he? Perhaps she was delirious or confused."

It feels like a half-answer, words designed to pacify rather than inform me. The woman didn't seem confused. She seemed sure of herself...and terrified.

Gram is waiting by the SUV. "Rory, check and see if the band has posted anything new."

Gunnar unlocks the doors and crawls into the driver's seat.

As he starts the engine, I check the @BADband666 feed again. "Nothing new."

"We should probably call it a night then," Gram says.

"I agree," Gunnar says. "Without more to go on, we could spend all night searching for them and never catch a glimpse. We're better off getting some sleep and then getting on the road early tomorrow."

"Sounds like a plan." I lean back in my seat and nibble on the rest of my sandwich.

Gram pulls out her phone. "Gunnar, do you want me to do a search for what's available?"

"That's all right, Ingrid. My grandfather gave me a short list of guest houses along our route that he felt would be suitable accommodations. At this time of year, all should have vacancies."

He drives to the edge of town and then turns into a gravel parking lot. It's another wooden building painted white, this time with two stories. We hop out of the vehicle and head inside. The owner tells us she has five rooms for rent, only one of which is occupied. Gunnar gets his own room while Gram and I decide to share. I'm still a little creeped out from dinner and it'll be easier for me to fall asleep if I'm not all alone. We're all on the second floor, with doors next to each other and a communal bathroom in the hallway.

There's only one bed in our room, but Gram and I have shared a bed before and this one is a queen, so there should be plenty of room. I kick off my boots and crawl under the covers in my jeans and sweatshirt. It feels amazing to stretch out after a full day of traveling.

"Sleeping in that?" Gram asks.

I shake my head. "I just need a minute to unwind. You can use the bathroom first, if you want."

"A hot shower sounds heavenly." Gram fishes some shampoo and conditioner out from her backpack. "I'm not sure if you're aware, but most of the water here is heated geothermally, which means the shower water can smell like sulfur."

"Ugh," I say, thinking of the noxious scent of sulfur from science class back when I was in school in Bangkok. "So we're going to smell like rotten eggs this whole trip?"

"No, silly," Gram says. "The scent won't stick to you, I promise. I just didn't want you to panic. You've seemed a little...flustered since we got here."

Jeez. Even Gram is picking up on my awkwardness around Gunnar. I'm going to have to get a handle on that.

"What did that woman in the restaurant say to you?" I ask. "She said something in Icelandic, right?"

"It was mostly gibberish." Gram's eyes are drawn to something outside the window. "A bunch of words strung together that didn't make much sense." She lowers the blinds and pulls the curtains closed.

She turns back toward me and I try to discern from her expression and body language if she's lying. She doesn't seem to be, but if she's not, then Gunnar is. And why would he make up a story about what the old lady said? He doesn't seem like the type who would lie just to scare me. Plus, his version of the story makes more sense with what I saw.

"It just seems odd," I continue, "her talking about evil when we're on this trek to retrieve a magical rock that allegedly leads people straight to hell." It also reminds me of the things my dad used to say when I visited him in the mental hospital, but I'm not going to bring him up right now. Gram's official position on my father is that the stress of my mom's difficult pregnancy wore him down, physically and emotionally. When Mom was dying in surgery, he had a psychotic break and started hallucinating demons and evil spirits. He hasn't ever recovered.

"You know," Gram says, "in Norse mythology, hell wasn't even a bad place. It was just where people went if they weren't lucky enough to die in battle."

"Yeah, I learned that in school. But these people aren't Vikings and that woman specifically said 'evil' more than once."

Gram pats me on the shoulder. "I'm sorry if she scared you, but I got the feeling she may have been mentally ill." She pauses. "And many Icelanders grow up very superstitious. Did you know that close to half the population believes in hidden people?"

"Hidden people?"

"Invisible elves, basically. We call them huldufólk."

"That's interesting," I say. "And a little disturbing. But why do I feel like you're trying to change the subject?"

"Not at all." Gram chuckles. "I just mean that when you take someone who already believes in supernatural things, and figure in advanced age, perhaps medications with side effects, or other issues, it's not that unusual for people to… have episodes."

"I guess."

Gram heads for the hallway with her shower stuff. "I wouldn't let it worry you too much."

Maybe Gram is right and I'm making too much out of this, but I can't stop thinking about the fact that she and Gunnar told me two different stories. As far as I know, my grandmother has never lied to me. Why would she start now?

6

Later I lie awake, my mind replaying each moment from the restaurant, my head spinning with questions: *What were we doing when the old woman came over to us? What were we saying? Could Gunnar have misheard her?*

Next to me Gram lies on her back, snoring peacefully. At least someone is getting some rest. Sighing, I slip out of bed and grab my tablet. If I can't sleep I might as well get some research done, but I don't want to risk waking Gram by turning on a light. I'll find a cozy corner of the guesthouse where I can sit and not disturb anyone else.

I fumble around in my backpack until I locate a pair of socks and something warm to put on over the T-shirt I'm sleeping in. It turns out to be the red-and-gray Icelandic sweater. I smile to myself as I pull it over my head. *Time to test you out.*

It's a little after eleven p.m., and my plan is to sneak downstairs and curl up in one of the chairs in the sitting room. When I slip out into the hallway, I see a narrow beam of light from under Gunnar's closed door. My heart revs up a little as I debate my next move. It makes total sense for me to try to clarify what happened at dinner, but I'm a little nervous about talking to him alone. What if he *does* hate me? What if he tells me to go away?

Just do it, a voice whispers in my brain. This voice has gotten me in trouble in the past, but for once I feel like it's giving me good advice. I lift one shaking fist and knock gently on his door. I hear Gunnar moving around inside, and then there's a pause and the sound of the deadbolt unlatching.

When he opens the door, he's wearing black and white plaid flannel pajama pants and no shirt. His damp hair is hanging over his shoulders, droplets of water clinging to his pale chest. "Hi," he says. "Is everything all right?"

Holy crap, I almost say aloud. Of course his chest would rival his cheekbones when it comes to chiseledness and general Louvre-worthy appearance. I train my eyes on the ground, hoping the dim lighting in the hallway is obscuring the blush I feel creeping across my face. "Uh, yeah. Sorry. I didn't mean to intrude."

"You're not intruding. I just got out of the shower. Come on in. I'm guessing you want to talk more about what happened at the restaurant?"

"Right." I lift my gaze to make eye contact, which involves taking in Gunnar's entire body, which sends another rush of heat to my face. I focus on one of his shoulders, but even that is so smooth, the muscle defined without being bulky. "Aren't you cold?" I blurt out.

"Not particularly," Gunnar says. "Aren't you warm in that? You're looking a bit flushed."

"It is warm," I say. "And comfortable. I was testing it out."

"Working your way toward that thank you." He grins as he shuts the door behind me. He goes to the far side of the room, bends down, and removes a folded piece of black fabric from his backpack. It turns out to be a concert T-shirt from a band I've never heard of. As he pulls it over his head, I'm just glad I don't have to avoid staring at his bare chest anymore.

"So," I start, "I feel like there might have been more to that story."

"There might." Gunnar sits on the edge of the bed. "It's possible that woman thought I was Einar."

"I don't understand. People think Einar is evil?"

"My brother is…troubled. He was doing all right for a while, but his girlfriend broke up with him a few months ago and he dropped out of school. My grandfather was upset, but figured he just needed time to heal and that he'd go back eventually. Instead, Einar started spending most of his time in his room on his computer, staying up until four or five in the morning and sleeping all day. That's how he met Lars, the lead singer of Black as Death. The two started messaging each other on some music board and then Einar starting working for the band. This whole pilgrimage to the doorway to hell was something the two of them came up with together."

"And that's why people think he's evil?"

"It's more than that." Gunnar sighs. "A few months ago, a church on the outskirts of Reykjavík burned to the ground. Satanic symbols were spray-painted in the parking area. Einar was questioned about the crime."

"Did he do it?"

"Possibly," Gunnar says. "But he wasn't arrested because the only evidence the police had was some eyewitnesses who saw someone they thought was Einar running away from the blaze. He acknowledged being there. Said he was out for a late-night walk and saw the fire and went to check it out."

"Didn't they ask why he didn't call 911?"

"It's 112 here, but yes. Einar said he didn't have his phone, and by the time he got home he could see online that the firefighters were already trying to put out the blaze," Gunnar says. "Also, not calling 112 isn't a crime even if they could somehow prove he was lying."

"If he wasn't arrested, how would people know he was questioned?"

"A local tabloid ran an article on the fire and mentioned my brother as a possible suspect." He pauses. "And someone from the church found one of his school photos online and put up a notice saying he wasn't to be allowed on the property. They also posted about their suspicions on the church website."

"So you think that woman saw a picture of Einar online and remembered what he looked like months later?"

"Or there may have been other articles or postings. Here, I'll show you." He holds out his hand and I realize he's waiting for me to give him my tablet computer.

"Okay." I tap in my password and hand the computer to him.

His lips purse as he taps at the screen. I walk around to the end of the bed so I can watch over his shoulder.

"You can sit down, you know?" he says, without looking away from the screen. "I don't bite."

That's too bad, I think. Gah, what is wrong with me? It's like I'm twelve years old again and getting flooded with puberty hormones for the first time. I lower myself gingerly to the bed, making sure to leave ample space between us.

Gunnar has pulled up what appears to be a church news feed with information about the fire. I consider the picture of his brother. Same long hair and high cheekbones. Einar's face is a bit sunken, though, and he has faint dark circles under his eyes.

He scrolls down to the comments. They seem to be a mix of alleged satanists praising the burning of the church and zealous parishioners pledging that God's vengeance would be swift and powerful.

"I don't want to hang out with either of these groups," I say.

"Same," Gunnar says. "This is not your ordinary Catholic or Lutheran church. It's a fundamentalist Christian church with a long list of 'sins' that require parishioner repentance by sending in donations."

"Church of the Holy Light," I murmur. "You think it's all a big scam?"

"Hard to know for certain."

"You really think your brother might have been the one who burned it down?"

"I saw him with spray paint that day. I asked him what he was doing and he told me to stay out of it, so I did."

"Did you tell the police that?"

He shakes his head. "I'm not in the habit of volunteering extra information to the police, but even if I were, I wouldn't implicate my brother. The church was empty. It's not like he killed anyone."

"So you don't think he's dangerous?"

"He wouldn't hurt me," Gunnar says. "And I don't think he'd hurt anyone else either, unless he was being influenced or coerced."

I start to ask what he means by *influenced or coerced*, but then he reaches out to hand me back the tablet and his arm brushes against mine. I flinch, visibly, even though there's a thick barrier of wool between us.

He turns his head sharply to face me, the ends of his hair splattering a few drops of water in my direction. "Why are you so...twitchy?" He cocks his head to the side.

I lick my lips and compose a lie in my head about too much coffee, but then I realize he sat across from me at dinner and might remember me ordering water just like he did. "You make me nervous," I admit.

"Nervous?" Gunnar snorts. "Why? I'm not exactly what people call intimidating."

I shrug. "I'm not very good around people my own age."

"Why?" he asks again.

"I don't know. They tend not to...like me." My voice wavers a little and I wish I could crawl under the bed and hide from my embarrassment. Why did I just say that? Why am I saying any of this?

"Ah." Gunnar's expression softens. "I know the feeling."

I would honestly rather everyone hate me than for people to look at me the way Gunnar is right now, with eyes full of pity. "Shut up. You do not."

He snickers. "You know, people might like you more if you didn't tell them to shut up."

"Come on. Look at you," I say. "You're ridiculously hot. I

bet everyone likes you. Unless they're jealous or something."

Gunnar's eyes widen. "You think I'm *ridiculously hot?*"

Oh God. I'm the one who needs to shut up. And yet, I keep talking. "I mean, yeah, sure, in a traditional, socially approved kind of way," I hedge. "I don't *personally* think of you that way."

But then I decide to be honest. Gram says that when you mess up, the power move is to own it. Backpedaling just looks sad and pathetic. And it fools no one. "You know what? Actually, I do think of you that way. I'm pretty sure every girl on this island thinks of you that way."

Gunnar shakes his head. "Untrue. Some of the girls at my school tease me. They say I'm too skinny and that my face is too smooth, like a girl's." He rubs at his chin. "They like men with big muscles and facial hair."

"Facial hair? Gross." I scrunch up my nose. "Well, if you ever get lonely, you should just drop by the US, because I'm pretty sure there they'd want to put you on magazine covers."

He laughs out loud. Lifting his chin, he crosses his arms, and leans slightly to the side. "You mean like this?"

"That looks like the cover of the worst rap album ever, but sure." My lips melt into a smile.

Gunnar reaches into his backpack and pulls out his traditional Icelandic sweater. "Maybe I should put this on."

"I don't know," I say. "You might even be able to make *that* look good right now."

"It looks good on *you.*" His eyes linger on me for a few seconds. "Also, you're cute when you're embarrassed."

This makes me blush even hotter. "What is happening right now?" I ask. "I never talk like this. I never *feel* like this. Are you some sort of Svengali?"

Gunnar laughs loud enough that I get the urge to cover his mouth with my hand. I don't, of course, because I have no idea what would happen if I touched him. I do get a great view of his molars, though. Cavity-free, of course.

"So now I'm ridiculously hot and…beguiling?" He blinks his long eyelashes.

I hop up from the bed and pace back and forth. "How about we just delete the last five minutes? My grandmother would kill me if she could see how unprofessional I'm being." I turn to face him. "I would appreciate it if you didn't say anything to her."

"I'm enjoying imagining how that conversation would go." He clears his throat. "So, Ingrid. I'm afraid we need to discuss your granddaughter's behavior. Her unwanted advances have been making me very uncomfortable."

"I have not made any *advances*," I huff. I look around the room. "This is a nightmare, right? Wake up, Rory." I pinch myself. I do not sit up in bed, safe under the covers. I am still in this room with Gunnar, who is still laughing at me.

"I don't want you to be nervous," he says. "Is there any way I can help? Maybe we should do like in the movies and just kiss right now to get it out of your system."

"Ahahaha." My breath catches in my throat. "Not funny." Is this flirting? Is this marble sculpture boy flirting with me? No, he's just screwing with me—feeding off my discomfort like some kind of Scandinavian succubus.

"Who says I'm joking?" he continues. "If there's some sort of…tension that's going to interfere with finding my brother, then I—"

Kill me now. Seriously. Stroke. Heart attack. Spontaneous combustion. "You want to help?" I say. "Tell me some of your flaws—let's hear all the reasons you suck. Your room is full of country music posters, you moonlight as a drug dealer, you think women belong in the kitchen, you hate immigrants. Something like that."

"I actually like to cook, but Grandfather is sort of traditional and insists on employing a housekeeper who cooks for us." Gunnar thinks for a moment. "I don't drink. I ride a bicycle to school."

"Okay, that's enough," I tell him. "You're not helping."

If this were anyone else, I would think he was manipulating me, that he had done some research to figure out exactly what to say to me. But this guy didn't even know my name a few hours ago. He just happens to be the kind of guy I thought existed only in books and movies—one who is both extremely hot *and* extremely cool.

The "just do it" parts of my brain light up again and I imagine taking him up on his offer to kiss. But if I do that I might get pulled even further into his orbit. Or get rejected. I'm not sure which would be worse.

Yes, I am.

That offer was a joke anyway, I remind myself.

"Oh, I know!" Gunnar's eyes light up. "I am bad at athletics."

"Really?" I ask, intrigued by the possibility of an awkward, fumbling Gunnar.

"I scored a—how do you say?—'own goal' playing football when I was younger. It was a big game. We lost by one. I got yelled at by my entire team...and some of their parents."

My insides go soft. Even I've never had an entire team of people mad at me. I'm seized by the urge to console him. "Okay, that story is sad, but it's getting late." I start backing toward the door. "I should go."

"I'm glad we had this talk." Gunnar smiles again.

"Ha, that makes one of us."

"Seriously, though. You're right that this job requires focus. But..." His voice drops low. "Maybe once we find my brother, I can show you around Reykjavík...if you want."

I can show you around Reykjavík. Is that code for something? I curse inwardly at myself for spending so much time reading about science and politics and no time at all reading about romance or dating.

"Sure. Yeah, maybe. Okay." I brush a bead of sweat off my upper lip. "Alternatively, we could just chalk this conversation up to extreme late-night awkwardness and pretend it never happened."

"I don't feel awkward." Gunnar grins in a way that both makes me want to slap his face and mash my lips to his.

"I meant me," I bark. "So, yeah, thanks for clarifying and good night and all that and I guess I'll see you in the morning."

Gunnar holds up the tablet. "Forgetting something?"

"Right." I snatch it out of his hand.

His eyes zero in on my bracelet. He reaches out to touch it with one finger, causing me to flinch again. "What's this? Do you have a medical condition I should know about?"

"It's not relevant," I say, backing toward the closed door. "I have to wear it because I'm highly allergic to certain anesthetic medicines that are sometimes used in emergency situations."

"I see. Is it made of iron?"

I shrug. "Stainless steel maybe? Why do you ask?"

"No particular reason. It just feels heavier than I imagined." Gunnar drops his hand to his lap. "Well…good talk, Rory. Sweet dreams."

"Thanks, you too," I mumble.

As I step into the hallway, he adds, "What do you have against country music anyway?"

I turn to look back at him. "I don't know. Everyone has something they don't like, right?"

I do know, though. I spend a fair amount of time convincing myself that Gram is all I need, that the fact I don't have a mom or a dad doesn't matter.

It does matter, though.

And sometimes all those country lyrics about loss and loneliness hit a little too close to home.

❧

Back in bed, I try not to focus on how I just totally em-

barrassed myself in front of a client's family member and I
try extra hard not to focus on Gunnar joking about kissing
me. At least I think he was joking. Oh my God, what if he
was serious?

My phone buzzes with a text.

Macy: Ooooh, pretty.

Me: Speaking of pretty, you would not believe the guy
traveling with Gram and me. He's the client's grandson,
but he looks like he belongs in a museum. Long hair, high
cheekbones. He should be the face of a VISIT ICELAND
tourism campaign.

Macy: Pictures?

Me: LOL. I would rather die than get caught taking
creepshots of a client's family member. He's like a mix of
Chris Hemsworth and Timothée Chalamet.

Macy: Wow. Is he nice?

Me: I think so? We sort of got into it when we first met,
but I just came back from talking to him and he doesn't
seem to hate me.

Macy: Got into it over what?

Me: An ugly sweater. Long story. I was rude.

Macy: OMG, do you LIKE him?

Me: No. Why would you think that?

Macy: IDK. I've never heard you call yourself rude before.

Me: I am rude sometimes, aren't I?

Macy: Hmm. Maybe a little snarky. Occasionally insensi-
tive. Or clueless.

Me: Thanks for the pep talk :P

Macy: None of those things are malicious. It's just who
you are. Tell me more about the guy.

I cave in and send her a few texts about Gunnar, including
a vague account of our casual bantering back in his room.

Macy: HE OFFERED TO KISS YOU?!?

Me: Pretty sure he was kidding. I mean, who does that?

Macy: IDK. Maybe hot Icelandic guys do that. I can't believe you didn't pounce on him. You're normally so impulsive.

Me: Ha! I'm trying to be less impulsive. Show Gram I can be helpful and all that.

Macy: Well, it sounds like the beginning of a hot vacation romance, if you want one. Keep me posted and send me a picture when you get one. And I'll let you know when I find a sexy Marine to sneak around with.

Me: Are there lesbian Marines?

Macy: Absolutely. There's an on-base LGBT group and everything.

Me: Sounds like you've been doing your research.

Macy: Heh, maybe. Okay, breakfast time. Be safe. TTYL.

Me: Bye.

A hot vacation romance. I giggle at the thought. Macy loves romantic comedies. I've always been more of a fan of action/adventure movies myself.

I can tell I'm not going to sleep anytime soon, so I log back onto the internet, intending to read more about Einar and the church he might have burned down. But I somehow end up Googling Gunnar to see if there are any stories about him I should know about. What pops up first are his social media feeds, including an Instagram account.

He doesn't have any active stories so I scroll through his image gallery, trying not to be relieved at each screen that passes without him posing with a pretty girl. There are a few girls in his feed, but those are all pictures of several people and look like they were taken at school or parties. I see that Gunnar is not one for selfies and wonder if maybe he really isn't aware of how handsome he is. Most of his pictures are of Reykjavík and the surrounding countryside. Apparently he works as an outdoor guide in the summer, and there are several pictures of him leading tourists through ice caves.

"Well, that'll come in handy," I murmur, wincing as I accidentally tap the heart button to add to a photo's fifty-seven likes.

My first thought is to undo the like and hope that Gunnar isn't paying attention to his notifications, but if he is and I undo it, it's going to be even more obvious that I was creeping through his feed. Swearing at myself for my rookie mistake, I decide to leave the like and just not mention it. At least it was on a picture related to our task at hand. I can play it off if I need to.

I plug my phone into the wall outlet to charge and notice it's after one a.m. Gram said something about getting up at six. Sighing, I roll over and bury my face in my pillow. Gunnar's Instagram pictures scroll through my brain one at a time. As I drift off to sleep, I realize there's something odd about them besides the lack of selfies. I scrolled through about fifty images and didn't see a single picture of Einar.

7

My sleep is restless and filled with dreams of the old woman in the restaurant. In some of them she morphs into a bright-red birdlike creature and catches fire like a phoenix. In others she is just a hunched-over lady in a plain black dress, and it's Gunnar who transforms. In one, we're sitting at the table, our dinners half eaten in front of us, when Gunnar turns to me with an impish smile. His hand caresses my thigh. I lean in to kiss him right in front of Gram and that's when his form starts to change. His pale skin goes red. His body grows in size until the clothes he's wearing are shredded into rags. He's not becoming a phoenix. He's morphing into a giant scaled being, like a mix of human and dragon, with horns and a spiked tail. *Like a demon*, I think, but I'm going to kiss him anyway. His mouth meets mine and at first his touch is soft, gentle. Then his teeth bite straight through my bottom lip.

I sit up suddenly, the heavy duvet falling away. The dream filters back. I lift a hand to my mouth, feeling my lips just to be sure. Exhaling deeply, I press my palm to my chest, as if I could manually pull back on the reins of my galloping heart.

"Rory?" Gram is curled on her side, staring at me. "What is it? Are you okay?"

"Bad dream," I say. "I'm fine."

"You haven't had one of those in a while," she says. "Do you want to talk about it?"

It's funny. Until my grandmother says this, I had somehow forgotten that I ever had bad dreams, let alone on a regular basis. But she's right. When I was nine I went through a period of night terrors where I was convinced I was a secret supervillain who killed people in my sleep. I used to make

Gram and Gramps barricade my bedroom door so that they would wake up if I tried to escape in the middle of the night. Luckily, that was just a phase, and I eventually got over it, thanks to a course of sleeping pills and some helpful suggestions from a child psychologist.

"I'm okay. I'm sorry I woke you."

Gram checks the time on her phone. "It's almost six— time to get up anyway."

"Seriously?" I slide out of bed and go to the window, peeking between the drapes. "It looks like it's three a.m."

"The sun won't rise until ten or so," Gram says. "But glacier trekking in the dark isn't safe, so it will limit the others just like it does us. We should hopefully be able to catch up with them by tonight."

After a quick breakfast of tea and toast, the three of us pack up our belongings and head out to the guesthouse parking lot. The area is completely quiet except for a few blasts of wind whistling through the tree branches and the gravel crunching under our boots. The sky is partially clear, the moonlight illuminating the glimmering layer of frost that's covering almost everything, including the front window of our vehicle.

Gunnar unlocks the back of the SUV, drops his gear on the ground, and mumbles something about getting the engine going. He starts the car, turns on the defroster, and then returns to the back to help Gram and me with our stuff. He's unusually quiet this morning and I'm wondering if being honest with him last night was a mistake.

Gram heads to the front of the SUV, but I linger for a few seconds as Gunnar lifts his backpack into the vehicle and does a little rearranging of our supplies. "We're cool, right?" I ask, wrapping my arms around my middle. Today would have been a good day for the fisherman sweater.

"What?" Gunnar lowers the gate and turns to look at me, his expression partially obscured by shadows.

"You're not…weirded out by me or anything?" I exhale a frosty breath into the early morning air.

His lips twitch. "Why would I be weirded out?"

"I don't know. You just didn't say much during breakfast."

He yawns. "Sorry, I didn't get a lot of sleep last night. Did a little extra research after you ran away, and then I tried messaging Einar and he didn't respond. I'm just hoping he's all right."

"I did not *run away*," I say. Then I add, "Sorry. Sometimes I forget it's not all about me. I hope your brother is okay too."

"Do you two need some help back there?" Gram yells out the side window.

"No. Sorry, we're coming." Gunnar gives me a slight smile. "And, yes, we're cool."

He jogs up to the front of the vehicle and slides behind the steering wheel. I climb into the seat behind Gram, wondering if I made matters even worse by asking if things were okay. I cringe as I replay last night's conversation in my head. No wonder people my age think I'm a freak.

Our tires spin slightly on the slick gravel as we turn out of the guesthouse parking lot and back onto Ring Road. I turn toward the window as I try to put last night out of my mind. It doesn't matter what Gunnar thinks of me. I'm only here for a couple more days anyway, and then I'll never see him again.

As the countryside flies by, the sky gradually begins to lighten. The coast is on the right of us and I catch a few glimpses of the dark blue sea. On the left are hills and mountains, mostly covered with green vegetation. A car passes by going in the other direction and I realize it's the first car I've seen on the road with us all day.

It makes me think about what would happen if someone had an emergency out here. You could wait hours before even seeing another person on this road, and then what if they ignored you and drove past? We're lucky enough to have a vehicle with Wi-Fi, but I'm guessing most people don't have that luxury, and huge chunks of the country have no cell service at all.

We continue along the two-lane highway, passing through a couple of small towns.

Gunnar peeks back at me over his shoulder. "You might want to have your phone ready. We're coming up to Skeiðarársandur."

"What's that?" I ask.

"A black sand desert," Gram answers. "Beautiful but desolate."

We're still probably thirty minutes from sunrise, but there's enough light for me to see what they're talking about. The mountains are still on the left, but everything in front of us is flat and black, save for the occasional tiny stream flowing down from the hills.

"It's like being on the moon or something," I say.

A few flecks of snow hit the front windshield. Gunnar looks up into the rearview mirror and frowns. "Do you know how long that car has been behind us?"

I turn around in my seat. The car is black and nondescript, a four-door sedan. "Sorry, I'm not sure," I say, kicking myself for sightseeing when I should have been staying alert. So much for being the observant one.

He drums his fingertips on the steering wheel. "There's a photo opportunity coming up on the right. They had to replace a bridge on this road. The old one got destroyed in a flood and all that's left are a couple of twisted girders, but the government has made it into a tourist attraction of sorts. Like a piece of modern art. Let's pull over there for a few minutes so you can take some photos." He glances up at the rearview mirror again. "I want to make sure that car isn't following us."

"Who would be following us?" I ask.

"I don't know. I'm probably just being overly cautious."

I turn to look behind us at the black car. It looks like there are two people in the front seat, but I can't make out any details about them. A chill runs up my spine. I remember the online articles Gunnar showed me. Would zealous churchgoers track us across Iceland? If so, to what end?

A couple of minutes later, the bridge appears on the right. If Gunnar hadn't told me what it was, I probably wouldn't have figured it out. It's two twisted pieces of metal, connected in the middle, that have come to rest against a pile of black rocks. From the highway it looks like a giant cross.

Gunnar pulls the SUV off the road, onto a stretch of sand with tire-track grooves in it. We all get out of the vehicle and start walking toward a metal sign with information about the bridge. The sky has gone pink and purple in preparation for sunrise. Snow flurries dance through the air. Along with the stark backdrop of black sand, the whole scene is otherworldly, as if the mangled girders are the remains of a crashed spaceship.

Gunnar spins around and watches as the car that was behind us continues along Ring Road without slowing. His shoulders slump in relief.

As I draw close to what's left of the bridge, I see it's covered with graffiti. One piece has been painted red, and people have carved names and spray-painted words and flowers.

I glance around. Gram is about twenty yards away reading an official display board about the bridge, and Gunnar is just down from me, studying the middle where the girders cross. As I watch, he jumps up, grabs onto a thick, twisted piece of metal, and starts doing chin-ups.

So much for being bad at athletics. At least his biceps are hidden beneath his winter coat. I'm sure they're sculpture-worthy too. Movement in my peripheral vision distracts me and I turn back toward the SUV. A black car is traveling from the opposite direction with its lights off.

The car pulls over in front of ours. It suddenly hits me that this looks like the same car that was behind us a few minutes ago. Two men get out of the vehicle, dressed in puffy black coats with knit caps pulled low almost over their eyes. One of them bends down behind the SUV. I see a glint of silver.

"Hey," I call to Gunnar. "I think those guys might be messing with our tires."

He drops to the ground and turns toward the SUV. "You there," he shouts, running for the gravel parking area. "What are you doing?"

The second man seems to be leaning against the hood of their car. It takes me a second to realize what's happening. "Is that a...crossbow?" I murmur to myself.

It is, and it's pointed at Gunnar. The man loads an arrow and retracts the string.

"Watch out," I scream.

8

Gunnar yells something in Icelandic. He ducks low behind a pile of volcanic rock. Pulling a firearm from under his jacket, he takes aim at one of the guys in black. I don't know what kind of gun he has, but I know enough about the weapons laws here to know it's illegal.

"What are you doing?" I shout. "What's happening?"

"Get down," Gunnar yells at me. "Both of you get down."

I spin around, looking for Gram. She's got her back pressed against the metal sign, a revolver clutched in her hand—yet *another* illegal gun.

As I turn to go to her, something whooshes past my head. An arrow hits the mangled bridge with a deafening clang. I drop to the sand immediately, uninjured but shaking, disoriented by the loud noise. My heart lodges in my throat. *What. Is. Happening?*

"Rory!" Gunnar starts running in my direction, firing shots at the black car over his shoulder. I head for cover next to Gram, crawling on my elbows and knees like a sniper.

"Come on, Rory," Gram says. "Almost there."

I end up ducking under the mangled bridge to make it to safety on the other side of the display board, where Gram is still standing. And then I hear Gunnar make a grunting sound and I know that he's been hit. I peek my head out from behind the display.

"Stay down," he yells. There's an arrow protruding from his shoulder. He's holding it to stabilize the shaft. His fingers are stained with blood.

"Oh my God." I fumble for my phone, but of course there's no service.

"Put it away," Gunnar barks. "I'm fine."

"You're not fine. You're—" My words fall away as my grandmother ducks her head around the side of the display board.

"We can't let them get ahead of us," she mutters. She takes off running toward the side of the road.

"Gram!" I chase after her, terrified that coming here was a horrible mistake, that I'll end up bringing my grandmother home in a coffin. I'm relieved to see that the guys in black have jumped back in their car and are speeding down the road.

Gram plants her feet shoulder-width apart. Bringing the revolver up to her eye, she braces it with her other hand and squeezes off three quick shots. The black car fishtails and drives off the edge of the road, scattering clouds of dust into the air. There's a shriek of metal and a flash of sparks as the driver pulls the car back up onto the pavement. The car disappears around the base of a hill.

"Holy crap. Did you just hit a tire at a hundred yards?" I ask. I knew my grandmother was a crack shot at the range, but I had no idea it translated to high-stress, real-world operations.

She turns to me. "Two tires, if I'm not mistaken." We both look back toward the disappearing black car. "They won't get far driving on the rims. They'll have to stop at some point."

"And, uh, who are *they*?"

"Not sure," Gram says grimly. "But I have my suspicions."

"What if they attack us again?" I ask. My mind is still reeling at the idea of my grandmother shooting at strangers.

"They won't attack us," she says firmly. "They've got bows. We've got guns."

As I start to ask a follow-up question, Gunnar groans loudly.

Gram and I turn to face him. He's sitting with his back against the base of one of the girders. He's yanked out the arrow and shucked off his coat, and he's holding pressure on his wound with his other hand.

We hurry back to his side. "Give me the keys." Gram holds out her hand. "I'll get the first aid kit."

"You can't be serious." My voice is shrill. "He needs a hospital."

"No hospital," Gunnar says between gasps of pain. He tosses my grandmother the keys. "I just need to rest for a few minutes and put a bandage on. It's not that bad."

"Stay with him." With the revolver in her right hand and the keys in her left, Gram turns and heads for the SUV.

"Will you help me get this shirt over my shoulder?" Gunnar's face is sweating, despite the freezing cold, and paler than usual.

"No, I will not. It'll be safer and easier to cut it off once Gram returns with the kit." I grab his jacket and use it to cover him like a blanket.

A gust of wind blows a small cloud of sand in our direction. I turn sharply, squeezing my eyes shut and tucking my chin to my chest. When I turn back to Gunnar, there are flecks of black trapped in the fine hairs on his jawbone. Almost without thinking, I reach up and brush them off with the fingertips of my glove.

"Thanks," he says weakly. "Is it me, or does it seem like it's getting darker outside?"

It's not snowing anymore, but it does seem dimmer than it did when we first arrived. I check my watch—according to what Gram said, the sun should be rising at any moment. A smudge of black off in the distance catches my eye. It looks like a plume of smoke. I peek around the corner of the metal girder for a better look.

"What is it?" Gunnar asks. "What do you see?"

I pause. My brow furrows. "It looks like...a fire," I say finally.

Gunnar peers beyond the edge of the bridge. "Oh no.

This is not good." He yells something in Icelandic at my grandmother, who has just found the first aid kit and is shutting the back of the SUV.

Gram lifts a hand to her eyes and squints into the distance. Then she hops behind the wheel and starts driving in our direction. The vehicle bounces awkwardly across the sand. At least two of the tires have been slashed.

"It's too late," he says. "We need to get under the sculpture, quickly."

I look back at the smoke. It's more spread out now, like a low-hanging cloud. It also looks a lot closer. Fires don't move that quickly.

"What is it?" I ask, my eyes transfixed on the swirling blackness.

"Sandstorm," Gunnar says grimly.

9

Gunnar shimmies under the twisted metal, pressing his back against the pile of black rocks the whole structure is resting on. I crawl under after him, but it's a tight space. He holds my body against his, burying my face in his rib cage.

"Don't turn your head until I tell you," he says.

"Okay." My single word is swallowed up by the fabric of his jacket. I smell the sharp tang of blood and pray that Gunnar was right when he said his wound wasn't that bad.

In seconds the storm is upon us. The wind howls and the metal girder groans above our heads. I can't help myself from sneaking a peek. I turn my head just slightly and end up with a face full of sand. It's everywhere now, blotting out the sky, painting the air around us an inky, endless black.

I turn my face back to Gunnar's chest, press myself tight against him as the storm rages. Sand and gravel-sized pieces of rock pummel my body. The wind blows my hair every which way. Gunnar tightens his grip on me as if he's afraid I might fly away. I hope Gram is safe in the car, that she didn't get out to try to help us.

After a few minutes, the wind goes from a howl to a whistle, and then, finally, just a soft murmur. I dare to sneak another peek. The air is still hung with gloom, but it's not dark anymore.

"Rory?" Gram calls softly to me. "Are you two all right?"

Gunnar releases his hold on me. My arms and legs quiver as I slide out from beneath the sculpture. I lift myself back to my feet and dust off the front of my jacket. I start to brush the sand from my face and hair.

Gram grabs my wrist. "Careful. You might get sand in your eyes. We can clean up in the car."

Behind me, Gunnar has crawled out from beneath the girders. He's hugging his coat to his chest. Black sand speckles his cheeks and jaw.

"Oh, hey. You've got that beard you said the ladies like," I tease.

He laughs, and then groans. "No jokes. Not even bad ones. It hurts to laugh."

"We'll get you fixed up in the car too," Gram says.

I look back and forth from Gunnar to Gram. "I really think he needs to go to a hospital."

"Honestly, Rory. I'm all right," Gunnar says. "There's no time to go back to Reykjavík, and the wound isn't that deep."

"Let me take a look." Gram opens the passenger side of the car and motions for Gunnar to get in. The first aid kit is open on the dash. She goes around to the driver's side and slides in next to him. I get in the second seat and pull the door closed behind me.

"I'm going to call Grandfather first and let him know that we're down two tires." Gunnar pulls his phone out of his pocket. "We've only got one spare, but maybe he knows someone who lives nearby who can lend us either a tire or a vehicle." He taps at the screen and then turns toward the side window of the car.

Gram hands me a towel from the first aid kit. "You can wet this and clean yourself off. Just blot, so you don't get sand in your eyes."

I pour water from my water bottle onto the cloth and hold the damp fabric up to my face. It feels heavenly. My skin is tingling as if I've just had the world's most vigorous exfoliating facial.

Gunnar and Henning are speaking in Icelandic, so I have no idea what they're saying, but it seems to be a heated exchange. Gunnar hangs up the phone and slides it back into the pocket of his coat. "He's upset that we were ambushed, but at this point he agrees we have to keep moving. He's got a friend in Vík who can have a replacement vehicle out to us in two hours or less."

"Well, I guess that leaves us plenty of time to take care of that shoulder then." Gram leans toward Gunnar.

He sighs. "I can't believe we're losing so much daylight. At this rate we won't make it out onto the glacier until tomorrow."

"It's only December 23rd though. So we still have time, right?" I ask.

"Yes, but time has a bad habit of slipping away when you least expect it," Gunnar says.

As I go to rewet the cloth, I sneak a peek at the front-seat proceedings. Gram has snipped away the sleeve and collar of Gunnar's shirt. His shoulder is stained with blood. She squirts a syringe of cleansing saline on it, exposing a dark, circular wound.

I flinch at the red, meaty tissue. "Looks deep."

"It's a clean shot, though." Gram probes the area gently. "No major vessels injured. Already starting to clot."

"And small-caliber tip," Gunnar adds.

I watch Gram work. "Do you want me to get the bleeding kit?" The worst-case-scenario kit includes some special fabric that's infused with thrombin to facilitate quick clotting.

"I don't think we need it," she says. "This isn't as bad as it looks."

"Do you think it was those Church of the Holy Light fanatics?"

Gunnar shakes his head. "They're more the mob and pitchfork type."

I look from Gram to Gunnar. "So then do you really not know who attacked us?"

Gram holds pressure on the wound. "There's a group of people called the Riftwatchers who feel that protecting the doorways to heaven and hell is their personal domain. They've been known to use crossbows in the past. If they saw the social media postings from Black as Death, they would have gone after the band."

I chew on my lower lip. "Okay, but we're not the band."

"No, but it's no secret my brother is close to them. They might have gotten me confused with Einar," Gunnar says. "Or they might have ambushed us just so they could get to Einar and the others first." He winces slightly as Gram lifts her hands from the wound.

"If they shot you with an arrow just to slow us down, what would they do to the others if they found them?" I ask.

"I'm not sure," Gunnar says. "And I don't want to find out."

10

Gram continues to work on dressing Gunnar's wound. She removes a small packet of gauze squares from the first aid kit and peels back the lid. She covers the wound and then wraps his arm with a roll of gauze, adding some strips of tape on top. "That should hold for a while. We'll make sure you're properly treated as soon as we find your brother."

"Splendid. Now I just need a new shirt." Gunnar glances back at me. "Would you grab something out of my pack for me?"

"Me? Okay." I undo the clips and drawstring holding Gunnar's backpack closed and pull the first cloth item I feel out of it, which turns out to be a pair of plaid boxer shorts. "Oh, I'm sorry." I feel my face go red.

"Good taste," he says. "But probably not the best choice to put on at this moment."

I find a black T-shirt and hand it to him. With Gram's assistance, he pulls the soft fabric over his head and shoulders. Then he slides back into his jacket.

"Like it never happened," he says breezily, shaking a couple of ibuprofen into his hand.

"Yeah, whatever." When I was ten, some kids in Thailand shot me with their dad's pellet gun and even that hurt more than Gunnar is letting on right now.

Gram closes the first aid kit and hands it back to me. I replace it in the back of the car next to our other supplies. Gunnar takes a sip of water to swallow the pills.

"I guess now all we can do is wait." Gram mops a bit of blood-tinged saline from the leather seat with a piece of damp gauze.

"But stay alert," Gunnar says. "Just in case those guys try to circle back around."

"Rory and I can keep an eye out," Gram says. "You should try to rest a little. Your body has gone through a trauma."

He opens his mouth to protest but then seems to think the better of it. "All right." He leans back against the passenger-side window, his eyes falling shut.

I watch him from the back seat for a few seconds, relieved to see the tightness fade from his jaw. His long eyelashes flutter. He exhales softly.

"You really think he's going to be okay?" I whisper.

"The wound seems to be clotting normally, and hopefully we'll be back to Reykjavík before infection is a potential issue."

"It seems crazy to risk it."

"I know," she says. "Believe me, if it weren't urgent for us to continue onward, I'd agree that we should take him to a hospital. But this is a manageable injury. His brother and the others are in danger."

I feel like we're all in danger, but I don't respond. If my grandmother thinks we need to continue, then I trust her. I settle back into my seat but scan the horizon repeatedly, looking for anyone—or anything—that might be a threat.

Gram is doing the same thing. To a casual observer, she's just an older lady sitting in a car, but I can see the subtle movements of her head and body as she keeps watch. Her revolver rests on the seat next to her.

Twenty minutes pass without a single car going by. My heart rate slows. I pull out my phone and decide to do a little additional research on the members of Black as Death. Here's what I learn:

Annika Lee's father emigrated from South Korea when he was a baby. He is now the first-chair violinist in the Gothenburg Symphony Orchestra. Her mother works for Ericsson Telecom. Annika got her start in music when her dad taught her to play the violin as a small child. Her parents added piano lessons when she was six. By the time she was ten she had taught herself to play guitar, and by the time she turned twelve it was her instrument of choice. She started her first band, Fatal Kiss, as a thirteen-year-old with some other kids from school. They were invited to play as openers for several heavy metal festivals in Gothenburg, where Annika eventually saw Black as Death play. She connected deeply to the band's sound and music and begged them for a chance to be their guitarist so Lars could focus on vocals. When they agreed, she left Fatal Kiss and moved to Iceland, where she's been living with Lars and working for his family's restaurant ever since.

Ragnar Jóhannsson is a twenty-five-year-old computer programmer who works for FRISK, a local antivirus software company. He grew up on the outskirts of Reykjavík with two older brothers, one of whom became a professional actor and moved to New York. Ragnar started playing bass in high school. He met Lars and Benjamín in a music class at Reykjavík University.

Benjamín Hansson, Black as Death's drummer, is a twenty-four-year-old grad student. He grew up in a family of fishermen but quickly decided that fishing was not for him. He studied physics at Reykjavík University and is now specializing in quantum mechanics. He started playing drums when he was eight and went on to play drums in both high school and college before eventually forming Black as Death with the others.

Lars Pétursson is a twenty-four-year old grad student studying chemistry while also helping out in his family's restaurant, a café located across from Halgrímskirkja. He auditioned for *Icelandic Idol* as a teen and was one of the finalists. After upper secondary school, his musical tastes went from mainstream to metal and he started a band called Nightmare Fuel. This band broke up after the lead guitarist was killed in a car accident and Lars took a break from singing until he later met Benjamín and Ragnar at the university.

I skim through a couple of Black as Death fan pages, comparing the biographical information with what the band has posted on their website, but there are no major differences. One of the sites has a link to an article called "Black as Death Arrest Scandal." I tap the screen to read what it's about. Lars and Annika were out drinking at a bar in Stockholm after a music festival when some tourists tried to hit on Annika and Lars stepped in to defend her. A minor bar fight ensued and Lars was arrested for drunk and disorderly conduct. The tourists tried to press charges for assault, but by the time the police arrived so many people had been hit, they couldn't sort out who the aggressors were. Apparently, drunk people don't make very good eyewitnesses.

Afterward, rumors swirled that Lars and Annika were a couple, but both maintained that their relationship was more that of siblings, with Annika telling reporters point blank, "I worked hard to become part of this band. I would never jeopardize my musical career with something stupid like a romance."

I smile. It sounds like something I might say, that is if I had something in my life I cared about as much as Annika cares about music.

About thirty minutes later, a black SUV and a tow truck pull up behind us. Two men get out of the SUV. One of them knocks on Gram's window.

Gunnar startles awake. He reaches for Gram's revolver.

"I think it's our new ride," I say.

Sure enough, the men say they're friends of Henning's. The three of us get out of the SUV and quickly repack our belongings. The tow truck driver starts to attach straps and chains to the disabled vehicle. Gunnar gives him the keys and we pile into the new SUV. In a couple of minutes we're back on the road and heading toward Hoffell.

"Look." I point ahead as we round a curve in the highway. The black car that presumably belongs to the Riftwatchers sits along the side of the road, both back tires obliterated by Gram's sharpshooting. The vehicle is empty and there's no one around. "I wonder if they had a friend in Vík too."

"I'm glad we slowed them down a little," Gram says.

"Me too." I'm still in awe of my grandmother's shooting skills under pressure. I thought I knew about all her special talents.

When we hit the outskirts of a place called Hof—which Gram says is more like a cluster of farms than an actual town—I offer to switch spots with her so she can have a break from driving. In the passenger seat Gunnar is reclined, his eyes closed, his breathing deep and regular.

"You're really not worried about him?" I ask, as Gram pulls over to the side of the road.

"He'll be all right," she says. "I know a lot of this doesn't make sense to you right now, but I believe Henning when he says this is an emergency."

"So you think there's really a doorway here that leads to hell? I didn't even know you believed in hell."

"Let's just say I'm open to the possibility." She shuts off the engine and turns to me. "But the important thing is to find Einar and get him home safely. If *he* believes there's a doorway to hell and goes through all this trouble to bring his friends there and then it turns out to be nothing, who knows what might happen."

I slide out of my own seat and jog around to the driver's side. "Gunnar said his brother might have burned down a church in Reykjavík . Do you think he's mentally unstable?"

"Perhaps," Gram says. "But I haven't seen him since he was a baby. All I know is that my friend is worried about his grandson and I want to help."

I slide into the driver's seat, being mindful to close my door as quietly as possible so as not to disturb Gunnar. He fidgets slightly but doesn't wake. I watch his eyelashes flutter for a few seconds. There's something delicate about him while he's asleep. I hope he's not in too much pain.

Shifting into drive, I pull the car back onto Ring Road. The vast wilderness of Iceland stretches out around us. The black sand gradually gives way to algae-covered lava, interspersed with patches of reddish dirt and occasional jets of steam billowing up from cracks in the ground. Above our heads a blanket of gray clouds stretches into forever.

"Imagine if you got lost out here," I murmur.

"It happens," Gram says.

We both fall into silence for a while.

My eyelids start to get heavy. I watch a mirage—a glassy puddle—appear on the center of the road and then vanish, only to appear again a few seconds later. Just when I think I'm going to have to turn off the heat and crack my window to keep from falling asleep, Gram says, "So have you thought any more about applying to colleges?"

Immediately my body goes tense. "This again? Can't I at least try my hand at working with you first?" I ask. "Or working *for* you, if you'd rather?"

"Can't you at least try college first?" she counters. "What if you really enjoy it?"

"What if I get kicked out? Seems more likely, given past experience."

A smile plays at Gram's lips. "Then you still tried."

"Why is this so important to you?"

"I just think it could be a good way to get some direction, explore options beyond doing what I do," she says. "Plus, you deserve to have some friends your own age."

"I have Macy," I protest. "And Alannah."

"Alannah is twenty-six and Macy lives in Okinawa most of the year. You deserve some friends you can hang out with."

"Hanging out is overrated."

The truth is, I tried hanging out with friends my own age when I was younger, but it never seemed to end well. I was hanging out in Sydney when I got expelled for underage drinking. I was hanging out in Seattle when Macy got grounded for the first time for trying marijuana. I was hanging out on an island called Koh Pha Nga when one of my classmates, Jessup James, decided to tell everyone I was a manipulative cock tease.

Hanging out is pointless at best, dangerous at worst.

"No man is an island," Gram says.

"I'm not all alone," I insist, angling my head so I can see her. "Do you just not want me to work for you? Is it because you think I'm unreliable or something?"

"No, heavens no," Gram says. "I would love to have you work with me. I just don't want you to settle for that because it's the safe option."

I laugh under my breath. "It's not exactly feeling like the *safe option* right about now."

"You know what I mean," she says.

I don't respond. I'm too tired to have this argument today. I turn my attention fully back to the road. As the sun starts to drop low in the sky, we pass a sign that says *Jökulsárlón 10 km*. I remember Henning talking about how beautiful something is there. "What's Jökulsárlón?" I ask Gram, doing my best not to mangle the pronunciation.

"Ah well, you see the patch of white up there?" She points up in the mountains at a slab of snow.

"Yeah?"

"That's Breiðamerkurjökull, which is a glacier that—"

"Wait. What was that name again?"

Gram repeats the name slowly, sounding out each syllable for me. "Anyway," she continues, "in Jökulsárlón there's a lake filled with pieces that have calved—broken off—from that glacier. The water is a mix of seawater and fresh water, which gives it an amazing color. It's quite possibly the prettiest place in the whole country. We're going to need to fill up on gas, so we might as well make a quick stop. We can grab some food at the same time."

"Sounds good." My stomach has been growling, but I know we lost time due to the sandstorm and the slashed tires, and I didn't want to suggest stopping for food and putting us even more behind schedule. Still, as Gunnar said, we won't get out on the glacier today anyway.

I drive over a bridge and gasp when I see the water below us—it's bright blue, almost turquoise. Chunks of white ice float in the gentle current.

Next to me, Gunnar stirs. He opens his eyes and looks around. "Jökulsárlón! Now you see why Grandfather was adamant we stop here."

Beyond the river lies a large lake filled with the same brilliant blue water. Larger chunks of white dot the surface like sailboats on an ocean. Only there's no wind right now, and the water in the lake is calm and clear enough that each iceberg is perfectly reflected. Henning was right. This is a once-in-a-lifetime photo op.

"It's incredible," I say. "And we're going to pull over for gas and a quick bite to eat."

"Good," Gunnar says. "Now that you mention it, I'm starving."

"How's your shoulder?" Gram asks.

Gunnar slides his arm out of his jacket and tilts his neck down to check out the bandage peeping out from the sleeve of his shirt. "I don't see any blood coming through."

"Glad to hear it," Gram says. "And your pain?"

"It's probably time for some more ibuprofen." He reaches for the bottle from the center console.

I take the exit for Jökulsárlón and turn left toward a small cluster of buildings that Gram tells me is a gas station, a small restaurant, and a tourist office where people can go out on the iceberg lagoon in the warmer months. Unfortunately, the restaurant has a sign that says CLOSED FOR THE WINTER. I pull into the gravel parking lot and park next to one of the gas pumps.

The three of us hop out of the vehicle. Gunnar heads for the gas pump while Gram and I duck into the small convenience store.

A middle-aged clerk greets us in Icelandic. Gram has a short conversation with him while I wander down a row of processed snack foods. Not exactly what I was craving. At the end of the row there's a refrigerated section with some yogurt, granola, and fresh fruit. I pick up a container of yogurt and an apple.

"Rory," Gram calls.

I find her at the back of the store, looking down into a silver kettle.

My mouth waters at the meaty smell. "Is that soup?"

"It's kjötsúpa, Icelandic lamb stew. Probably better from a restaurant than a gas station, but right now it'll do."

I look dubiously at the oily liquid. "Well, it smells good. Definitely the best choice in here."

We each get a small paper container of the stew. I show the yogurt and fruit to Gram, who helps herself to a yogurt too. The front door chimes happily as Gunnar ducks in from outside. "I asked the pump attendant if my brother and the band stopped here recently, and he said he saw them late last night, after 22:00. He's a fan and he recognized Annika Lee right away."

"The cashier said she hadn't seen them, but she was off yesterday," Gram replies. "I can't believe they drove this far last night, especially considering the weather. Let's hope they slept in."

"How long has it been since we've checked their social media?" Gunnar asks.

I pull out my phone and check the Black as Death Instagram feed. There's an image of them posed next to two snowmobiles at the edge of the Vatnajökull Glacier.

Gunnar peers over my shoulder. He frowns. "That image is from 13:00 today. We're going to be almost an entire day behind them. No one will rent us snowmobiles this late."

"Good thing we've got all day tomorrow to catch up," I say.

"Yes, good thing." Gunnar pushes his hair out of his face. His blue eyes are tight with worry.

We bring our food up to the counter and he pays for everything with a credit card. "You sure you don't want anything else? Grandfather doesn't care how much money we spend on food."

"In that case..." I reach toward a chocolate bar displayed next to the register. Just as my hand closes around the wrapper, I freeze. I squint at the small price tag, trying to remember the conversion rate for Icelandic money. "Wait. Is this... almost nine dollars?"

I knew everything in Iceland was expensive but a nine-dollar chocolate bar is next level.

"Hmm." Gunnar picks up the bar and flips it over. "It's a bit pricey because all of the ingredients are organically grown and ethically sourced. No rainforest destruction or child slavery."

"I do like ethically sourced things," I say. "But I don't *need* chocolate."

"Sure you do." Gunnar hands the bar he's holding to the cashier and picks out a second one. "Let's go with one dark chocolate espresso and one sea salt and caramel."

"Well, if you're going to twist my arm," I say with a grin. "I am happy to support a local company on your dime, or in this case dozens of dimes."

The three of us return to the car to eat. The kjötsúpa tastes even better than it smells. The broth is silky smooth and seasoned with just the right amount of herbs. I bite into a hunk of lamb, expecting it to be tough or greasy, but it practically dissolves between my teeth. The same goes for the potatoes and carrots—they're firm enough to hold their shape in the stew, but they melt like butter in my mouth.

"This is one of the best things I've ever tasted," I say.

Gunnar smiles. "I don't think I know anyone in Iceland who doesn't enjoy a hot, steaming cup of kjötsúpa in the winter."

After we've all cleaned our paper containers down to the last drop, Gunnar collects our trash in the paper bag that we got from the store clerk. "Let's take a quick walk by the glacier lagoon so you can see the icebergs up close."

I'm busy peeling back the bronze wrapper on the dark chocolate espresso bar. There's nothing like the perfect dessert to top off the perfect meal. "I don't need—"

"I'm talking five minutes." He looks down at his watch. "We have plenty of time to find a place to stay tonight before it gets completely dark. You should see this because you might never get the chance again."

"Okay." It's cute how much Gunnar loves Iceland and how he wants to show me all the pretty things here. I tuck the candy bar in my pocket and follow him down to the edge of the water. I snap a couple of pictures of the icebergs, which are even more gorgeous up close. I thought they were white from a distance, but now I see that they're translucent. Some of them are tinted blue like the water.

Gunnar motions for me to stand next to him for a selfie. "I need evidence for when I go back to school and tell all my friends I spent part of my holiday with an American girl."

"You're going to tell your friends about me?" My voice rises in pitch.

"Sure." He grins. "I'm going to tell them how you said I was *ridiculously hot.*"

"I have no idea what you're talking about," I say. "Maybe

you heard that in your dreams."

His smile widens. "Right, that must be it."

I imagine him putting this photo on his Instagram account. "Do you have any pictures of you and your brother together?"

"I don't." Gunnar's smile fades. "Einar has never liked having his picture taken, not even with me."

11

At around eight p.m., we reach the turnoff for the Hoffell area, which Gunnar explains isn't an actual town but an expanse of land that is home mainly to farmers, guesthouse owners, and tour operators. Gram has called ahead and reserved two rooms at a small guesthouse a couple of kilometers past the turnoff. She figured if the Riftwatchers are looking for us, it's safer if we don't stay right next to the glacier.

Unsurprisingly, we're the only guests. "You're the first people I've seen all day," the owner says, tossing her wavy black hair back from her face. She's wearing a sweater almost exactly like the one Gunnar bought for me, even though it's plenty warm in here.

"Well, I'm glad you don't close up for the season," Gram says.

"My husband and I live in the side wing so it's no trouble to stay open. I get the occasional winter tourist bus full of people coming out to ride snowmobiles or sit in the hot springs."

"Hot springs?" I perk up. Maybe I can have that night at the spa after all.

"There's a geothermal pool right on the property," she says. "Nice and hot. Go out the back door and right down the incline if you're interested."

I make a mental note to ask Gram more about geothermal pools. I wander around the main room of the inn while she registers us and Gunnar pays for the night. Clusters of wooden pedestals stand in each corner, displaying a variety of painted pottery and carved sculptures. I lean in to read the tiny print on a display card and learn that all of these items are from Greenland.

I lift up what looks like a seal carved out of ivory, admiring the detailed craftsmanship.

"Careful now," the woman says from behind the registration counter. "Those are really fragile."

"Are you from Greenland?" I ask.

"Yes. My father moved us over when I was eight and I've lived here ever since."

The woman gives us each a key and the three of us head to our rooms. I'm sharing with Gram again. The décor is best described as rustic minimalist—or maybe college student on a serious budget. Thin mattresses sit on box springs without bed frames. The only other furniture in the room is a table between the two beds, empty except for a small wooden lamp shaped like an owl.

"I'm going to hop in the shower, unless you want to go first?" Gram says.

"You go ahead."

She ducks into the bathroom. I decide to go next door and check on Gunnar.

"Hey," he says. "Is everything all right?"

"Yeah. I just came to see how you were doing." My eyes scan his room. It's set up the same as mine—two small mattresses on box springs, the table between them. His lamp is shaped like a seal. "Is your shoulder okay?"

He opens the door wider and ushers me in. "Actually, if you wanted to help me out with a sponge bath, that'd be marvelous."

My eyes narrow. "What exactly does—"

He snickers. "I'm joking, but you should see your face."

"Very funny." I pull the door shut behind me. "I still can't believe you got shot with an arrow. How bad does it hurt?"

"A lot," he admits. "Sort of like a cross between stabbing and burning."

"I knew it. And you pretended to be fine all day?"

"I wasn't *pretending*. Mind over matter, you know?"

"Mind over matter is easier said than done," I say. "You're tough."

"Tougher than I look?" He grins.

"Definitely tougher than you look, Icelandic Ken doll," I tease.

Gunnar cocks his head to the side. "Who's Kendall?"

"No. Ken doll. You know Barbie, the doll? Ken is her boyfriend."

"Ah, so you're making fun of me in my time of crisis. Got it."

I shrug. "Well, you know how Americans are."

"Wretched, dreadful people," he says solemnly.

"The worst," I agree.

For a few seconds we just stand there facing each other. Gunnar offering to show me around Reykjavík flashes through my head. Did that conversation even happen? It feels surreal now. I have no idea how we went from talking about the woman at the restaurant to basically flirting.

I pull the other half of the chocolate bar out of my pocket. "Do you want some?"

"No, thanks. I don't have much of a sweet tooth."

"Oh, good. There's that deal-breaker I was looking for last night," I say. "Anyone who doesn't like chocolate is seriously deranged, or perhaps an alien."

"Which am I?" he asks, his lips quirking into a smile.

I pretend to consider the question carefully. "I'm still deciding."

"Let me know when you figure it out."

He strolls across the room and I resist the urge to fixate on the graceful way he moves, the way his hair swishes when he walks, the slight curl of his long fingers. Whoops, maybe I am fixating a little. I swipe at the screen of my phone so he won't see me staring at him in the reflection of the window glass or something. He peers out into the dark for a few seconds and then turns around. "Are you checking out my Instagram feed again?"

"Hardly," I scoff. "I was looking up information on the Northern Lights."

"It's a clear night. Would you like to go see if we can find them?"

"Sure." I slip my phone into my pocket and turn toward the hallway. "Just let me get my jacket and hat."

"Wait." He reaches out and grabs my arm just beneath my shoulder. My muscles tense instinctively. The warmth of his hand is radiating right through my thermal pullover. "I figured we could go for a dip in the pool out back. That way we'll stay warm while we search the sky." He releases my arm and tucks both of his hands in his pockets. "Have you ever been in a geothermal pool? It's very therapeutic."

"I, uh, I'm actually not much of a swimmer." In all my spa daydreaming, it was always me and Gram, not me and Gunnar. Sharing a geothermal pool with a guy feels…intimate.

"Well, it's not much of a pool," Gunnar replies. "According to the owner, it's less than two meters deep. No danger of drowning."

"Says the one of us who is greater than two meters tall," I say pointedly.

"I'm one point nine at best. But we can stay where it's shallow. I don't want to get my bandage wet." He rotates his shoulder around in a circle, grimacing slightly. "You did say you like to try new things, right?"

"I meant new foods." I pat my stomach. "You really think the water is warm enough to keep me from freezing?"

"Yes. You might even find it too hot for your taste." He claps his hands together. "Come on, Aurora. Let's go look for your namesake. The pools are just a few meters from the building. We'll dash and dive."

I clear my throat. "Are you wearing a swimsuit under those clothes?"

Gunnar laughs, more of a guffaw really. As if I've said something especially hilarious.

"What's so funny?"

"You don't need a *swimsuit*. The water is usually cloudy enough to keep all your good bits covered. And you don't have anything I haven't seen before."

I snort. "Oh well, that's a relief."

He laughs again. "You're more than welcome to wear your underclothes, or your jeans and jacket for that matter. I was simply saying that the Icelandic people, of whom you claim to be a descendant, aren't ashamed of their bodies."

"I am *not* ashamed!" I suddenly remember that I'm wearing my least sexy pair of grandma underwear. Okay, maybe I'm a little ashamed of those. "But give me a couple minutes. I'll meet you out there."

"Don't chicken out on me." Gunnar winks and then heads for the hallway.

"Don't worry." I head back to my room and peek in on my grandmother. She's propped up in bed reading something on her phone. The wooden lamp is casting a creepy shadow on the far wall.

"Everything okay?" she asks.

"Yes." I set my backpack on the ground and bend low so she can't see me going through my underwear options. "Gunnar and I are going to check out the geothermal pool. You want to come?"

"Sounds tempting, but I'm going to get some rest. You go ahead. The water feels wonderful on tired muscles." She glances up from the screen. "You know, I've always felt a bit guilty whisking you away from this land as a baby and speaking so ill of it. It's true this country holds horrible memories for me, but for many other people it's a source of great happiness. I'm glad you're getting to experience some of Iceland's joys."

"Well, it's just hot springs or whatever. I'm not sure *joy* is on tonight's schedule." My brain reminds me of the way Gunnar looked last night when he opened the door to his room shirtless, his wet hair dripping over his chiseled chest. Fine, maybe a little bit of joy.

Gram coughs gently, as if she can read my mind. Gah, that would be the absolute worst. "Well, if it should rear its head, all I'm saying is that it's okay to have a good time, even when we're working."

"Thanks, boss," I tell her. I duck into the bathroom and change into a dark blue bra and underwear. It'll work well enough as a makeshift bikini. I put my pants and thermal back on and give myself a quick once-over in the mirror, running my fingers through my hair to smooth out a bit of frizz. My skin has a bit of natural rosiness to it, probably from being out in the wind and cold. *Probably from Gunnar,* my brain informs me. I tell it to shush.

Back in the room, I give my grandmother a little wave. "All right. I'm off to benefit from the therapeutic properties of volcano water or something."

Gram smiles. "Have fun."

12

Fun is not the word that pops into my mind when I step outside. It's cold—breath-seeing, bone-blasting, hide-under-a-blanket-and-read-a-novel-until-spring kind of cold. And I'm still fully dressed.

The back porch leads to a patio with a couple of metal picnic tables that have seen better days. I stride across the concrete and hurry my way down a path of circular stones that ends at the edge of what looks like a miniature pond, only without any kind of vegetation. Steam is rising from the surface, but the water beneath is dark and clear.

"Aurora!" Gunnar waves from the far side of the pool. "Come on in, the water feels tremendous."

"It better," I mutter.

He approaches the edge of the pool, submerged up to the middle of his chest, his bandage hovering just above the water's surface. "Sorry, I didn't catch that."

"I thought you said the water would be cloudy."

He shrugs. "Sometimes it is, sometimes it isn't. Depends on the minerals. But come on, it's plenty dark out." He gestures to his own body. "I mean, you can't see anything, can you?"

My eyes flick low for a second, my cheeks coloring immediately.

"Don't panic. I left my briefs on so I wouldn't offend your delicate sensibilities."

"How thoughtful," I say. "All right, I'm getting in. Turn around."

"I thought you weren't ashamed of your body."

"I'm not. But that doesn't mean I'm going to show it to just *anyone*."

"Fair enough." Gunnar makes an elaborate swish of the water as he spins around so his back is to me. He lifts his hands up to cover not just his eyes but his whole face.

I untie my shoes and step out of them. Then I hurriedly peel off my jeans and thermal. After doing a quick check to make sure everything that needs to be covered is covered, I slide into the dark water, swallowing back a scream at the shocking change in temperature.

"Does that bird sound mean you're finished and I can turn around?" Gunnar's voice is as musical as ever.

I lower my body so that I'm kneeling on the bottom of the pool and only my head and neck are exposed. "It wasn't a *bird sound*. It was shock. You didn't tell me this water was a million degrees."

"I did tell you it was quite warm." He still has his hands over his eyes. "It's about thirty-eight degrees. I'm not sure what that works out to in Fahrenheit."

"Well, lucky for me I was raised in countries that use the metric system, so I know exactly how hot thirty-eight degrees is and holy crap that's hot." I splash a handful of water in Gunnar's direction. "You can look now, dummy."

He drops his hands and turns around. He starts moving in my direction.

I submerge myself all the way to my chin. "How do you know if the water gets *too* hot?"

"If your skin starts blistering or you smell burned flesh, it's time to get out."

"What?" I know he's messing with me, but I lift my arms out of the water to check them anyway—they're red, but no blisters.

"Kidding," he says. "Are you always so…tightly wound?"

"Just on days when someone tries to impale me with an arrow."

"If it makes you feel better, I'm fairly certain they were only aiming for me." Gunnar leans his head back and wets his hair so that it falls like a pair of smooth blond curtains across both shoulders. He checks his bandage to make sure it's still dry.

"That does not make me feel better," I snap. But even as the words escape my lips, I realize they're not true. I'm becoming used to the heat now. It's enveloping me like a warm blanket. "I can't believe you're so blasé about what happened. Have you been shot at before or something?"

"I have not," he says. "It was terrifying, but I'm all right now, so I'd rather focus on finding my brother." He pauses. "And since we can't do much of that at the moment, I'd rather focus on enjoying the night."

"Makes sense."

Gunnar moves away from the edge of the pool and I follow him, rising from my knees to my feet. He's right that it's not too deep for me to be able to touch the bottom. The water laps against my skin as I pass through a cooler pocket.

"Why is it hotter in some places than others?" I ask. "And do not tell me it's because you peed."

"It has to do with where the actual geothermal vents are located." Gunnar's form is hazy in the steam rising off the surface. "But also I peed a little."

"Gross." I use my arms to propel myself through the water after Gunnar, who is heading to the far side of the pool. "Where are you going?"

He stops next to a floating pallet of wood on the other side of the pool—almost a miniature dock. "So what do you think?"

"It's pretty nice." I lean my arms across the wooden pallet. "What is this for?"

"Probably a place for people to put their drinks."

"They've thought of everything." Turning around, I rest my neck against the wood so my body can float. My toenails peep through the surface of the water, but my feet quickly grow cold so I resubmerge them.

Across the pool an underground vent sends a jet of steam into the air. Holding tight to the wooden pallet with my hands, I lean back and let the warm water heat up the back of my head. I scan the sky, hoping for the Northern Lights, but all I see is darkness, punctuated by a thousand tiny pinpricks of light. I sigh happily. "This is incredible."

"It is," Gunnar says. "I thought I might have to dare you to get in."

I think back to the time a girl in Vietnam dared me to pick up a wild monkey. Eight stitches, and my left thumb still feels tingly on occasion. And then the guy in Australia who dared me to jump from the roof of our building onto the next roof. That dare scored me a severely sprained ankle and a week's worth of walking on crutches. If you've ever seen other kids with crutches and been jealous of the attention they get and the way they can be late to every class, let me inform you that it's not worth it. My armpits ached for weeks, in ways I didn't even know armpits could hurt.

I made the jump, though.

"I have been known to take dares," I say. "Though after the last one I promised my gram I would stop." I return to my feet so I can look Gunnar in the eye. He's leaning back against the wooden pallet, one hand fiddling with the medallion he wears around his neck. "What is that?" I point at the chain.

"St. Benedict." He holds the medallion out in my direction. "It's supposed to have protective powers. My grandfather had them made for the three of us after my parents died."

"So you guys are really into protective amulets and stuff?"

"You could say that."

"Sometimes I wish I believed in something like that. Even if it isn't real, just having faith could be a sort of placebo effect."

"What *do* you believe in?" Gunnar asks softly.

"My gram, mostly. And myself."

"It's good to believe in yourself." He looks past me, out into the dark countryside.

"I'm sorry," I say. "I didn't mean to make you think about your parents."

"It's okay. I barely remember them. I was just a baby when they died."

I move closer to him. "What happened?"

"They got swept away in a massive avalanche. It was so big it buried an entire village, killed almost a hundred people."

"Wow. Does that happen a lot here?"

"Not as much these days. A few years ago, a company created these metal barriers that serve as avalanche guards. They catch the snow on dangerous slopes before it can engulf whole towns." He pauses. "It can still happen if you live far out in the countryside, though."

"It must have been hard for you and your brother, growing up without your parents."

"It was." His eyes meet mine. "I figure you understand the loneliness. Henning told me that your mother died in childbirth."

"She did."

"And your father?"

"My father is…unwell. We've never really had a relationship." A shiver moves through me. I duck lower in the water so that only my face is uncovered. "How exactly does one get out of a pool like this without freezing to death?" I ask, eager to change the subject.

"As quickly as possible," Gunnar says. "Are you wanting to get out already?"

"Not necessarily. Just thinking ahead."

"The only answer I have is that you wrap up in the biggest towel you can find and run like hell back to the guesthouse."

"I knew there was something I forgot to bring with me."

Gunnar chuckles. "I didn't bring a towel down either. I

guess we'll have to freeze together. But hey, don't let thinking about the future keep you from enjoying the present."

"Good point." I inhale a deep breath of air, lean back, and look up at the stars again. A greenish light peeks out from behind the dark silhouette of a faraway mountain range. I lift one arm out of the water and gesture at the sky. "Is that the Northern Lights?"

"It sure is." Gunnar points lower to the horizon. "You can see them even brighter over there."

The pulsing blue-green light arcs like a rainbow. I trace the path with one finger. A second stream of pale green spills across the night, this one vertical, like a thin plume of cigarette smoke. "Wow. I had no idea."

"Not too bright tonight, at least not yet. Sometimes it's like the sky is awash with green fire. Occasionally you can see other colors too—reds or purples—but I mostly see green. It's rare to see them at all in Reykjavík because of all the ambient light." He pauses. "You know what they are, right?"

"Particles from solar flares hitting other particles in the Earth's atmosphere," I say.

"I like the Viking explanation better than the scientific one."

"Oh yeah? What did the Vikings think?"

"I've heard a couple of different things. One is that the Vikings believed the Northern Lights were reflections of the Valkyries' armor as the bravest among them traveled to Valhalla to help Odin prepare for Ragnarök, which was a big end-of-the-world battle. Other stories say the Aurora was the final breath of brave soldiers who died in combat."

"Those *are* better explanations." I look up at the sky again. "Man, they're so pretty!"

"They are." Gunnar brushes a lock of hair back from my face. "I know you like Rory, but the name Aurora, it suits you."

My body goes tense at the gentle pressure of his touch.

Why am I so...affected by him? *Because he's hot.* Okay, but besides that. We're close now, close enough for me to see his perfect cheekbones and the soft blue of his eyes, close enough to see the tiny grooves in his lips. If I were to imagine the perfect place for me to have my first kiss (by which I mean my second first kiss, because the full-moon party on Koh Pha Nga where I drank something that turned out to be more than just fruit punch and sucked face with Jessup James, who I was friends with but absolutely not interested in, does not count), it would totally be here, in the warmth of a natural pool, underneath a sky filled with glowing ribbons of light.

With Gunnar.

It's both unprofessional and irresponsible for me to want to lock lips with a client's grandson, but I want to. And unless the stew we had for dinner was spiked with cheap rum like the fruit punch from Koh Pha Nga, it's not because I'm drunk. Also, the way Gunnar is looking at me makes me think he feels exactly the same as I do.

But all he does is look.

So maybe he's shy. I remember something Alannah told me about shy boys: that they fall into two groups. Half of them want girls to make the first move, and the other half want girls to make the first move, but in a way that makes the guy think that *he* made it.

As I'm trying to decide which of these descriptions fits Gunnar, he lets out an epic belch. "Sorry." He grins. "I blame the kjötsúpa."

Or maybe he's *not* shy. Maybe I'm just drunk on hormones and misreading the situation. "Aurora suits me, huh?" I say, keeping my voice light. "Is that some roundabout way of telling me I'm pretty?"

"Maybe. In a traditional, socially acceptable kind of way, of course." Gunnar chuckles to himself. "Truthfully, I find you compelling. You have a...strong presence."

"Strong presence sounds like something my grandmother would say. In fact I think she has said it."

"Well, it's decided then."

"So wait. I'm *not* pretty?" I scrunch my face into a pretend pout.

"I was trying to say that you're *more* than pretty. Are all American girls so needy?" His eyes flash with amusement.

I smirk. "Are all Icelandic boys utterly incapable of saying what's on their minds?"

Instead of responding, Gunnar leans toward me. I swallow back another teasing retort, focusing on the seriousness of his expression. We exhale at the same time, the fog of our breath mingling in the cold night. I look up at the Northern Lights, trying to imprint this moment on my brain—not just the sky, but every sensation: the warmth of the water, the chill on my skin, the sharp stillness all around us. And Gunnar, looking at me like I matter—like I'm important to him.

I lift one hand to his shoulder and drag my fingertips just below the edge of his bandage. Touching him sends another rush of desire through me. I think back to this morning, our bodies pressed together under the sculpture. I hunger for that closeness, but I also have no idea what I'm doing right now. What is the protocol here? Am I allowed to kiss him? Am I supposed to ask him to kiss *me*? What if I mess things up between us? What if I mess up this entire trip?

Gunnar watches me closely, his eyes full of questions.

"Is it still hurting a lot?" I say finally.

"Sometimes," he says. "But you were doing an excellent job of distracting me there for a while."

"Sorry." I look away. "I got scared for a second. This whole day has been so scary, you know? I think Gram and I might be in way over our heads."

Gunnar shakes his head. "You are the perfect people for this."

"Why do you think that?"

"Because you're skilled hikers with tracking experience," he says. "And I trust my grandfather's judgment." His lips curl into a grin. "Plus, you've got me to help."

I reach out and splash warm water at him playfully. "Help? You're just the chauffeur."

"Take it back!" He grabs me around the waist and pretends as if he's going to dunk me. "Take it back or drink the sulfur water."

I squirm in his embrace and try to get away, but not really, because if this is the only kind of touch I can get, I will take it and enjoy it. I lift my chin, turn my face toward his. Our breath is melding together again. His eyes are still bright with playfulness. But then he loosens his grip on my body and lifts one hand to the side of my face.

I turn my head so my lips are against his palm and give it the gentlest kiss, so gentle he might not even have noticed.

"Rory," he says quietly, drawing his hand away.

Whoops. So much for not noticing. "I'm sorry," I say.

"Stop apologizing." Gunnar wraps his good arm around my ribs and pulls me into a loose hug. I extend it probably longer than I should because I can't remember the last time anyone has held me like this. Even Gram only hugs me on special occasions. It's weird to go through life hardly ever being touched. It's…lonely. Maybe Gram and I will recover the pentacompass and return to Paris and then head back to the States and I'll never see Gunnar again. I know that's how it usually works when you meet someone on a trip. But maybe there could be something more between the two of us. Gram did say I should explore all my options so… I reach out and trace the silver chain of Gunnar's pendant with one fingertip, his chest muscles tightening under my soft touch. I tilt my head back to look up at him.

He rests his chin against my forehead. "We should go inside. There's something I need to talk to you about."

"An inside conversation, huh?" That can't be good.

"There are some things I need to show you as well."

There are definitely a few things I'd like Gunnar to show me right about now, but I can tell by the tone of his voice that the romance is over for the night. "Lead the way."

He moves gracefully through the water. I follow behind him at a slightly slower pace, keeping my feet on the bottom of the pool as much as possible. He waits for me at the edge. When I draw close, he leans in to brush a damp strand of hair out of my eyes. He gives me a gentle peck on the forehead. My brain informs me that this absolutely counts as a kiss. Strangely, it feels more intimate than the tongue in throat action I got from Jessup James three years ago. *Maybe because you actually like him.*

But that's crazy. I can't *like* him. I barely know him.

13

Gunnar is kind enough to run up to the guesthouse in his underwear and grab a towel for me while I wait at the edge of the water. It's hard to argue with that voice in my brain telling me I like him when he does stuff like that. Not that it's that big of a deal, but it's just the right-size deal, if that makes sense. I've never been a fan of grand gestures—those are red flags, like someone is compensating for something. All I want is for people to accept me and care about me, at least a little. And okay, if someone wants to freeze their butt off getting me a towel so I don't have to turn blue alongside them, I guess I want that too.

I decide to return the favor by making Gunnar some tea once we're both safely inside and wrapped in the fluffiest towels he could find. I put the kettle on and pace back and forth in the kitchen, checking out all of the spices and browsing through a cookbook full of soup recipes. It's in Icelandic, so I can't read any of it, but the photos make my mouth water.

When the tea is ready, I fetch a couple of mugs from a cabinet. Gunnar and I sit across from each other at the dining room table.

"What a night," he says finally.

"Yeah, it was...fun."

He sips his tea. "You say that like fun is a new concept for you."

"No. My gram and I have fun all the time. We were actually baking Christmas cookies when she got the call from your grandfather." I lift my mug to my mouth and blow on it gently before taking a drink. The warm liquid floods through my insides, making me think of that initial moment when I went from the frigid air into the geothermal pool.

"What about friends?"

"What about them?"

"What sort of fun do you have with your friends?"

"I only have one friend and she lives in Japan." I regret the words as soon as I say them, but I don't want to lie to Gunnar. Lying should be reserved for critical moments, not for something trivial like saving face.

He arches an eyebrow. "Only one friend?"

I shrug. "I told you people my age don't like me."

"I know. I'm just not sure if I believe you." He leans back in his chair. "Maybe it's because you don't try."

"How would you know whether I try?" My right hand grips the handle of my mug so tightly I'm worried it might snap off in my palm.

"Sorry, I didn't mean to upset you."

He's right. I am upset. Angry. The sensation rose up in me out of nowhere, and I take a few seconds to experience it, explore it a little like my therapist recommended, rather than react instinctively. It's like a knot in my chest, a tangle of wet rope where my heart should be. Gunnar is also right that I don't try. But what he doesn't know is that I used to try. Too hard, maybe, because it never worked.

"It's fine. Please go on." I struggle to keep my voice even. My fingernails dig into the palms of my hands.

"All I'm saying is that when I first met you, your energy was kind of...guarded," he says. "Maybe *other people* don't try...because they're afraid to."

"Yeah, well, I'd rather they be afraid than treat me like crap."

"Makes sense." He sips his tea. "But it's hard to be open to friendship if you're expecting everyone to treat you like crap."

I clear my throat. "I feel like I've been pretty open with *you*."

"You have. But I sense that I'm an anomaly."

I don't say anything at first, because he's right again. I've given him more attention in two days than I've given any other person my age besides Macy in the past year. Then I narrow my eyes at him. "Did you bring me inside just so you could lecture me about my personal failings?"

"No," he says. "You're right. I'm sorry. This is not my business. And it's definitely not what I wanted to talk to you about. Wait here. I'll be right back."

Gunnar heads upstairs and comes back a few minutes later, dressed in pajama pants and a long-sleeved T-shirt. He's carrying a leather-bound book in his hand. The serious look on his face makes the hairs on the back of my neck stand up.

"Are you going to let me read your diary?" I joke.

He slides back into the chair across from me. "It's actually the Riftwatcher manual."

"Seriously? How do you have that?"

"Henning used to be a member, a long time ago."

"Is it weird to you that he believes in stuff like demons?"

"No," Gunnar says. "I know you think this is all family folklore or superstitious nonsense or whatnot, but…it's real. I need you to understand that it's real."

I arch an eyebrow. "*What* is real?"

"*Demons* are real. A lot of people might be in danger if my brother and his friends open that doorway."

He pushes his mug of tea to the side and lays the book on the table between us. The cover is branded with what I'm assuming is the Riftwatcher insignia, a stylized R overlaid across a telescope.

I study Gunnar carefully for a moment, looking for any hint that he's putting me on, that he's going to laugh and call me gullible if I decide to take him seriously. "So you believe there's a doorway to hell located at the bottom of a volcano that's buried under a glacier?"

"Yes."

"So you've…seen this?"

"No. But I know my brother was possessed by something not of this world. I saw that."

"You saw what?"

"I saw the demon in him. I saw it manifest. I saw its strength."

I snicker. "Come on, man. You're messing with me, right?"

"I'm not." Gunnar's jaw tightens. "At least let me show you a few things before you close your mind completely."

Ouch. "Okay. I'm sorry." I hold up my hands in mock surrender. "Show me the book."

He unties a strand of rawhide and opens the Riftwatcher manual. "The first chapter is the biblical folklore. Riftwatchers are Christians. They believe demons are fallen angels that God banished to hell at the time of the Great Flood. According to their research, all demons are stronger than humans, but they also possess different powers depending on the type of angel they were prior to the fall."

Gunnar points at a short list of bold printed words. "The major types of demons include dream-walkers, mind-readers, telekinetics, persuaders, and destruction demons."

"What is Einar?" I ask.

"A mind-reader," Gunnar says. "As far as I know." He flips back a few pages in the book. "Here's a list of famous figures from history who were confirmed as possessed at some point in their lives."

I scan the list. Several of them are historical dictators, familiar to me from my homeschool studies—everyone from Julius Caesar to Mussolini to Idi Amin. There are also political figures like Machiavelli and Rasputin that I could see being possessed. But some of the names come as a complete shock. "Joan of Arc?" I protest. "But she wasn't evil."

"The Riftwatchers suspect that Joan of Arc was possessed by a powerful persuader. Not all demons present as evil. They're chaotic and self-serving, but some of them are just impulsive. And they're eager for new experiences, especially ones where they can witness a variety of human emotions."

"I'm not sure I'd describe Joan of Arc as self-serving either," I say. I find another unlikely name on the list. "Amelia Earhart?"

"The Riftwatchers believe she didn't die on her voyage— she just used it as a way to escape her life."

I can tell by the tone of Gunnar's voice that he believes it too. Of course the first guy I've ever been seriously attracted to believes Amelia fricking Earhart was possessed by a demon. It's like falling for a conspiracy theorist, only worse.

"Okay, so this is all very interesting, and let's say I believe you. Is there anything in this book that can help us? How do we protect ourselves against demons? How do we fight them?"

Gunnar flips to a different section of the book. "Defense against demons includes protective spells, enchanted items, circles of iron, and holy water. The recommended plan when you're facing an angry demon is to flee, if possible. But my handgun has iron bullets and the rifle I brought shoots cartridges of holy water."

I shake my head. "I'm trying to be open minded but it all sounds completely insane to me."

"I understand. I wouldn't be such a strong believer myself if I hadn't witnessed Einar's behavior firsthand while he was possessed."

"*Was* possessed? As in past-tense?"

"Yes, he underwent an exorcism."

"And it was successful?"

Gunnar nods. "As you probably know, there are two parts to an exorcism—casting out the demon and banishing it back to hell. Neither part is easy, but there have been cases where practitioners successfully completed the first part and failed at the second part."

"Meaning they left a pissed-off demon roaming around without a body?"

"Essentially," Gunnar says. "In order to prevent that, most responsible exorcists prepare a backup entity to force the demon into. This is often a cat or a bird, because demons are naturally drawn to these animals, and once inside the new body, the exorcist can control the demon by controlling the animal."

"The cages in your living room," I say. "Are they—?"

"Yes. My grandfather is the one who performed Einar's exorcism. The empty cage held a raven that he used as a failsafe during the ceremony. Einar's demon ended up in the bird."

"Henning told me the bird had been released."

"We're not sure what happened. She was locked securely in the cage. Grandfather thinks Einar set the demon free into the streets of Reykjavík."

"And you?" I prompt.

"I think Einar let the raven go, but kept the demon for himself."

14

Kept the demon. Why would he—?"

Gunnar drops his chin. "It's a sad story, but the gist is that Einar was seeing a girl who started to pull away from him. He really liked her and thought maybe it was the demonic presence inside him that was repelling her. He was willing to risk his life if it meant she would give him another chance."

"So he got the exorcism and then she ditched him anyway?"

"Exactly." Gunnar sighs. "Apparently she told him he should try to be more like me."

"Ugh," I say.

"Indeed. He's never confirmed that he let the demon back into his body, but there'd be no reason to let the bird go otherwise. When I asked him about it, he said it was none of my business, but that I had no idea what it was like to go from being 'a powerful freak' to 'just a freak.'"

"Double ugh."

"Right. I should have been more supportive of him when he was struggling. I should have been more supportive of him my entire life, but I always felt this distance between us, and it didn't go away after the exorcism. Maybe I was blaming it on the demon, but it was me."

"You shouldn't blame yourself—"

"Shouldn't I?" Gunnar cuts me off. "When Grandfather told Einar the truth, he acted like it was no big deal. Some part of me had to recognize he was devastated, but I just nodded and went back to my studies when he said he was fine. And after the whole issue with the church fire, I was relieved when he told us he wanted an exorcism, even though I knew doing it for a girl was a bad idea. I just wanted my twin brother to be normal," he finishes bitterly. "As if that's even a real thing."

"Did he start acting differently after the bird disappeared?"

"It's hard to know," Gunnar says. "By this time, he had already befriended Lars and the others. He spent more and more time with them and less with us."

"That is a sad story," I murmur. I'm still not sure how much of it I believe, but I can tell this is all real for Gunnar. His eyes look so wounded that I decide it's time to change the subject. "I appreciate you sharing all this with me, and I promise to take things more seriously from now on." I gesture at his shoulder. "How's your pain?"

"It's not too bad, but I'm definitely going to need a dressing change in the morning."

"I could help you now," I offer, not wanting this night to be over. "I watched Gram bandage your wound earlier today."

"You don't mind?"

I shake my head. "If you get the first aid kit from the car, I'll throw on some pajamas and be right back."

I run upstairs and change into a pair of sweatpants and a long-sleeved shirt. By the time I get back to the dining room, Gunnar has removed his shirt. His bandage is damp with pinkish-red fluid.

He watches me closely as I loosen the tape around his shoulder and remove the soiled gauze. The wound has scabbed over, but the skin around it is puffy and red. I open a tube of antibiotic ointment and smear some across the surface. He flinches slightly as I rub the goo on his skin.

"Sorry, I'm trying to be gentle."

"You're doing fine," he says. "I'm just a sensitive man-baby, or that's what the girls at school would say."

I open a package of gauze and cover Gunnar's wound

with the soft white squares. "I think I might like to meet these girls. They sound awesome."

"I think you'd all get along. You're almost as mean as they are."

"Almost?" I scoff. "Them's fighting words."

He whistles under his breath. "You trying to fight me when I'm injured?"

"Nah. I need at least a little bit of a challenge. I mean, come on." My lips quirk into a smile. The knot in my chest loosens a little. I'm relieved that Gunnar and I have found our way back to joking around. "Hold that in place so I can reinforce it." I layer some rolled gauze on top of the gauze squares, then wrap the shoulder with tape.

"Not bad." He moves his shoulder from side to side. Then he says, "Hey, I'm sorry about earlier. Sometimes I overthink things."

"What do you mean?"

"I felt like it wouldn't have been right to kiss you without being upfront about my beliefs. But maybe all I did was wreck the moment."

"Oh, you think we had a *moment*?" I tease.

"Arrogant, I know." His lips twitch. "Maybe when this is over, if you want, you and your gram can stay in Reykjavík until New Year's and I can kiss you properly."

"Or improperly." I arch my eyebrows playfully.

Gunnar blushes hot enough that I can almost feel the heat radiating off him. Gah, when it comes to keeping it professional, I am completely striking out.

"Sorry," I say quickly. "I don't even know what I meant by that."

He coughs. "I have some thoughts, but I'm going to keep them to myself for now."

I smile. "You should know that Gram and I are planning to have New Year's Eve in Paris. Not sure New Year's Eve in Reykjavík would measure up."

"Challenge accepted," he replies. For a moment neither of us speaks. Part of my brain is telling me it's crazy to like someone I've just met, someone who believes in demonic possession. Another part is telling me that I do, in fact, like Gunnar. "We should probably try to get some rest," he says finally.

"Right. Long day tomorrow," I agree, a little disappointed but also relieved. I remind myself that I'm trying to behave in a way that will encourage Gram to hire me. Whatever is or isn't going to happen with Gunnar can wait until we find his brother.

The two of us rinse out our cups and head for the stairs. Gunnar gives my shoulder a gentle squeeze as we reach the door to the room I'm sharing with Gram.

"Thanks, Rory," he says, "for the bandage change and for listening. I know it all sounds crazy and there are more details that might help explain things better, but it's not all my story to tell."

"I understand," I say. "I'm trying to anyway." I'm not sure whether more details would change anything, to be honest, but I respect the fact that he's concerned about his brother's privacy.

"I'll see you tomorrow."

I turn to him, my body aching to give him a hug, possibly more than a hug. Instead, I hold back. "Goodnight, Gunnar," I say softly. I slip into the dark room and close the door behind me, my mind awash with emotions.

15

The next morning we pack up our things and bid our hostess farewell, or *bless* as they say in Icelandic. The snowmobile rental place is about a mile down the road, so it takes us only a few minutes to get there. The parking lot is empty and there are no lights on in the building. There's a piece of paper taped to the outside of the glass front door.

"Maybe he's opening late." Gunnar puts the car in park and jogs across the lot. He's back about thirty seconds later. "Bad news. The shop is closed until December 27th."

"So there's no one who will rent us a snowmobile?" I ask. "Should we just break in?" My eyes scan the surrounding area, looking to see if there are any nearby houses.

"We could," Gunnar says. "We could borrow one and have it back before anyone even noticed. I'm not sure if they keep them full of gas or not, but we—"

"I have a different idea, one that doesn't require felony theft. And bonus, it's better for the environment." Gram points at a billboard just down the road. It's a picture of dogs—a whole pack of them. Even if the printing weren't in English, I'd be able to figure this out.

"Dogsledding!" I exclaim. "Do you think they'll be open?"

"Only one way to know for sure." Gram winks.

"Excellent idea, Ingrid," Gunnar says. "Let's pay them a visit."

The three of us pile back into the SUV. I tap both of my feet against the floorboard as we drive. Dogsledding sounds way more fun to me than snowmobiling and there's also probably less chance of us getting into a wreck.

When we arrive at the dog farm it's still dark outside, but

warm lights glow through the windows of a small cottage. A sign on the front door reads: DOGSLED TOURS: IN-QUIRE INSIDE.

Bells jingle from the top of the door as the three of us step into a cozy little room with pictures of dogs and dog-sleds on the walls. One side of the room offers sweatshirts, socks, books, and postcards for sale.

A woman in a brown dress and a headscarf appears from a back room. "Hello. I'm Taslima," she says in softly accent-ed English. "I wasn't expecting any tourists until after the holiday. Did you want to book a dogsled ride?"

"We were actually wondering if we could pay someone to take us up on the glacier," Gunnar says. "We're looking for some friends of ours. They headed out on a trek yesterday and we're worried they might be in trouble. We can pay dou-ble your hourly rate."

The woman's dark eyes widen slightly. "The dogs can only go so far on the glacier. After that, the terrain gets uneven and dangerous for them. I don't mush myself, but my daugh-ter could take you about three kilometers out."

"That would be a great help," Gunnar says. "Would it be all right to leave our car parked in your lot for a night or two?"

"That would be fine," Taslima says, "as long as you're back around for it in the next couple of days. I'll let Nasrin know you're here so she can start getting the dogs ready. I imagine you have some gear to bring along?"

"We do," Gunnar says. "Give us a few minutes. We'll get everything packed up and organized."

"Bring it directly around the back. There's a gate in the southeast corner of the yard." She points off to the right. "Oh, and you'll want to dress very warmly, with hats and face masks if you have them. We can provide eye protection."

"Eye protection?" I ask.

"For the wind and snow," she explains.

"Oh, I see."

Gram, Gunnar, and I head back outside. The sun is just starting to creep over the horizon, fading the black sky to a deep blue. Gunnar opens the back of the SUV and pulls out our packs. He sets mine and Gram's on the ground. He opens his own pack and starts adding things from the vehicle, including what looks like a tent and the padded rifle case.

I unbuckle the top of my pack and loosen the drawstring. I decide to trade the fleece I'm wearing under my winter jacket for the red and gray Icelandic sweater. Time for that monstrosity to earn its keep.

Gunnar smiles when he sees me putting it on, but he doesn't say anything.

"Let me take some of that gear." I hold out my hands. "I can carry more." It won't be easy, but I don't feel right letting Gunnar haul our heavy load, especially considering his injury.

"It's all right. I can manage. And you'll both need one of these." He hands us each a small sleeping bag and a bungee cord so we can lash it to the bottom of our packs. Then he pulls a long black rope and a pair of climbing harnesses from a duffel bag and adds them to the top of his pack.

"You're sure you don't want help with any of that?" I gnaw at my bottom lip as I watch him cinch his overstuffed pack tight.

"I'll let you know if it gets too heavy," he says. "Oh, I almost forgot." He reaches into the back of the SUV one more time and retrieves three helmets, each with a built-in headlamp. "We'll need these for the glacier. Might as well put them on for the sled ride just in case."

"Why do we need helmets to walk on a glacier?" I hate wearing a helmet—it messes up my hair and makes my forehead all sweaty.

"Because there's always a danger of falling and cracking your skull," he says. "And once we're in the caverns, we'll need to watch out for ice falling from above our heads."

"Fair enough." I hate head injuries even more than fore-head sweat and bad hair.

I slide my helmet on and adjust the size so it fits comfortably over my winter hat. I snap the strap under my chin. Gram and Gunnar do the same. Then the three of us head around to the back of the house. There's a tall wooden fence blocking the view of the kennels, but Taslima stands at the gate. We go through one at a time, careful not to let any dogs escape.

It turns out there's a second set of fencing back here— chain link that is taller than me—keeping the dogs in their enclosures. There are four separate areas, each with a big wooden doghouse. The frozen ground is littered with bones and chew toys. Most of the dogs are up and running around, excited at the thought of an excursion.

My jaw drops a little. "There are so many!"

"We have sixteen dogs right now," Taslima says. "With a litter of pups on the way."

About half of the dogs are white and fluffy, like the ones you see in movies about dog sledding. The others are a mix of different colors and breeds.

A younger woman wearing coveralls and snow boots is untangling a mess of ropes and dog harnesses on the far side of the yard. Behind her sits a sleek and modern sled.

"Come. I'll introduce you to Nasrin." Taslima starts to cross the yard.

The three of us follow her, staying on the outside of the kennels. The dogs continue to trot around, shooting us curious glances. I bounce up and down on my toes. I've never been in a place with so many animals. I want to pet every dog here.

Nasrin looks to be in her early to mid-twenties. Her skin is a soft brown, like her mother's. A thick black ponytail protrudes from the bottom of a bright blue snow hat.

Taslima speaks to her softly in what I think is Arabic.

Then she tells her our names and that we're looking to go out on the glacier.

"Pleased to meet you," Nasrin says, looking from Gram to Gunnar to me. "Is there a special reason you want to go out there today? The weather report says there's a chance of snow. It could be an uncomfortable journey."

"We're looking for my brother," Gunnar says. "He and some friends headed out yesterday without proper gear and I just want to be sure he gets back safely."

"I see. It's frightening how many people go glacier hiking without the necessary equipment." Nasrin considers our oversized backpacks. "It looks like the three of you came prepared. I should have just enough space for your gear."

Taslima fishes a cell phone out of the pocket of her winter coat. "I need to make a call, but my daughter will take good care of you. I wish you a safe trip. I hope you find your brother quickly." She gives us a little wave and then heads back inside.

The closest I've come to dogsledding is photographs in books, most of which show animals hooked to primitive structures carved from wood. Nasrin's sled is made of what looks like black fiberglass with royal-blue padded interiors. There are two rows of seats, each big enough for two people, and then a cargo compartment covered by a tough nylon shell. The base is mounted on thick all-terrain wheels, with sleek runners elevated a few inches above the ground. In the back is a spot for the musher to stand, and also a big lever that slides back and forth.

"That helps me steer." Nasrin points at the lever.

She unzips the cargo hold and gestures for us to give her our backpacks. She heaves the packs one by one into the space, refusing Gunnar's help. "I am estimating weight so I can decide how many dogs we will need. More dogs mean more power, but it can make for a slower ride if we have to

stop frequently to untangle them or because someone needs
a break."

My eyes skim across the yard. Some of the dogs are sitting
now. Others are still bounding back and forth, their bright
eyes shining.

"Wait here." Nasrin ducks inside the back of the cottage.
I take the opportunity to pull out my phone and send
Macy a quick text.

Me: I'm going DOGSLEDDING!

Macy: Very cool. Is that part of your gram's official work?

Me: Believe it or not, yes.

Macy: And how are things with Sir Cheekbones?

Smiling, I slip my phone into my pocket as Nasrin returns
with an armful of silky blue fabric. Several of the dogs start
to bark.

"They know when they see their boots that some of them
are going on an excursion," she explains.

"It seems like they all want to come." I look hopefully at
her. "Can we bring them all?"

She laughs. "That would be a disaster. They do all love to
run. It's in their blood. In this way it's different from horses,
many of which have to be broken and beaten before they
become successful racers."

"They're quite thin, though, aren't they?" Gram asks.

She's right. These dogs are shaped like greyhounds, with
muscular chests and tight, raised stomachs. When they walk
I can see the outline of their ribs beneath their fur.

"It might appear so, but keep in mind that the average
pet dog is overweight. Also, these dogs are exercised every
day. They eat thousands of calories of food, but as they are
in excellent shape, they have a high metabolism that keeps
them lean." Nasrin's voice takes on a softness. "My mother
and I bought this business from an Icelandic man a year ago,
but before that I worked here as a musher for three years.

I assure you, these dogs have never been mistreated. I love them like family."

"If it's just you and your mother, I bet this place keeps you busy," Gram says.

"We have a few employees, but everyone wanted off for the holidays, and we saw no reason not to accommodate their wishes." Nasrin tugs at her ponytail. "Give me a few minutes to get everyone into their boots and finish organizing the ropes in front of the sled."

"Do those keep their feet warm?" I point at the thin fabric booties.

"No. They are more for protecting them from getting scrapes and cuts if they run across sharp sticks or rocks. Even ice can cut them if a paw lands on it wrong."

While the three of us watch, Nasrin makes quick work of selecting six dogs to be part of our team and securing the cloth boots over their paws.

I pull my phone out and reply to Macy's text.

Me: Ha. We had an interesting night. I'll tell you more about it later.

Macy: Don't leave me hanging!

Me: It's too complicated to text.

Macy: I can't believe you're all hornt up for a guy you just met.

Me: AHEM. I am not hornt up. I am simply…intrigued.

Macy: LOL. Whatever. Did you kiss him yet?

"Is something funny?" Gunnar asks. He's watching me with his pale blue eyes, a smile playing at his lips.

"Nope." I slip my phone back into my pocket. "Just telling my friend that I get to go dogsledding."

Nasrin buckles the dogs into the harnesses one at a time. The dogs selected yip excitedly, waiting for their master's command.

"It's a good thing our closest neighbors live two kilometers away," she says wryly. "The dogs make enough noise to wake the dead." She points at the sled's wheels. "For the first two kilometers, we'll be on wheels since there's no snow on the roads right now. Once we hit the glacier, the wheels actually fold upward and then the runners will take over."

"Clever," Gram says.

"Do you have everything you need out of your vehicle?" Nasrin asks. "Phones, food, medicine?"

"I think we're all set," Gunnar says.

"Then it's light enough to head out." Nasrin hands us each a pair of skier's goggles. "These will protect your eyes from wind and snow. Hop on when you're ready." She jogs up to the front of the sled to give each of the dogs a final check.

Gram takes the front seat and Gunnar and I sit next to each other in the back. My insides are spinning like a runaway carnival ride. This is the coolest thing I've done since Gram and I found Devin Blackrock's hidden treasure.

"You look more excited than they do." Gunnar bumps me in the leg with his knee and points at our lead dogs who are both jumping up and down while waiting for Nasrin to board the sled. He and I are both bundled up in several layers of winter clothing, but I can still feel the heat of his leg against mine.

"I think I am more excited than them," I say. "I never dreamed I'd ever get to do this."

Before Gunnar can reply, Nasrin hops on the runners at the back of the sled. She hollers a word in Icelandic and the dogs trot through the open gate. My head snaps around to face the front. I still can't believe this is happening.

But once the dogs make their way through the gate, they stop again. I peek back at Nasrin.

"One moment." She hops off the sled and closes the gate behind us. Then she calls out to the dogs again and we're off.

16

It's not the immediate rush of air that I'm expecting. The six dogs trot across the terrain at a leisurely pace, matching their gaits to one another. We run a couple of yards off the shoulder of the road to protect them from cars, not that there's much traffic all the way out here.

Once we get away from the buildings, the dogs pick up speed. It's still slower than I'm expecting, but quick enough that the wind freezes my lips and cheeks. I tug the thin neck gaiter I'm wearing up over my nose and mouth. My body is occasionally jolted from side to side. I peek back at Nasrin again, amazed by how she manages to stay upright despite the rough ground beneath us. She gives me a thumbs-up with her left hand as she leans her body to the right.

I turn back around and take in the whole scene. My eyes are everywhere: on the dogs, on the sun peeking over the horizon, on the moss-covered lava rocks passing beneath the wheels of the sled. My cheeks ache slightly from the stupidly large grin I have on my face. Gram is an even-keeled person—I never really see her extremely happy or sad. I'm the opposite. I tend to experience emotions intensely. Right now I feel like my skin is literally glowing beneath all the layers of outerwear. I'm seized by the urge to stand up and throw my arms wide, as if I'm perched on the front of the *Titanic*. Instead I laugh, a deep throaty noise that comes from far down in my gut.

"What's so funny?" Gunnar asks, his voice just loud enough to hear over the wind.

I shake my head. "Just giddy."

Gram peeks back over her shoulder. She gives me a

thumbs-up with one gloved hand. I lift my own thumb in reply.

We cross a bumpy area and the sled bounces slightly. Nasrin slows the dogs.

Gunnar reaches out for my arm to steady me. His cheeks have that rosy thing going on again, this time from the cold. I've never thought of myself as a person who cared about physical appearances, but some animal part of my brain is clearly less enlightened than I would like. Maybe it's all just pheromones. Lust.

"Why are you staring at me?" he asks.

Trying to decide if I actually like you. "No reason."

I look away from him. The sun hovers low over the land. The sky is a mix of pink and purple. I pull my phone out of my pocket and snap a picture. Then I get a couple of photos of the dogs, their furry bodies working hard to transport us. Gunnar reaches for my phone and I give it to him. He reverses the camera and leans in close to take a photo of the two of us, one arm looping around my back.

He nudges me and points off in the distance at a rounded peak topped with snow. "That's Grímsvötn," he says. "Our most active volcano. When it erupts it not only affects towns around here, the smoke and ash in the air can travel all the way to Spain."

"Whoa," I say, trying to imagine what it would be like to live in a country with active volcanoes. Not much different from any other country, I guess. After all, the US has floods and fires and tornadoes. Other places have sinkholes and tsunamis. And then there are all the unfortunate places where dodging bombs and drone attacks is part of their way of life.

The world is sad, when you stop to think about it.

Sad and dangerous.

I turn my attention back to the dogs. The two in front run close to each other, as though they're sharing fun anecdotes while they work. The middle dogs are completely focused, eyes forward on the dogs in the lead. And then there are the dogs closest to the sled, one of which has managed to get a back leg on the wrong side of the rope connected to the sled.

Nasrin whistles and the dogs slow to a stop. "Everyone doing okay?"

Gram turns around to face her. "I'm finding the ride very refreshing. How about you two?" she asks Gunnar and me.

"This is seriously one of the best days of my life," I say.

"Glad to hear it," Nasrin says. "I just need a minute to fix the lines." She jumps off and jogs up to the front of the sled. We watch her help the brown-and-white dog get its leg back on the right side of the rope.

Gram smiles impishly. "Who knows, maybe after you get your diploma you'll decide you want to come back here to go to college. University of Reykjavík is a phenomenal school."

"Several majors taught in English too," Gunnar adds.

"I'm not sure if college here would be as fun as this." I keep my voice light, but a current of anxiety moves through me. My brain cycles through a series of reasons Gram is so obsessed with me going away to college: she's tired of me living with her; she wants to be able to date again without me knowing; she's terminally ill and is trying to prepare me for life without her.

Or she just wants you to be happy.

It's probably the last one, at least I hope it is, but why can't she see that I'm happy with her?

Nasrin has finished fixing the lines. "Silly Salmon," she chides, giving the dog a scratch behind the ears before heading back to her spot on the sled.

"Did you say that dog's name is Salmon?" I ask.

"The old owner had a habit of naming each litter of pups by themes. So Salmon was born two years ago, and he has siblings named Tilapia, Herring, Mackerel, Sturgeon, and Sardine." She smiles. "Sardine was the runt of the litter, of course, not that you'd know it now." She points. "She's up in the middle with Jigsaw, one of our pups from the Power Tools litter."

"Why do they have English names?" Gunnar asks.

"Because our farm has always accommodated tourists, and have you ever tried to teach anyone from outside Scandinavia to say Icelandic names?"

"Good point," Gunnar says. "Reminds me of last summer when I was leading a hiking excursion and none of the tourists could come close to saying 'Eyjafjallajökull.'"

"Hey, I think that was the name of our plane," I say. "And I can't pronounce it because Icelanders somehow make twenty letters into three syllables. It's like half of the letters are silent."

"Oh, we say them all." Gunnar grins. "Just very quickly."

Nasrin laughs. "I did my best to learn basic Icelandic my first year here, but even though I can read it well enough, my pronunciation will always be terrible. Good thing most of the tourists speak English."

She calls out and the dogs take off running again. I wonder what it's like to live here and take tourists dogsledding for a living. The idea of specializing in something so niche feels risky, like you'd always be dependent upon others for your survival. I guess some people might say that about what Gram does, but there will always be a market for people who are able to find lost items.

When the edge of the glacier comes into view, I gasp. I was expecting a pristine white sheet of solid ice, heavy and flat, like the snow blanketing the lawn in front of Notre Dame. Instead, the gray dirt of the road leads into a gentle sloping bed of ice, speckled heavily with rocks and bits of dark clay. It reminds me of the snowdrifts that form in the corners of city parking lots, jagged and uneven, soiled by pollution.

Nasrin stops the sled. "Here we are," she says brightly. "Vatnajökull Glacier."

I slide out of the sled. "Wow, it's so…"

"Dirty?" Nasrin offers with a grin. "Some tourists think that's because so many people use this land for recreation, and to be sure we bring some soil with us. But a lot of the sediment you see is part of the natural process. Glaciers grow in size from snowfall, but also from the bottom up. Bottom-up growth traps dirt and sediment in the layers of ice which is then exposed when the sun melts away some of the top layers."

Gram scans the field of ice. "I never knew that."

Salmon woofs loudly as if agreeing with Gram. Jigsaw and Sardine sniff around looking for good places to pee, while other dogs collapse to the dusty ground, their tongues protruding from smiling mouths.

"I'll need a few minutes to switch from the wheels to runners." Nasrin pulls what looks like a tire jack out of the storage compartment. "If you three could remove your packs temporarily, that would help speed things along."

"Oh, sure." I help Gunnar remove all three of the packs from the cargo area.

Gram screws the lid off the small thermos she keeps clipped to her waistband and pours herself a cup of tea. I shake my head when she offers me some. I'm more interested in getting to know our furry companions. They've all flopped down now, either stretched out on their bellies or curled on one side like cats.

"Are you sure they're not too tired to keep going?" I ask Nasrin.

"They'll get a few minutes of rest, but I normally run all of them longer than this each day, so they're not as tired as they look, I assure you. Probably they're just angling for you guys to pet them."

"We can pet them?" My voice rises in pitch.

Nasrin adeptly removes the wheels from the front corner of the sled. "Sure. Why wouldn't you be able to pet them?"

"I don't know. I guess I thought they were working dogs."
I make air quotes around the last two words.

"They are, but they're also very friendly dogs, and they're not working at this moment. And most of them love attention. If you want, you can give them a drink while I reorganize things for the glacier portion of our trip." Reaching into the cargo area, Nasrin returns with a two-liter bottle of water and a bowl. "Two dogs can share the bowl at a time. All six need to split this water so I have enough for them to get us back to the yard."

I start at the front of the sled. Both dogs here are the traditional black-and-white Siberian Huskies. One of them has vibrant blue eyes that remind me of the glaciers at Jökulsárlón. The other has one pale blue and one brown eye. Both dogs are stretched out on their bellies. I drop to a squat and pull off my gloves. I give each dog a good pat and scratch behind the ears. I find the tag at each of their throats. One of these dogs is named Mercury and the other is called Saturn. They must be littermates.

The dogs hop to their feet when I set the bowl on the ground. When I start to pour, they both rush for the water so quickly that I fall backward onto the packed snow.

"Oof." The padding of my ski pants cushions the blow.

The other four dogs are barking now. They pace back and forth and jump up and down, their attention focused on their running mates.

Nasrin looks up from her work at the back of the sled. "Told you they weren't that tired."

When Mercury and Saturn have licked the bowl dry, I move back to the middle dogs, Sardine and Jigsaw. They yip and whine while they wait for me to pour the water into the bowl. Gunnar keeps a hold on each dog's collar until I'm finished pouring. Then I back up and he lets the dogs loose.

After both dogs are done drinking, he gives the remaining two dogs water while Gram and I give Sardine and Jigsaw a thorough petting. I bend down to stare into Sardine's brown eyes.

"You're a good dog, aren't you?" She licks the tip of my nose and I laugh.

Gunnar looks up from where he's capping the empty two-liter bottle. Our eyes meet.

"What?" I ask.

"Nothing." He shakes his head, but his eyes linger on me for a few beats before I eventually look away.

Nasrin hops back to her feet and strides across the ground. She does a quick check of the ropes and harnesses, giving each dog a quick pat on the head. "Looks like we're ready to head out. Once we're up on the glacier, we'll be traveling a bit faster, so be sure to zip up your coats and tighten the straps on your eye protection."

Gunnar, Gram, and I pile back into the sled. I tighten my goggles and pull my gloves back on. I lift my neck gaiter back over my nose and mouth.

The dogs dance sideways, yipping and barking with anticipation. Nasrin shouts a command and the sled starts moving. The dogs clamber from the hard ground onto the snow-packed glacier with ease and agility. As we draw away from the road, the glacier is whiter, more like I envisioned, but it's still not flat. The surface is sloping and ridged, like a wrinkled bedsheet tossed over a pile of laundry.

My head swivels every which way as the dogs pick up speed. To the left is a greenish-gray mountain range. Another glacier stretches between two of the peaks. Beyond it the blue sky is painted with wispy white clouds. They fan out above our heads like long, straight brushstrokes. The sun is high in the sky now. It's gone from pink to yellow, reflecting off the ridges of the glacier.

Gram glances back at me again. I can't read her expression through her goggles and gaiter, but the wind has taken her shoulder-length gray hair, blowing it straight out behind her like a flag. It makes me want to take down my own hair, which is secured in a ponytail that's tucked down the back collar of my jacket.

"Isn't this great?" she yells. "No better way to travel."

"Totally," I agree, bobbing my head.

I settle back into the seat. For a while I just watch the scenery pass by. Snow stretches out in all directions. The world is quiet except for the dogs' heavy breathing and an occasional yip or bark when one of them steps out of formation. My own breath is silent, trapped by my rapidly dampening neck gaiter. I pull down the fabric to expel a couple of warm puffs of foggy air, blotting moisture from my cheeks.

Something wet slaps against my goggles. At first I think it's a splash of snow from the sled's runners, but I get hit a second time and then a third. With my gloved hand I wipe the moisture away so I can see.

Gunnar points upward at the sky. The white wisps have been replaced by ominous gray clouds. It's snowing.

17

Nasrin stops the dogs and hops off the runners. "Looks like a storm is rolling in. We're going to have to head back soon."

"You can turn back whenever you need to," Gunnar says. "We'll continue on foot. I need to make sure my brother is not in danger."

She frowns. "If you keep going, *you're* going to be the ones in danger. Why not return to safety and call in a rescue team?"

"We're not sure if he needs help," Gunnar explains. "And we're qualified to handle these conditions."

Nasrin pulls a lip balm out of the pocket of her parka and applies it liberally. "You are prepared for emergencies? You have a way to call out if you get into trouble yourselves?"

"We've got the right gear. And we have someone at home who knows where we're headed and will send help if we fail to check in."

"I hate to leave you three out here, but I need to get my dogs home safely."

"We understand," Gram says.

The three of us step down from the sled onto the surface of the glacier, which is slicker than I imagined. I hold out an arm for balance. Mercury and Saturn turn around and look expectantly at Nasrin.

"Check in with me when you get back in range. I can come pick you up, or if nothing else at least I'll know you're safe." Nasrin tucks her thick black ponytail into the back of her parka. "If I don't hear from you by the day after tomorrow, I'm going to alert the local search and rescue that you're out here."

"Let me also give you my grandfather's number, if you don't mind," Gunnar says. "He can arrange for a search team if needed." Gunnar pulls a wad of cash out of his pocket and gives it to Nasrin. "Here's a little extra for your troubles."

"Thank you. This is…quite generous." She pockets the money.

She and Gunnar unload our packs and, while I say a quick goodbye to the dogs, Nasrin pulls some meat out of the cargo area and gives each of them a snack. They tear into the meat as though they haven't eaten in weeks.

"Will you be able to make it back safely?" Gram asks.

"Yes," Nasrin says. "The dogs have a lot of stamina. And having a bit of fresh snow on the glacier will actually make the trip quicker. And then once I'm back to the road it'll just be a matter of getting home. I'll have them snuggled down in their beds long before this storm gets too bad."

All of the dogs have inhaled the meat she gave them. Saturn is hungrily licking at the drops of blood that remain in the snow. Nasrin turns the sled around and the dogs automatically find their spots at the front again. She jumps onto the back of the sled and heads out with a wave.

Above our heads, the gray clouds twist and swirl. So far the snowfall is light, but there's no guarantee it will stay that way. Gram, Gunnar, and I all dig sets of crampons out of our backpacks. Gunnar helps me attach them to my boots. The first step I take nearly lands me flat on my face as the edge of the metal crampon collides with the snow and I pitch forward.

Gram grabs me by the shoulder and holds on until I regain my balance. "You might have to lift your feet a little higher than you're used to." She demonstrates by taking a few steps across the ice. As much hiking as we've done together, none of it has ever been on a glacier. My grandmother looks like a straight-up pro, though. I'm impressed.

"This will help too." Gunnar gives each of us a collapsible ice axe that doubles as a walking stick.

I grip the tool in my palm. It's made of some kind of lightweight metal—titanium perhaps. Tentatively I take a couple more steps, the end of the axe serving as a third point of contact on the ice. The metal spikes of my crampons dig into the glacier. "Oh, now I get it." I turn and walk back toward Gram, increasing my speed a little.

"Try to be light on your feet if you can," Gunnar says. "Sometimes snow or ice will cover up cracks in the glacier. People have died by falling into hidden crevasses."

"Lovely," I mutter.

"Just step where I step," he says. "I've done enough glacier hiking that I can usually find a safe path."

We continue walking in the same direction as we were heading in the sled, which Gunnar tells me is northwest based on the locations of the mountain peaks around us. I look for evidence of other traffic, but it's difficult because the hard-packed glacier wouldn't have picked up a lot of tracks, and anything that is there is rapidly being covered by new snow.

It's slow moving on foot. Gunnar is quicker than Gram or me, but instead of urging us to hurry, he stops every few minutes to check the ice in front of us for cracks and weak spots.

I walk beside Gram, my eyes trained on the ground. We reach a place where a deep crevasse cuts the glacier in two. We're going to have to choose which side of the crack to walk on. Dropping to a squat, I brush away some fresh snow to expose the ground beneath. There are some parallel scratches here that look like tracks from snowmobile runners. Orienting myself in the same direction as the grooves, I walk forward and find additional marks on the right side of the crevasse.

I show the scratches to Gunnar and Gram. "If this is them, they definitely stayed right."

"Good eye," Gram says.

Gunnar continues to lead as we veer to the right of the crevasse. The snow is coming at us from an angle, finding its way down the cuff of my left glove and the side of my collar. I pull my sleeve down and the edge of my glove over it, and then keep moving. There's not much I can do about my collar. My neck gaiter is rolling up slightly from the bottom, leaving a tiny sliver of my neck exposed. Every twenty yards or so we stop to look for the telltale grooves of the snowmobile. By the time it's one p.m., the snow is almost three inches deep.

We're heading up an incline now. It's subtle enough that I can't visualize the change in altitude, but I can feel it in my burning leg muscles and my pounding heart. I turn around briefly to make sure Gram is doing okay. She's very fit for a sixty-three-year old, but if she were to fall, she'd be at a higher risk of injury than Gunnar or me.

"Sorry to slow everyone down," she calls through labored breaths.

"I was just thinking I could use a break," I reply. I stop so she can catch up with me, pulling my water bottle from where it's clipped on the side of my pants and taking a small swig. It's about half empty.

Gunnar stops too, bending over to brace his hands against his thighs. He yanks his gaiter down under his chin. Tiny clouds spew from his lips as he catches his breath.

Gram leans on her ice axe. "I forgot what good exercise glacier walking was."

"It's a full body workout," I agree.

"We are going to sleep well tonight," she says with a grin.

I shudder just thinking about spending the night out here. Some people are simply not built for the cold, and I am unapologetically one of them.

Gunnar slides his pack off his shoulders. "Huddle together."

The three of us face inward, making a tight circle. Gunnar unbuckles the top of his pack and pulls out some foil-wrapped protein bars. Gram and I each take one. I have to pull off my gloves to open the package.

Gram grabs the thermos clipped to her belt loop and offers me a drink. The tea isn't hot anymore, but at least it's not ice cold. We have a stove we could use to heat it, but none of us want to go through all of that trouble right now in the middle of a storm.

"If this keeps up, we're going to have to stop for today," Gunnar says between bites of protein bar. "It's not safe."

"But then we'll get even farther behind," I protest.

"Not as far behind as we'll be if someone falls and breaks a leg."

"Good point." I finish my bar and take a long swig from Gram's thermos. "You doing okay walking?"

"Sure," she says, chewing slowly. "What is it about protein bars where no one has figured out how to make them taste good?"

Gunnar laughs. His breath is warm against my face. "I think they purposely make them taste bad so people won't eat too many at one time."

Gram grimaces. "No danger of that."

While Gram finishes her bar, I scout around to find more snowmobile tracks. I find some parallel grooves a few yards to the north and gesture for the others to follow me. The terrain continues to grow steeper. Gram shows me how to dig the point of my axe into the snow if I start to slide and need to self-arrest. I'm pretty sure if I slip I'm just going to roll all the way to the bottom of the hill.

Hiking on a glacier in a blizzard is a weird feeling, like being trapped in a snow globe that someone keeps shaking. It's a desert of white, where everywhere I turn things look almost the same. I imagine what's going on beneath my feet, a thick layer of ice spread on top of a volcano. I am climbing a volcano. How cool is that? I envision the jets of steam that hit the ice from below, causing it to melt in places, forming caves and caverns that we'll soon be exploring. It's exhausting, but it's also pretty awesome. I am lucky to be on this journey, even if all I want is a nice warm bowl of lamb stew. *Or a dip in a geothermal pool.*

My heart starts pounding again when I think about my time with Gunnar last night. I really thought he was going to kiss me. *You wanted him to kiss you.* I did. But instead he took me inside and told me his brother was possessed by a demon, that he saw this, that he believed it completely.

It seems so outrageous, like something you'd hear from some radical preacher or on a fringe YouTube channel. But Gunnar strikes me as sensible and—

The tip of my crampon catches on a rough piece of ice and I trip forward, flailing out with my ice axe. I recover my balance just before my feet slip out from under me. Gunnar doesn't notice my near-fall and Gram doesn't say anything. I wonder if we're all lost in thought.

I try to clear my mind and focus on the task at hand. I take slow, even breaths after every two steps, inhaling through my nose and exhaling through my mouth. Just when I'm thinking I'm going to need another break, I catch sight of something familiar in front of us.

"Hey!" I point into the distance. "Is that a mirage?"

"If it is, I see it too," Gunnar says.

A pair of black and red snowmobiles are rapidly filling with snow. Gunnar hurries over to the closest one. He wipes off the side of it with his glove. Metallic red letters read HOFFELL ADVENTURES.

Gram and I catch up to Gunnar. Gram lowers herself into the front seat of one of the snowmobiles. She pats the seat behind her. "Might as well take a quick rest while there's a good place to sit."

She's got a point. I plunk down in the second seat.

"If my brother and Black as Death left these here, we must be close to the entrance to the ice caves," Gunnar says.

"Or maybe it was getting too steep here for them?" I look back at the hill we've ascended. I would hate to roll down it in a snowmobile.

"Well, if they walked from here, we should be able to find footprints," Gram says.

"Right." Gunnar looks up at the sky. "It looks like the snow is tapering off a little."

I watch for footprints as we continue up the incline. I stay close to my grandmother, on her left side, the one where she doesn't have an ice axe to support her. If she fell, I wouldn't be fast enough to catch her, but maybe she'd be quick enough to grab onto me.

It's probably silly of me to worry about her since she's the one with mountaineering experience and I'm the newbie, but I don't know what I'd do if anything happened to her. My brain has played this song regularly ever since my grandfather died—Gram slipping in the shower; Gram bald and weak from chemotherapy; Gram buckled into a mangled car on some Parisian thoroughfare; Gram sleeping soundly in her bed but just never waking up. Even though my mother died in childbirth when she was twenty-four, I somehow always saw my grandparents as immortal until I lost one of them.

A fluttering above my head snaps me out of my reverie. A solo bird, with brown and white feathers, soars across the sky. "Hey, is that a falcon?"

Gunnar peers up at the sky. "Ah. That's a gyrfalcon. It—"

His words are drowned out by a sharp cracking sound. My head swivels left and right. I'm terrified that someone is shooting at us. I look back toward Gunnar just in time to see his body start to sink into another crevasse, this one hidden beneath the snow.

"Gunnar!" I scream.

All I can do is watch him fall.

18

The crevasse isn't wide enough for Gunnar to fall all the way through the ice. If it weren't for his bulky backpack, he might have plummeted who knows how far down. Instead, he's stuck, dangling in mid-air.

"Oh my God!" My heart beats wildly, a terrified baby bird locked in a cage.

Gunnar spreads his arms flat across the glacier, his ice axe still clutched in his right hand. "I'm afraid to try to anchor myself," he says. "If the surface is fragile, I could make the hole bigger."

I look over at Gram, praying she's had some kind of training for these situations.

"No one panic," she says, her voice maddeningly calm.

"Too late," I reply.

"Let me take a closer look." Gram moves slowly toward Gunnar.

"Hold on," I say, again envisioning a life without my grandmother. "The ice might break."

"Trust me." She scans the situation. Around us the entire world has gone quiet. Deathly quiet.

"I feel securely wedged right now," Gunnar says. "And I don't see any cracks in the ice."

"Maybe I can pull you out," Gram says.

"With what?" I ask. "Gunnar has all the rope in his pack."

"I suppose that was bad planning on my part." He swears under his breath. "You were right, Rory. I should have split the safety gear among us."

"It's okay. This is all my fault." My voice wavers. "I shouldn't have distracted you by asking about a stupid bird."

"It's not your fault," Gunnar says. "I should have been less easy to distract."

I gnaw on my lower lip. It's nice of him to say that, but my brain still logs this as one more time my behavior has gotten someone I care about into trouble.

Gram lowers herself to her knees. "I'm going to crawl toward you and then try to pull you with my hands."

"All right," Gunnar says.

"No, wait." My voice is sharp with fear. "Gram, let me go. I'm lighter."

"Rory, I don't—"

"Please, let me do this," I insist. She weighs probably thirty pounds more than I do, and I would rather die than live without her.

"Okay," Gram says. "Stay low. Take your time. Keep breathing."

I slide my backpack off my shoulders. Slowly, I lower myself to my knees in the snow. The ground beneath me feels sturdy and solid. I drop down to my belly to further distribute my weight.

I start to shimmy toward Gunnar. My heart is still slamming against my rib cage. It's a full-grown bird now, trying to beat its way right out of my chest. I pause and force myself to take a couple of deep breaths.

Gunnar is perfectly still as he watches my approach. When I get close enough to him that I can grab his hand, I remove my gloves. He does the same. Our fingers touch and I am comforted by the momentary warmth. I grab both of his hands, lock my fingers around his.

"Hi," I say softly. "God, I am so sorry about this."

"Me too, but we're going to figure it out," he says. "Now scoot backward, very slowly. Don't try to pull too hard."

I do as he instructs, but instead of him coming toward me, it feels like he's pulling my arms out of my sockets.

"Here, I'll pull on your legs," Gram says, from behind me.

It sounds like a bad idea, but we don't have a lot of options.

Unfortunately, Gunnar isn't able to use his lower body for leverage, and Gram and I aren't strong enough to pull him out of the hole, especially not knowing whether we're on stable ground. My entire body ends up being stretched like a medieval prisoner being tortured on the rack.

"New plan," I say. "I'm going to try to get into your backpack, get the rope and a harness. You can put it around your chest. Then Gram and I can back up and use our whole bodies to pull from a safe distance." My heart rate slows slightly as I focus on the revised task, my brain mentally taking me through each step.

"Good idea." Gunnar is breathing hard. Snowflakes are gathering on his eyelashes.

I wipe some flecks of snow from his face with my thumb. "I can do this," I tell him.

"I trust you," he says. "You'll need to unclip the main compartment and then undo the drawstring. The gear should be close to the top."

I creep around to the back of Gunnar, where all but the lowest compartment of his backpack is accessible. I slowly rise back up onto my knees.

So far so good.

I reach up with my right hand and undo the buckles on Gunnar's backpack. Then I loosen the drawstring and reach inside. My bare hand immediately comes in contact with the rope.

"Got it," I say.

Beneath the rope is a nylon harness used for rock climbing or belaying. With shaking fingers, I attach the rope and harness with a bowline knot, one Gram taught me when we first started hiking together.

"Excellent work, Rory," Gram says.

A surge of pride moves through me, but now is not the

time to celebrate. Adjusting the harness's leg straps, I help Gunnar slide his arms into them and then buckle and tighten the main strap underneath his armpits. It's not ideal, but it's the best we can do right now.

Gripping the rope with both hands, I shimmy back to my grandmother. I wrap the rope around my hand once and have Gram do the same. We both crouch low, one foot in front of the other.

"On three we're going to pull, okay?" I call.

"All right," Gunnar says.

"One…two…three." Gram and I use all of our weight to pull back on the rope. Gunnar's upper body slides forward ever so slightly. He leans forward so that his face is almost in the snow.

"A little farther," he yells.

Gram and I pull again. I grit my teeth, imagining that this is a tug-of-war competition and the prize is survival. The textured rope digs into the flesh of my palms, but I don't let up.

We pull a third time and then a fourth. My upper and lower body muscles are burning by the time Gunnar's waist appears through the hole in the ice. One more pull. His entire backpack is visible again.

"I think that might be far enough." He uses his elbows to inch his body forward.

Gram and I watch silently. Gunnar's feet emerge from the crevasse and the pain in my chest starts to fade. My hands are shaking—I'm not sure if it's from cold or adrenaline. I'm expecting Gunnar to shimmy over to us, as fast as his knees and elbows will take him.

Instead he yells, "Don't let go of the rope yet." He reorients his body so his head is facing the hole. Flipping on his headlamp, he peers down into the chasm.

"What are you doing?" I holler.

Gunnar doesn't respond. A few seconds later, he turns

away from the hole, flicks off his headlamp, and slides on his stomach toward Gram and me.

When he's about fifteen feet away from the break in the ice, he slowly lifts himself up on his knees and then rises to his feet. He unties the rope from the front of the harness and slides his arms out of the straps. Reaching into his pocket, he pulls out his phone and swipes at the screen, his forehead furrowing as he studies the display.

"What are you looking at?" I ask, pulling my gloves back over my trembling fingers.

It takes him a few seconds to reply. "Now hear me out before you start yelling," he says. "But I think we should lower ourselves into that crevasse."

19

A re you kidding me?" My voice is almost sharp
enough to start an avalanche. "I just risked my life
to get you out of there."

"I know, and I'm grateful," he says. "But it looks like the chasm connects to the ice caverns. By my calculation, we should be right on top of them. Sure, we could hike another kilometer in the snow, looking for where Einar and the others entered, but it's going to be dark soon. If we're going to stay on the surface, we need to start thinking about setting up camp."

"He's right, Rory," Gram says. "It'll be safer to camp down in the caverns than up here. And warmer."

"Warmer?" I repeat dubiously.

"Warmer," Gunnar says firmly. "And drier. There's no wind or precipitation down there. Just an occasional glacial stream we might have to cross."

"Okay, you've convinced me," I say. "But are we going to be able to fit through the hole? Trying to make it bigger seems risky."

"I'll be able to fit if I take off my backpack," Gunnar says. "I'll go down first and make sure everything is safe. Then I'll call up and you can hook the backpacks onto the rope and I'll lower them."

"And then how do Gram and I get down?"

"I'll belay both of you from the bottom." Gunnar glances around. "I'll need to put in a couple of ice screws since there's nothing to anchor to around here."

"And we won't get hopelessly lost?" Part of me is dreading the portion of this mission that takes place underground. I've seen too many horror movies filled with people trapped in tunnels. My chest goes tight as I look at the hole in the glacier. I can almost feel the walls closing in on me, the ice collapsing, my lungs filling with snow.

"Don't worry about getting lost." Gunnar digs in his backpack and comes out with a couple of long metal screws the width of pennies. "I brought breadcrumbs."

"Breadcrumbs?"

"Cave markers. They're glow-in-the-dark plastic tabs that we can stick into the ice to mark our way."

"Oh, cool." I didn't even know such things existed.

"Grandfather and I planned for everything," Gunnar says. "We're going to be fine."

"I don't mean to question your—"

"I know. You and your gram are just used to doing things for yourselves." Gunnar flashes a smile at Gram and then taps hard on the surface of the glacier with his ice axe.

"Would you like me to put in the anchors?" Gram asks. "You've had quite a scare, Gunnar. Perhaps you'd like a moment to…regroup."

"I'm all right, Ingrid. Honestly, it's best if I keep my mind occupied, I think."

"How is your shoulder?" she asks.

"It's not bad," he says. "The wave of adrenaline I just got is probably helping."

Gunnar taps the ice again. Satisfied, he places one of the screws perpendicular to the ground and then turns the handle until it disappears deep into the ice. When the plate of the screw is flush with the snow, he tugs on the handle and nods to himself.

"It's that easy?" I ask.

"Well, the secret is that you have to have ice thick enough to bury the entire screw. If you hit rock, or air, then your anchor isn't safe. So it's always a good idea to place at least two anchors." He positions a second screw about a yard away from the first one.

I watch closely. "So each screw by itself should hold us, but you're using a backup in case one of them turns out to be insecure?"

"Exactly." Gunnar uses nylon straps and carabiners to connect the two anchors. He pulls hard on the nylon. When it feels secure, he straps himself back into the safety harness.

"How deep is the hole?" Gram asks.

"Not sure, but it widens out considerably and I could see the bottom, so we shouldn't run out of rope. Maybe ten meters." He reaches up to turn on his headlamp.

Gram and I stand back as he crawls to the edge and lowers his body into the darkness. "It's beautiful down here," he hollers up as his face vanishes beneath the glacier's surface.

After about three minutes, the rope connected to the anchors starts to move. Gunnar pulls all of the rope down into the hole except for one end with a carabiner clipped to it. I attach his backpack and then yell out, "Lowering your bag."

The bag disappears and then the end of the rope comes back up. Next I lower Gram's backpack. When the end of the rope comes up again, Gram has donned the safety harness. She clips into the locking carabiner and sits at the edge of the hole. "Ready to come down," she calls down to Gunnar. I see the rope go tight against her midsection. Slowly she disappears into the darkness.

Next I send my backpack down, but not before I pull out the small pink lunch box. (Never let yourself get separated from your lifesaving gear—that's a rookie mistake.) Finally, the rope comes up again and it's my turn to descend.

I sit down and dangle my feet into the hole, waiting until Gunnar pulls the rope taut before I push my body forward, into the darkness. Below me, I see the soft glow of a moving headlamp. Gram must be exploring. Reaching out with both hands, I grasp only air. I get no feel for how big the space is that I'm descending into.

"You all right?" Gunnar's voice calls up to me. He's closer

than I thought. His light is focused on the floor, probably so he doesn't accidentally blind me.

"I'm fine." I run my fingers across the back of my helmet. I want to turn on my headlamp, but I can't seem to find the switch.

"You're almost down. Just a bit farther."

I expel a heavy breath as my crampons scrape against solid ground. My legs go wobbly beneath me and I nearly pitch forward onto my knees as Gunnar lets out the last bit of rope.

He reaches for my arm. "I got you."

I blink hard. "Sorry, I got dizzy there for a second. I think I was holding my breath."

Pulling off a glove, I reach up and turn on my headlamp. A beam of white cuts across the cave. It's more of a cavern, really—over fifty feet high in some places and about half that across or more. I gasp when I see the walls. I expected them to be white and gray—hard-packed snow like what we've been walking on. Instead they're a mix of clear to blue, mostly transparent.

"Otherworldly, isn't it?" Gram asks, coming to stand beside me.

"It's like being inside of a sapphire," I say.

"I've been in some ice caves where instead of sharp corners like this the edges are rounded and it feels like you're in a soap bubble," Gunnar says. "Very surreal."

"What makes them different?" I ask.

Gunnar thinks for a few seconds. "They're formed by geothermal activity from the volcano below, so I suppose it has to do with how the steam hits various parts of the glacial walls, how hot it is, the angles of the earth."

"But I thought this volcano was dormant?"

"Dormant just means it hasn't erupted in a long time. It doesn't mean there's no magma present," Gram explains.

"But it won't erupt anytime soon, right?" I shift my weight

from on foot to the other. "Especially if we're looking for a way to get *inside* of it?"

"Scientists here get warnings prior to eruptions, sort of like with hurricanes. We don't have to worry about Huldulogafell erupting," Gunnar says.

The words should be comforting, but they're not. Gunnar has had two near-death experiences in two days. I shudder to think of what other dangers might lie before us.

20

Gunnar points at a passageway in the north wall of the cavern. "This way."

I shine my headlamp on our rope, still dangling from the hole above our heads. "What about all that?"

"We're going to leave it set up, so we have a way to climb out of here once we've found my brother."

I gnaw on my lower lip. Leaving gear behind seems like a bad idea. "What if we don't find our way back here?"

"We will." Gunnar bends low, his headlamp shining into the depths of his backpack. He pulls out something small and orange that turns out to be a package of reflective tabs. "Breadcrumbs, remember?" He holds the package out to me and then swings his pack back onto his shoulders. "You can be in charge of them. Be sure to mark our path every time we make a turn."

I take the package, then cinch down the strap on my helmet. I step into the tunnel behind him and Gram. *Here we go.*

The walls here are the same crystalline blue, but they're closer together, and that makes them feel less majestic and more foreboding. We inch through the passageway, the world silent except for our boots crunching across the icy ground. I train my headlamp on Gunnar's lean frame, his blond hair hanging below the bottom of his helmet. He picks his way gingerly, every step calculated and measured. As I focus on his slow and steady progress, my breathing slows. I exhale deeply, my muscles relaxing somewhat. But then Gunnar bends low and pulls something out of his boot—his handgun. I haven't seen him with it since yesterday morning, back in Skeiðarársandur.

"We should probably be prepared for anything down

here," he says. "I have weapons for everyone, but you don't have to carry one if it makes you uncomfortable."

I think back to our conversation from last night, how he told me his handgun had iron bullets that could weaken demons. I still can't wrap my head around that. If he's right—if demons are real and Einar is actually possessed—we might have to fight him to get him to return to Reykjavík with us. I did not sign up for that.

"I'm going to stick with the ice axe for the moment," Gram says. "For me, the biggest danger right now is probably breaking a hip."

"Me too." I'm not thrilled about the idea of trying to shoot anything in a dark cave with my grandmother and Gunnar in close proximity. It would be way too easy for the wrong person to get hurt.

I shine my light around the walls and then down at my feet. Water pools in natural depressions in the ice. I step carefully around them, in no hurry to test the water-resistance of my boots. With no wind and no wet snow slapping me in the face, it's almost cozy down here. I pull my neck gaiter down and leave the fabric bunched around my collar. My breath makes soft clouds in the air.

"Why is it so wet here?" I ask Gunnar.

"Because there's a volcano below us," he says.

"Well, that's comforting." I imagine what it would be like if the volcano did decide to erupt. Would we be scalded to death by steam, swept away in a flood of melting glacier, or incinerated by boiling lava? Sometimes there is no good choice.

The tunnel narrows until both sides brush against my quilted jacket. I pause again to catch my breath. Gunnar notices the absence of my footsteps immediately. He turns around and I get blasted in the face with his light.

"Ow." I close my eyes but the light burns right through my eyelids. I lift an arm up to shield my entire face.

"Sorry." He tilts his headlamp down at the ground. "I just wanted to be sure you were still with us."

"At least you didn't point the gun at me," I mutter. "I'm fine. I just don't like tight spaces."

"I'm hoping it's not going to get much tighter," he says.

"Me too." A rustling sound by my feet makes me jump. When I look down, I see it's just a couple of dead leaves tumbling one over the next. "How did leaves get down here?"

"Perhaps they were stuck to someone's clothing or backpack?" Gram suggests.

I angle my headlamp toward the leaves, which have been swept up against an outcropping of ice. The dried stem of one wiggles in an invisible breeze. "But why are they blowing?"

"There's probably an opening out onto the glacier somewhere ahead of us," Gram says.

Sure enough, another twenty yards down the tunnel, we find a hole leading back to the glacier above our heads. The wind whistles, loosening new snow and sending it spraying down on top of us like a miniature blizzard. Snowflakes dust my cheeks and coat my eyelashes. I blink hard and blot my face with my gaiter. The edges of this hole are smooth and well-worn. Not necessarily man-made, but it's been here for a while—probably the entrance we were searching for.

"Look." I catch a glimpse of a silver carabiner at the edge of the hole. It's part of a rappelling setup. "Someone else came down this way."

21

D o you think it was Einar and the band?" I ask.
"It's difficult to be certain," Gunnar says. "No way
of knowing how long that equipment has been up
there."

I scan the ground, but I don't see any obvious boot prints.
Just snow and ice and, wait—something shiny catches my
eye. I bend down and retrieve a black-and-white candy wrapper that was half-buried in loose snow. "Draumur," I sound
out. "What's that?"

Gunnar takes the wrapper from my outstretched hand.
"Draumur is chocolate mixed with black licorice. It's my
brother's favorite candy bar."

"Chocolate and licorice?" I scrunch up my nose. "Why
would anyone do that?"

"It's actually quite good," Gram says. "And the printing
on this wrapper is still bright. It can't have been down here
for too long."

"True." Gunnar bobs his head. "It could definitely have
been Einar's."

"Hopefully we'll be able to pick up a real trail at some
point." I sweep my headlamp from the ground to the walls
as we continue moving.

The tunnel starts to slope downward and I take smaller
steps, my free hand extended out to one side to maintain
balance. Gram and I lag behind Gunnar, who strides con-
fidently across the slick ground. He stops occasionally to
look back at us but doesn't say anything. After what feels like
about an hour, we come to our first fork in the tunnel. Ahead
of us is a wall of solid ice. We can veer either to the left or
to the right.

"See if you can find any tracks, Rory," Gram says.

"Okay." I read somewhere that when faced with a choice, most people who are right-handed will go right, and since the majority of the world is right-handed, I start with the obvious choice.

"I'll come with you." Gunnar grips his axe in one hand and his gun in the other as he follows me into the right passageway.

I angle my headlamp at my feet, looking for any partial boot prints or scuff marks. The ground is composed of hard ice dusted with bits of snow that must have blown in from openings up to the glacier. I find no obvious tracks.

Gunnar hovers behind me. "I don't see anything," he says. "I'm going to check the other tunnel."

"I'll be there in a minute." It's easy to miss stuff if you're in a hurry. Slowly, I rise back to a standing position, examining the walls, looking for telltale places where someone might have rested a glove or carved a notch to mark their path. Again there's nothing. I'm just about to turn back and find Gunnar when it hits me that both Einar and Benjamín are tall—so tall they'd have to stoop down in places to protect their heads. I scan the ceiling of the tunnel and find what I'm looking for almost immediately. "This way," I call.

Gram and Gunnar duck into the tunnel. "Are you sure?" Gunnar asks.

"Somebody came this way." I angle my light up at the ceiling. "They bumped their head against that cluster of icicles and broke off some of the tips." Looking back at the ground, I find some jagged shards of ice hidden in the snow that seem to be remnants of broken icicles.

"Good find," Gunnar says.

Gram pats me on the shoulder. "I told you your powers of observation would come in handy."

I smile to myself as we continue walking. This passageway looks almost the same as the last one, except it's a little bit wider, which I'm grateful for. Eventually the tunnel ends at a large open cavern. It's not as wide as where we descended and the ceiling is lower, maybe eight feet or so, but it's a relief to be able to stretch my arms to either side. I roll my head in lazy circles, willing some of the tension to leave my body.

The three of us scout the perimeter of the cavern and find two new passageways, one that continues straight and another that veers off to the right.

"I could use a break," Gram says. "Especially since there's enough space to stretch out here. What time is it?"

Gunnar checks his watch. "It's a little after nineteen hundred."

I swallow back a yawn. "It feels like midnight to me. I can't believe I'm tired at seven. I don't suppose you packed any Red Bull, did you?"

Gunnar chuckles. "No, but that espresso chocolate bar might give you a little kick."

"I am hungry, now that you mention it."

"Might as well have a quick snack to keep up our strength." He pulls a foil-wrapped package out of his pack, along with a couple of apples.

The three of us sit in the center of the cavern. Gunnar distributes what turns out to be cheese sandwiches on rye bread. Gram and I split the dark chocolate espresso candy bar.

"Are you sure you don't want any?" I hold the shiny wrapper out in Gunnar's direction.

"Maybe just a square," he says. "If you can spare it."

"I knew it," I say. "Everyone likes chocolate, at least a little."

Gram yawns. "Maybe I shouldn't have stopped moving. I could fall asleep sitting up."

"We can take a longer break if you need," I say. "Right?" I look to Gunnar for confirmation.

"Black as Death didn't give their fans an exact time for

when they plan to open the doorway, but it won't be Christmas for five more hours," he replies. "We could rest for an hour or two. I'm actually more tired than I expected to be myself."

"Probably from the scare of almost falling through the ice," I say. "You could have died, you know that?"

"I'm trying not to think about it," he admits.

"How much farther do you think is it to the…doorway?"

"Not more than three hours, probably, assuming all the tunnels are like this. And we should be transitioning from the ice caves to the lava tubes soon, which means we'll be mostly going downhill." He pauses. "But one of us should keep watch."

"You two can rest. I'll keep watch," I say. "But what do I do if I see someone?"

"Wake me up," Gunnar says.

"Wake us both up," Gram agrees.

"Other than that, use your best judgment." Gunnar pulls the handgun out of his ankle holster. "Take this. If anyone shoots at you, shoot back."

"Solid strategy," I say dourly. As much as I've trained with a gun, two days ago in Skeiðarársandur is the closest I've come to being shot at, and I've never remotely come close to firing a weapon at anyone.

"I aim to please." He holds the grip of his gun in my direction.

Wordlessly, I take the weapon from him. I wrap my hands around the grip, keeping the barrel pointed downward.

Gunnar nods approvingly. "Wake me up if you get tired, and I can take over."

"Sure," I say, but I'm not going to wake him. He's injured and my grandmother is old. They both need rest more than I do.

I watch a little enviously as Gunnar and Gram zip themselves into their mummy sleeping bags. They look so cozy, the tops of their bags pulled tight around their heads, only small circles of their faces exposed to the air.

There's a soft dripping sound coming from somewhere off in the dark. I count the drips for a while, just to have something to do. By the time I get to five hundred, the cold ground has radiated all the way through my pants and long underwear. Reluctantly, I lift myself back to a standing position, Gunnar's handgun clutched awkwardly in my hand. I tilt my head to the left and right to crack my neck. I check the time on my watch—it's been only fifteen minutes.

I wish I had a book. I wish I had anything. I debate getting my phone out of my backpack. There's no signal, of course, but at least I could mess with some of my apps or play a game. I don't do it, though, because I don't want to waste my battery or shirk on guard duty.

I start counting the drips again, but this leads to a new problem. They're making me have to pee. I switch tactics and try to ignore the sound, going back over everything in my head that I know about our mission.

I wonder what condition Einar and Black as Death will be in when we find them. They'll probably be exhausted, maybe hurt or sick. I shake my head. I understand the idea of trying to come up with a viral publicity stunt, but all the album sales in the world will be meaningless if the band members die of hypothermia.

Speaking of freezing to death, my hands feel like two blocks of ice. I pull my gloves off and blow on my reddened fingers. The only way I'm going to make it is to walk laps around the cavern. I start in front of Gram and Gunnar, walk down to the passageway where we came from, and then turn and walk all the way to the opposite end, where passageways lead straight and to the right.

I shine my light into the straight passage. Holding the gun out in front of me, I imagine what it would be like to have someone come at me, to pull the trigger, to see a person die.

That definitely does not feel like real life. I've never seen a dead body, aside from my grandfather, who was all made up to look pretty in his casket.

I find the source of the dripping sound—it's a melting stalactite. By now, each plink of water is like a tiny jab to my bladder. I knew I shouldn't have drunk so much tea today. Grumbling, I take a quick look around the cavern to make sure no one is lurking in the shadows.

Then I tiptoe into the passage that veers to the right. Using my headlamp to guide me, I walk until I find a wide spot in the tunnel. Leaning my back against the hard wall, I tuck the gun into my pocket, undo the drawstring on my pants, and pull everything just far enough down for me to do my business. The cold air bites into my exposed skin. Reflexively, I clench all of my muscles, including the ones that make it possible for me to pee.

I exhale slowly and rub at the exposed skin of my thighs, forcing myself to relax. Mid-stream, it occurs to me that I should have done this in the tunnel we came from and definitely won't have to walk back through for several hours at least. Oh well, too late now. I blot myself dry with a tissue, yank my pants up, and turn to head back to Gram and Gunnar.

Just as I'm about to re-enter the cavern where Gunnar and Gram are sleeping, I come to a stop. Gunnar is standing in the tunnel opening. He's not wearing his helmet. He's not even carrying a flashlight.

"I was looking for you," he says.

22

oly crap. You scared me." I check my watch.
"What's the matter? Can't sleep?"
One side of his mouth curls up slightly. His eyes
look almost silver in the glow of my headlamp. "I want to
show you something."

"What is it?"

"It's a surprise."

"I hate surprises."

"You'll like this one."

"You're acting weird," I say. "Is everything all right? You're
not getting hypothermia, are you?"

"Just come with me."

I expect Gunnar to take me back to the main cavern, but
instead he pulls me back down this offshoot tunnel, away
from Gram. I shine my headlamp around in front of us so
that we both can see. "Where are we going?" I whisper. "I
was just down this way. Do the two tunnels connect or something?"

He ignores my questions. "Come on. Follow me."

I hurry after Gunnar, mentally cataloguing the route we
take since I don't have any of the cave markers with me.
When he turns into a smaller passageway, I reach out for his
arm. "Stop. We're going to get lost."

"Actually, we're here."

I shine my headlamp around again but here just looks like
everywhere else to me. The ice above our heads is clearer
than in other places, reflecting the vibrant blue of the glacier.
Is this what he's trying to show me?

"It's pretty," I start. "But—"

"Shh." He touches one gloved finger to my lips. He smiles

that crooked smile again, his eyes glinting with mischief. "Turn off your light."

"Why?"

"Just do it."

"But someone could sneak up on us," I say.

"I *dare* you."

I turn off my headlamp and plunge both of us into total darkness. Gunnar's hands find my waist. He presses me back against the wall, icy cold brushing against the nape of my neck.

"What are you doing?" I hiss.

"Kissing you."

"Seriously? Now? Are you delirious or something?"

Gunnar reaches up and unsnaps the chin strap on my helmet. Gently he removes it from my head. He runs one hand through my hair. "That's better."

I cringe at the thought of how sweaty and knotted it probably is. "Weren't you the one who said we needed to keep the helmets on at all times so we didn't get KO'd by a falling chunk of ice?"

"Five minutes won't kill us...probably." He drops my helmet on the ground and then unzips the top of my jacket, his fingers stroking the neckline of my wool sweater.

I am paralyzed, the higher-level parts of my brain trying to figure out why Gunnar is suddenly so touchy feely and the animal parts telling me to shut up and enjoy it.

Gunnar leans in. His cheek brushes against my jaw. His breath is hot on my neck. Then his lips find mine.

He's gentle at first, like he's waiting to see how I'll respond. He tugs off his gloves and buries his fingers in my hair.

I wrap both of my arms around his neck, pulling him tight against me. This is crazy, a crazy thing to do at a crazy time, but I don't care. Gunnar nuzzles his way up my neck, nipping gently at my earlobe. My insides are suddenly ablaze with heat.

"Why isn't it working?" he mumbles into my hair.

"Oh, it's working." My knees are about to give out. I pull his mouth back to mine.

He unzips my jacket, one hand sliding up under my sweater to rest against my stomach. His fingertips are impossibly warm, almost hot enough to burn me.

An image flashes in my head: the woman from the restaurant talking about the evil at our table, evil that will kill us all. I remember my dream: Gunnar kissing me and then morphing into a monster.

"Hold on." I pull away from him and my MedicAlert ID bracelet catches in his hair. He reaches up and starts to undo the clasp.

"No," I say. "I told you I never take that off."

Gunnar's face twists into something ugly and unfamiliar. He starts to speak, but suddenly I hear footsteps in the tunnel.

"Rory?" Gram's voice echoes off the walls of the passageway.

"We're coming," a second voice calls. It sounds like Gunnar. But that means...

23

E inar!" I pull my arm free. "I knew there was something—"

"Off about me?" he says, his voice sharp. "Not right? Go ahead, I've heard them all. Every reason why my brother is perfect and I'm just a defective copy. A freak."

His words cut more deeply than I expect, because I've heard them too. People referring to me as the 'weird girl.' Classmates whispering. Parents telling their kids to stay away from me.

"I was going to say *different*. You—" Before I can finish the thought, Einar spins around and disappears into the darkness.

I lift a hand to my mouth. My lips pulse with the memory of his kisses. I can still feel his hands on me, his entire body pressed against mine. Why would he do that? Was it just a random impulse when he realized I thought he was Gunnar?

"Rory?" Gram's voice again.

"I'm okay," I holler. I feel around in the dark until I find my helmet. I switch on my headlamp and shine it in the direction Einar went. There's nothing but ice and emptiness.

Gram and Gunnar appear from the other direction. Gunnar is carrying the rifle. Gram has her ice axe clutched in her right hand.

Gunnar points his weapon around the passageway, his finger dangerously close to the trigger. "I heard voices."

I gesture down the dark tunnel. "Your brother was here, but he's gone now. I—I thought he was you."

Gunnar lowers the gun to his side. He shines the light of his headlamp at me, starting at my feet and trailing upward.

He doesn't comment on my flushed skin, my disheveled hair, but I can see his jaw tighten. "Did he...hurt you?"

I slide my helmet back on my head. "No. He just scared me a little."

"Come on," Gunnar says. "Let's get back to our equipment."

"But he's probably still close," I say. "We should go after him. He seemed...sad."

"Sad?" Gunnar's eyes narrow. "My brother can be very charming when he wants to be. You can't trust him."

"You think he came here to lead us into a trap?"

"Maybe. Or maybe just you." Gunnar turns back toward our camp. "Regardless, we can't leave all our belongings. We're heading in the right direction—that's what matters. We'll find him."

Gram walks next to me as we head back to camp, close enough that our shoulders brush. She reaches out and holds my arm, letting Gunnar get a few yards ahead of us. "Are you really okay?" she murmurs.

"I'm fine. I didn't mean to run off. I got up to go to the bathroom and then he found me when I was heading back. I thought it was Gunnar so—"

"Did he seem dangerous to you?"

"No. Just different. A little angry. A little sad."

"Well, I'm glad we found you before anything bad happened," she says.

"Me too," I say, thinking again of the way he kissed me. It feels wrong to keep that a secret, but it doesn't feel right to talk about it either.

We return to the area with our sleeping bags and equipment. Keeping his back to the wall, Gunnar checks out the other tunnels—the one that leads straight ahead and the one from where we first came. "We're alone," he says finally, holstering the gun.

It's meant to be a comforting statement, but there's a big difference between being alone and being safe.

"I'm sorry I worried everyone," I say. "I just went off a little way to go to the bathroom."

Gunnar paces back and forth. "I should have clarified how much my brother and I look alike, that we have the same kind of winter gear."

"I knew you were twins. Plus, you showed me a picture. This isn't your fault." I lift my gaze to Gunnar's. "Something felt wrong from the moment I saw him. I should have trusted my gut." But I didn't. I followed him because I liked the way he was looking at me. *And then you stayed because you liked how he was touching you.*

"What do you mean felt wrong?" Gunnar asks.

I shrug. "It was just something about his eyes. They were almost…reflective in the dark. Your eyes didn't do that when we were in the geothermal pool at the guesthouse. Does he have different color eyes than you?"

Gunnar and Gram exchange a long look. "Somewhat," Gunnar says.

"How does someone have somewhat different colored eyes?"

Gunnar ignores my question. "What did he say to you?"

"He didn't really say much," I reply. "Once I heard you guys call my name, I figured out who he was."

"Let me ask you this," Gram says. "Did Einar try to take off your MedicAlert ID bracelet?"

"Sort of," I say. "But only because it got caught in his hair."

Gunnar's face contorts. He swears under his breath.

"Rory." Gram's voice is firm. "It is very important, now more than ever, that you keep that bracelet on."

"What does the bracelet have to do with anything? You're not making sense."

Gram starts to answer but then pauses. "You know, I think we could all use a cup of tea to settle our nerves."

I frown at my grandmother. "Why are you both acting so weird? I don't need tea. I need *answers*. It's obvious you both know things that I don't."

"Rory is right," Gunnar says. "I think it's time we tell her everything."

"Let me just heat up some water and we'll have a long talk." Gram starts digging through her backpack. "You might not need tea, but I do."

"Whatever," I say, my voice sharp. How is it that my grandmother seems to have secrets with Gunnar, a boy she hasn't seen since he was a baby? How come any time I'm with two or more other people, I always end up feeling like they're part of some special club and I'm on the outside?

Gunnar gestures at the grip of the gun that's sticking out of my pocket. "Get that ready. When in doubt, shoot."

I shake my head. "I'm not shooting anyone who isn't attacking me."

"Fine. Just know that they move fast—faster than we do."

"Who are *they*? The band members?"

"Demons," Gunnar says.

"So now you think *all of them* are possessed?" I ask incredulously.

He glances furtively around the cavern. "I hope not."

Five minutes later, Gram has poured each of us a fresh cup of herbal tea.

"Rory, I want to start by apologizing," she says. "Some of what I'm going to tell you will be difficult to believe. I knew if I shared everything up front that you'd have a lot of questions, and that would end up delaying our progress in searching for Einar."

I look from Gram to Gunnar. "Gunnar told me about

Einar being possessed, about his exorcism, about how maybe he took the demon back. Am I to assume you believe him?" I wrap my hands around my mug of tea, absorbing the warmth.

"Yes, but this goes much deeper than that." Gram exhales deeply. "You don't have malignant hyperthermia. Neither do I. And your mom didn't either. That was just a story I concocted."

"What?" I ask, my brain initially rejecting my grandmother's words. "What do you mean? Why would you do that?" Gram has harped on about malignant hyperthermia since I was a small child. She's been obsessed with me keeping my bracelet on twenty-four-seven.

"Demons are repelled by iron, and the MedicAlert bracelets are manufactured entirely of iron. I had them made specially to protect us."

I remember Gunnar translating the Riftwatcher manual the night before, saying that circles of iron offered protection against demons. That's probably why he asked about my bracelet in the first place. "So it's not just Einar. You both think there are...demons running around everywhere?"

"I don't know," Gram says. "Most demons exist in a non-manifest state. Unless they show themselves, only certain people can identify them. One of the ways is by seeing their eyes reflect silver."

"Wait, so I have the ability to recognize demons?"

"Yes. I thought you might. Your mother did as well."

"It's genetic?"

"I'm not sure," Gram says.

My mind reels as I try to process all of this information. "If what you're telling me is true, does that mean my father is in a mental institution for no reason?"

Gram frowns. "Of course not. Some people respond better than others to witnessing supernatural things. Your father saw a manifested demon before you were born, and he couldn't handle it. The experience made him paranoid. He sees demons everywhere now, which is why he's in the psychiatric facility."

"So if my mother didn't have malignant hyperthermia, then how did she die? Are you saying a demon killed her?"

"Indirectly," Gram says. "Your mother was possessed. She died during an exorcism."

24

Her words hit me like a jolt of machine-gun fire. "My *mother* was *possessed*? How could that happen?"

Gram sips her tea. "About eighteen years ago there was a minor earthquake in this area, which we suspect unearthed the doorway to hell. The village of Leyndarmálsstaður, which no longer exists, was overrun with demons. Your parents were unlucky enough to be hiking nearby. One of the demons possessed your mother, who was pregnant with you. Later, back home, it manifested while she was with your father, and he…did not handle it well. I started treating your mom with medicinal herbs and holy water to keep the demon at bay, but your father refused to see her. He called her a monster and claimed both you and she were touched by the devil."

I think back to the last time I tried to visit my father at the state hospital. I think I was seven or eight. Gram and I flew to Seattle so I could spend a couple of days with my other grandparents and they suggested that I visit. I remember the nurses saying they had reduced my dad's medication dosage because it had been a long time since he'd shown any hint of agitation. Until he saw me.

The minute our eyes met, he started screaming about devils and demons. His features contorted; spit flew from between his lips. The staff ended up having to pin him down and give him multiple injections. No one ever suggested that I visit again.

"Your mother begged me to help her get an exorcism— she thought if she did that your father would take her back. But she was weak from the pregnancy and an exorcism can kill even a strong, healthy person." Gram pauses. "Still, it was what she wanted, so I hired the best man for the job."

"Henning," I say.

"Right. We both knew the risks beforehand. I wanted her to wait until after you were born, but your father was threatening to go back to the States and she feared she might never see him again. She made me promise that I would never let harm come to you. From the moment you were born, I bound you with iron to keep you safe. Demons cannot cross an iron boundary."

I pull up my sleeve and consider my bracelet. I never put a lot of thought into what it meant to have malignant hyperthermia. To me, it felt similar to the kids who carry EpiPens because they're allergic to bee stings. The chances of my needing emergency surgery felt even less likely than some kid from my class getting stung by a bee. I never really understood why Gram was so militant about insisting that I keep the bracelet on. Even now it doesn't quite make sense. We've lived in several different countries. Did she think *all* of them were overrun with demons?

"What happened to the village after the demons got to it?" I ask.

"The Riftwatchers were notified of the breach. They trekked to the doorway and used magic to seal it. But they found so many demons in Leyndarmálsstaður that they decided the safest move was to destroy the entire area. They set explosives and caused a massive avalanche. Given the recent earthquake, people expected that the mountain snow would be fragile. No one suspected human meddling."

"An avalanche can kill demons?"

"If you kill the host body of a demon, the demon dies with it."

I turn to Gunnar. "Is this how your parents died?"

"It is." He looks down at his mug of tea.

"Gunnar's parents were Riftwatchers, but they didn't

agree with the draconian methods employed by some of the senior members. They weren't convinced of the number of demons supposedly present. They tried to help rescue workers at Leyndarmálsstaður, but another avalanche hit the village and they were killed as well."

"So these Riftwatchers murdered an entire town of people just because some of them *might* have been possessed?"

"Yes. To them, no amount of collateral damage is too high when it comes to protecting the Earth from demons."

"And Einar? How did he get possessed?"

Gram sighs deeply. "Henning served as an exorcist for the Riftwatchers. He ended up possessed during a botched procedure. Rather than attempt to exorcise him and possibly kill him, the Riftwatchers taught him to control his demon. That way they could study him, and he could use his demonic powers to hunt other demons at their behest. Having someone who could read minds was very useful to them. It worked for over thirty years, until one day when he was playing with Gunnar and Einar on the front porch, Einar yanked off the iron pendant Henning always wore. Henning felt the demon leave him and assumed it ended up in Einar."

"Why Einar?"

"My grandfather made both of us iron cuffs that we wore around our ankles as children," Gunnar says. "The clasp malfunctioned on my brother's, but Grandfather didn't realize that until later."

"Henning told the Riftwatchers the chain on his pendant broke when he was out shopping and the demon left him. He didn't want to tell them the truth for fear that they would take Einar away, or harm him," Gram says. "Instead, Henning has been giving him the same herbs I gave your mother—they weaken a demon's power and prevent it from having influence over the host body."

"So you took a job knowing we might have to fight *de-*

mons? Gram, this is insane. Why would you think we were capable of handling this?"

"Because the plan has always been to find Einar and the others *before* they got to the doorway."

"But if Einar is already possessed—"

"We're not sure if he is, but we can handle one demon," Gunnar says.

"How? By killing him? Your own brother?"

"No." Gunnar lifts his chin, his blue eyes bright. "The rifle shoots holy water. The bullets cause burning and pain to manifested demons, but the shell exteriors are fragile enough that they'll fracture on impact instead of penetrating flesh. We can use it to subdue my brother, and then I have iron chains we can use to bind him and control his demon. I think from here on out, it's best if all of us are armed. You can carry the rifle, Rory. You have enough training to be a decent shot, and I think you'd prefer a non-lethal weapon, correct?"

That's for sure. "Okay. What about Gram?"

"Ingrid can take the handgun. She's already shown us she's skilled with small firearms." Gunnar pulls a small case out of his backpack. He removes a dagger made of shiny black rock, not unlike the pentacompass. The blade curves and then tapers down to a jagged point. "I'm going to carry this. It's a djöflablað, a demon slasher."

"So you're going to stab your brother."

"Not if I can avoid it. But if we run across other demons, this will provide adequate self-defense."

"It looks sharp," I say skeptically. "But it also looks like you'd have to get really close to use it."

"That is the one drawback. It's effective, though. If you hit the neck or the heart, it's usually fatal."

"Demons have hearts?"

"Demons are parasites," Gunnar says. "They invade every cell of a human host. Humans have hearts, so demons have hearts."

"Is there any way to kill them without killing their human hosts?"

"Unfortunately no," Gunnar says. "The only way to save human hosts is to exorcise the demons and banish them to hell, but that doesn't always work. So now you see my grand-father's urgency. If Einar and his friends open the door, there's no telling how many demons might be let loose in the Icelandic wilderness. There's no telling how many people might die."

25

I exhale deeply. My entire belief system rests on science, on facts and observation, things that inherently make sense to me. If it were just Gunnar and Henning telling me this story, I would have already rolled my eyes and left.

But this is my grandmother, whom I have lived with my entire life. I've never seen her give credence to myths or superstitions. She's always believed in evil, sure, but as far as I knew, it was the kind of evil perpetrated by human beings.

"So you saw my mother possessed by a demon?" I say to Gram. "You *believe* this? Are there really no other explanations for how she died?"

"I grew up Christian," Gram says gently, "believing in heaven and hell, but not giving much thought to the comings and goings from either of those places. I thought it a one-way transport. But what I saw with Katrín was not of this world."

"How can you be so sure? What did it look like? Did her head spin around like in *The Exorcist* or something?"

"I'm not certain whether these details are helpful," Gunnar interjects.

I narrow my eyes at him. "I need to hear this. If I was born from a monster, I want to know."

"You're not understanding, Rory," Gram says. "Being possessed doesn't make someone a monster. It makes them a monster's *victim*. Katrín was just in the wrong place at the wrong time, and simply not strong enough to fight off the invader, because—"

"Because of me," I finish.

"I was going to say because of her condition." Gram

looks kindly at me. "You can't blame yourself. You didn't choose when to be conceived."

Tears well in my eyes. "I don't— This is too much." I bury my face in my hands.

"Just breathe," Gram says. "Do you have more questions?"

I take a couple of deep breaths and exhale slowly. I will the tears away, swallow down the panic that is rising in my throat. I have a million questions, but there's no time to ask them now. This whole day has been a nightmare and it keeps getting worse. I just want to do whatever we have to do so we can go home.

"My questions can wait." I look from Gram to Gunnar. "What happens next?"

"We continue onward," Gram says. "Find Einar, find the pentacompass, make sure the doorway is sealed."

Gram and Gunnar roll the sleeping bags tightly and lash them to the bottom of their packs. Gunnar helps Gram and me lift our backpacks onto our shoulders before donning his own.

"Let's do this," I say.

The words come out more confident than I feel, but I have nothing but the utmost respect for my grandmother. She's been on this earth for a lot of years. If she says demons are a thing and my mom died during an exorcism, I'm going to try to be open to the possibility until some other explanation—a scientific one—presents itself.

Gunnar takes the right passageway, the one where Einar found me. Gram and I follow close behind him. The slope here is a gentle decline, but the path is full of slick spots and frozen debris. Gunnar holds his left arm out for balance, his right hand clutching the curved dagger. Gram is in the middle, still using the ice axe for support, her weapon holstered. I bring up the rear, the rifle slung over my shoulder, easy enough to grab if I need it.

I flash back to the dream of Gunnar turning into a demon again. What would a real-life demon do if it caught me? There have been plenty of TV shows about stuff like that—demons who maul people, monsters who drink blood and leave hollow corpses tossed about. I've never thought much about dying before, but that's not how I want to go, mutilated and abandoned in some lonely ice cave where my body might never be found. And it's sure as hell not what I want for my grandmother.

My chest goes tight again. I inhale sharply, but can't get enough oxygen. Suddenly every streak of blue in the cavern walls feels like the last bit of color I might ever see.

Gram glances back at me. "Are you all right?"

I blink hard. "Yeah, why?"

"It sounded like you were breathing heavy."

"It was probably just a big sigh," I say, trying to keep my voice light. "I can't believe we gave up Christmas in Paris for *this*."

"Me neither," Gram says. "I can't wait to get back to our cookies."

"Did someone say cookies?" Gunnar asks. I didn't realize he could hear us.

I start to jokingly tell him he's not invited to our cookie party when a drip of something cold and wet lands on my cheek and I let out a little scream. Both Gunnar and Gram spin around so quickly that I have to put my hands out to keep from bumping into them.

I lift a gloved hand to my face. "I think it was just water," I say. "Sorry."

Gunnar angles his headlamp at the ceiling above our heads. Sure enough, water is dripping from some of the stalactites.

"What are the chances these tunnels get so wet that the ceiling caves in on us?" I ask.

"Greater than zero," he says.

I give the chin strap on my helmet an extra tug. "Well,

we'd better hurry up, then." The rifle bounces against my
back as I walk, a constant reminder of the danger we're in.

When we reach a place where the tunnel again forks into
two passageways, Gunnar and I split up to check them out.
He takes the left tunnel and I take the right one. As before, I
find a couple of stalactites broken off from the roof of the
cave. "This way," I call.

The tunnels seem to go on forever. Occasionally there are
narrow passageways forking off to one side or another. At
each intersection, we search for clues as to which route Einar
and the others have taken. If there aren't any obvious clues,
we keep to the main tunnel.

As we continue walking, the passageway widens again. It's
maybe ten feet across and fifteen feet high. The ice around
us slowly becomes peppered with bits of stone and dark gray
sediment.

"We're getting closer to where the glacier ends and the
volcano begins, aren't we?" Gram runs one gloved hand
against the tunnel wall. Her glove comes back smudged with
gray.

"We are." Gunnar unzips his jacket halfway. "From this
point on it should be a little warmer."

She reaches for her thermos and takes a couple of sips.

"Is that still tea?" I ask.

"Yes. Would you like some? I'm afraid it's not warm anymore."

I reach out for her thermos and take a long swig. "Maybe
it'll calm me down," I mumble.

Ahead of us Gunnar pauses. "How about you two take a
quick break while I scout ahead?"

"Okay, but don't go far," I say.

Gram and I watch Gunnar's back disappear down the
tunnel. "I owe you an apology," she starts. "I shouldn't have
brought you with me without telling you everything."

"I still have no idea what to believe."

"It's a lot to take in, I know."

The tears rise up again without warning. "Gram, I'm scared," I whisper.

"Me too," she says. "But we'll get through this."

"How can you be so sure?"

Before Gram can reply, Gunnar's headlamp bobs back down the tunnel. "There's a partial cave-in about fifty meters up. It's basically a wall of ice chunks. It looks impassable, but if we can climb to the top, I think there's just enough space for us to squeeze through to the other side."

I cringe. Yay for more tight spaces. "What's on the other side?"

"I don't know. I didn't want to go up there without you two because the climb is going to take a few minutes, and I'm going to be vulnerable until I can get through to the next chamber."

I inhale deeply and let out another long, slow breath. I can be scared later. Right now I have to focus. "Gram and I can cover you while you check it out. Let's go."

I stick close to my grandmother as we continue down the darkened passageway until we arrive at the cave-in. Sweeping my headlamp across the rubble, I swallow hard. The space at the top looks impossibly tiny.

Gunnar starts making his way up the steep pile of ice. He's faster than I am, but I do my best to follow his technique, stepping where he steps and placing the tip of my axe and my crampons in the same spots. I turn around frequently to check on Gram. So far she's doing okay, following me the way I'm following Gunnar.

About halfway up, he executes a maneuver where his long legs support him over a crevice between two slabs of ice. My legs aren't long enough to reach.

"Hold up," I call to Gunnar, who is almost at the top of the heap. I dig my axe into the ice, looking for a handhold I can use to pull myself up. "I need help," I finally say.

Bending low, Gunnar reaches down and grips my fingers, pulling me up onto the next ledge.

"Thanks," I say. "Not all of us have your super-long legs."

"That's right. I forgot that Americans are, on average, quite a bit shorter than Icelandic people. It must be hard to be so...maladapted for everything." He grins to show me he's kidding.

"The struggle is real," I tell him. He bends down to help Gram up on the ledge, but her left hand slips out of her glove. Gunnar lunges for her as she dangles in the air by the tip of her ice axe. No luck. She loses her grip and falls to the ground, landing hard on her tailbone.

"Gram!" I peer down from the ledge. "Are you okay?"

Her face contorts as she tries to get back to her feet. She reaches out toward the wall of ice for support but ends up lowering her body back to the ground. "It's my ankle. It twisted when I hit the ground."

I climb back down to her level and slide my backpack from my shoulders. I pull out the first aid kit. "I can help you wrap it."

Gram winces as she removes her boot. She folds her sock down to expose her ankle.

"What if it's broken?" I ask, unrolling a tan compression bandage.

"We can't know for certain without an X-ray," she says. "Either way, I don't know how I'm going to keep going. Even if you two could pull me back up this pile, I can't put very much weight on that side."

"What if you use the ice axe as a crutch? We could lash two of them together maybe?" I circle the bandage around her ankle in a figure-eight and secure it with a silver clasp.

"That could work, but I would be slow. Too slow." She tugs her sock back on and then gives Gunnar a long look. "As much as I don't want to send the two of you onward alone, I don't see another solution."

I shake my head. "I'm not leaving you."

"I can continue on my own," Gunnar says.

"No." Gram shakes her head. "The greatest dangers lie ahead. The two of you are going to need each other."

"I need *you*," I say.

"Not for this," Gram says. "And I'll be here, I promise. I'm going to have some ibuprofen, elevate my ankle, and take advantage of the cool environment to hopefully prevent much swelling. I'll do my best to be ready to walk again when the two of you return."

"But, Gram—" My voice wavers.

"Rory, it is imperative that the doorway remain sealed. We cannot allow anyone to open it."

I can tell by her steely expression that this is a battle I'm not going to win. I swallow back a sob. Leaving her side feels like a terrible mistake, like tempting fate, like if I turn away from her now I'll never see her again.

But I've also spent my whole life trusting her. Her judgment has never steered me wrong in the past. "You're sure Gunnar can't do what needs to be done without me?" I ask.

"Positive." Gram reaches out and squeezes my hand. "I know you're scared. I need you to do this for me. I need you to do this for everyone."

I am paralyzed for a few seconds, but then the part of me that doesn't want to disappoint her wins out over the part of me that doesn't want to leave her. "Okay, but if you die I'm going to be really pissed off," I say, trying to hide my terror behind humor.

"Likewise." Gram smiles faintly. She exchanges another meaningful look with Gunnar. "Take care of her," she tells him. "Trust your gut." She turns back to me. "You too. Be quick but be safe. Take care of each other."

I reach out and give her a hug. She holds me tight for a few seconds. "Good girl," she whispers in my ear. "Remember, you are stronger than you know."

I swallow hard and blink back tears for the third time in less than an hour. I hope she's right about that.

If Gunnar sees my distress, he doesn't comment. "Let's go," he says.

We turn back to the pile of ice chunks and retrace our path. We're both breathing hard by the time we make it to the top. The space between the top of the pile and the ceiling of the passage is just big enough for us to crawl through one at a time. We duck down, listening for the sound of anyone on the other side. As I stay low and point my gun through the opening, Gunnar pokes his head up.

"I don't see anyone," he says.

"Good." I rise up just far enough to see what's on the other side. We'll have to make our way down the other side of this pile. From there a single tunnel leads farther into darkness.

Staying low, Gunnar crawls through the opening on his stomach and elbows like a sniper. I hold the rifle in both hands, scanning back and forth across the dark tunnel with my headlamp as he slides his way down the jagged mound of ice. Pressing his back to the nearest wall, Gunnar wields the demon slasher before him, angling his light around the passageway.

"Who's there?" he shouts.

I search the area with my headlamp, but I don't see anyone. "Gunnar? What is it?"

"Stay there." He walks quickly down the tunnel, disappearing from view when it curves slightly.

"Gunnar?" I aim the rifle, my finger dangerously close to the trigger.

"False alarm." He reappears in the beam of my headlamp. "Sort of."

"Sort of?" My voice rises in pitch.

"Come through and I'll show you."

I crawl through the hole and fumble my way down the

chunks of ice, sliding down most of the pile on my backside.

"This way." Gunnar leads me down the passageway.

Just beyond the curve, a dead man is sprawled across the damp ground. Two crossbow arrows protrude from his body—one embedded in his chest and another in his neck.

I recognize the skull tattoo on his left temple. It's Ragnar from Black as Death.

"The Riftwatchers are here," Gunnar says grimly.

26

We need to warn my grandmother," I say.

Before Gunnar can reply, something whizzes past our heads. Shards of ice explode behind me. We drop to the floor of the tunnel. "Lights off," he hisses.

I turn off my headlamp and the whole passageway is plunged into darkness. "Are they shooting arrows again?" My face is smashed against the wet ground. My heart pounds in my throat, but all I can think about is Gram. She's all alone on the other side of the cave-in.

"I don't think so," Gunnar says. "My brother used to have this slingshot—"

Before he can finish his reply, an unfamiliar voice shouts, "Get them!"

Gunnar leaps to his feet. I can just barely see the outline of the curved knife slashing back and forth in front of him. I rise up, aim the rifle into the darkness, and prepare to shoot.

Something slams directly into my chest. It's like being punched by an angry robot. I fall backward, my head connecting hard with the ground. I feel a little woozy, but I'm pretty sure that helmet I didn't want to wear just saved my life.

"Rory!" Gunnar is beside me in an instant, his lanky form pressed against the ground. "Are you all right?"

"I think so," I choke out. Lifting a hand to my chest, I feel where the projectile slammed into my winter coat. It didn't break the skin, but it hurts like hell.

"Aw, did I hit a girl?" a voice calls out playfully. This one I recognize.

"Einar, we came to help," I yell. "You and your friends are in danger."

A chunk of ice breaks off from the ceiling and crashes around us. A baseball-sized rock lands next to my foot. Clearly the rocks here are providing useful ammunition for Einar's slingshot.

"You are the danger," Einar calls back.

Gunnar rolls me onto my stomach and shelters my body with his. Sliding the rifle off my shoulder, he whispers in my ear, "If I provide cover fire, can you crawl to the left? There's a natural alcove where we can take shelter."

"Yeah," I say.

Gunnar fires a couple shots down the tunnel while I crawl to safety. In a few seconds we're both tucked securely behind a lip of rock. We're trapped, though.

"The Riftwatchers are here," Gunnar yells. "We just want you to come home. You know what'll happen if they find you first."

Icy shrapnel rains down from above us. "I don't have a home," Einar yells.

"Who's with you?" Gunnar asks. "We found Ragnar. Are the rest of the band members safe?"

"Don't pretend to care about us," the unfamiliar voice calls—perhaps Lars or Benjamín.

Gunnar grips one of my hands in his as he speaks to his brother in Icelandic. Kind, gentle words, at least that's how they sound. Einar does not respond.

Gunnar hands the rifle back to me and pulls the curved blade from his waistband. "On the count of three," he says quietly, "I'm going to point my headlamp down the tunnel. Hopefully it'll blind them. Shoot anyone you can, all right? Remember, you're not going to kill them. We just need to immobilize them temporarily."

"Then what?" I whisper back.

"We use the iron bindings I brought to restrain them. I'll handle that part."

"Okay." I suck in a sharp breath and aim the rifle down the dark passageway.

"One, two...three." Gunnar flicks on his headlamp. Surprised by the sudden light, Einar lifts his hand to protect his eyes. I aim for his midsection and pull the trigger twice. His slender body contorts, and he stumbles backward. A growling sound comes from behind Einar, and a figure starts running toward us. I see a flash of pale skin and a red beard—Benjamín. He doesn't seem to be carrying a weapon, and his head is lowered as if he were a bull about to gore us. His body starts to glow with a silvery light. I squeeze off a third shot. He's close enough for me to see the bullet hit the top of his head, water droplets and metal shavings spraying out from the point of impact. He lets out a roar that sounds inhuman. He's still moving toward us at full speed. As I prepare to fire again, Gunnar steps forward with the curved knife.

As Benjamín reaches us, Gunnar slams the curved blade deep into his chest. Benjamín's eyes widen, his mouth opens, and blood flows from his lips. Gunnar twists the knife and lifts his arm sharply, opening Benjamín's body from his heart to his throat.

Something warm and wet splatters across my face as Benjamín crumples to the ground. Blood. Demon blood. I don't even want to think about what terrible side effects could befall me if I accidentally ingest any of it. I swallow back a surge of bile as I wipe my mouth with one of my gloves.

Gunnar's light shines down the passageway, and we see Einar raising his slingshot again, pointing it at me. *Crap.* My breath catches in my throat as I take aim with the rifle. My finger dances on the trigger. Two more shots. Two more hits. Einar screams in pain, his body falling to the ground.

27

I slump back against the wall in relief.

"Come on." Gunnar hurries down the passageway toward his brother. I take a deep breath and follow him, praying he was right about my rifle not being lethal. Luckily, when we reach Einar's side, he lets out a slight groan.

Gunnar unzips a compartment on his backpack and pulls out something silver. It's a chain the width of a shoelace. "It's stronger than it looks," he explains. He binds Einar's wrists behind him. "Let's go," he tells his brother. He hauls Einar to his feet and herds him back down the passageway.

Einar makes a strangled sound when we pass Benjamín's body. "He was one of my only friends."

"I had no choice," Gunnar says.

"There's always a choice," Einar replies, his breathing labored. "Speaking of choices, brother, do you think she'll still choose *you* once she knows everything?"

"I don't want to hurt you, Einar," Gunnar says, through clenched teeth. "But I will knock you out if I have to."

I look down at Benjamín's body, his insides spilling out onto the cold ground. Clearly Gunnar has no problem using lethal force. I try to reconcile the laid-back, easygoing guy he's presented himself as this trip with the ruthlessly efficient killer I watched a few moments ago.

He recognizes the horror in my eyes. "I know it looks bad," he says. "But he could have killed both of us."

"It was just hard to watch," I murmur.

The three of us head back toward the cave-in, but then Gunnar stops abruptly. He gestures toward his brother. "Shoot him again if he tries to run. I need to check something."

Einar and I watch as Gunnar returns to Benjamín's mutilated remains and starts rifling through his pockets. He
doesn't seem remotely fazed by the carnage splayed out in
front of him. I don't have quite that strong of a stomach. I
swallow back a surge of bile and look away.

Einar laughs lightly. "What's the matter? Are you worried
now by how adept my brother is at killing? Having second
thoughts?" He turns his attention to Gunnar, who is still bent
over Benjamín's corpse. "I wish he could have heard what
you were thinking when the two of us were alone together.
Pity we were interrupted."

"What are you talking about?" I ask, rage building beneath my skin as I think about the kisses Einar stole from
me. Then I remember Gunnar telling me about the different
types of demons, that Einar was a mind-reader.

"Yes," he says. "I can hear your thoughts. It's a gift be-
stowed on me in exchange for being a vessel for a higher
power. And right now, you're thinking I'm insane to consider
a demon a 'higher power.' And before that you were wondering if there's something wrong with my brother, since he
shed Benjamín's blood so easily."

"Enough," Gunnar calls. He returns to the two of us and
hauls Einar to his feet. "Walk or we'll drag you."

"Where are we going?" Einar asks.

"You're going to stay with someone who can guard you
for a while. Rory and I are going to make sure no one unseals
the doorway to hell."

Einar chuckles again. "Too late. We already opened it."
His eyes flick to Benjamín's corpse. "But you know that,
don't you?"

"Einar, why?" Gunnar pushes his brother back toward
the pile of ice. "Why would you want to let demons out into
the world? Why would you want other people to become
possessed?"

"Do you really have to ask? For the first time in my life I

had friends who accepted me, friends who actually *liked me* for who I was. I'd never force them to become the same as me, but when they said they wanted to, it seemed like a way to guarantee that they'd always be in my life."

"I guess. Except now two of them are dead."

"Thanks to you," Einar says coldly.

"I didn't kill Ragnar," Gunnar says quietly. "And Benjamín was self-defense."

"Part of you enjoyed killing him."

"That's not true. I did what—"

"You forget I can read your mind, brother. Do you know what it's like," Einar continues, "to be able to hear the thoughts of your own family and realize you're a problem, a burden, someone they're ashamed of?"

"I am not ashamed of you," Gunnar says firmly.

"Maybe not, but you were relieved when I started to keep my distance."

Gunnar is silent for a few moments. All three of us know this is true. He shines his headlamp down the passageway. "We're going to be climbing up that pile of ice. There's space at the top where we can squeeze through one at a time."

Einar pauses. "I'll need my hands to climb."

"No chance. I'll pull you." Gunnar grabs the front of Einar's winter coat. "And if you try to run, we will shoot you again." He glances back at me. "Rory, can you help me from behind?"

"Uh, sure." I slide the rifle onto my shoulder and make my way up the jagged pile behind Gunnar and Einar, giving Einar's back some gentle shoves to help with momentum.

Gunnar ducks Einar's head down so he can squeeze through the hole and back to the cave where we left Gram. I grab the rifle and cover them while Gunnar helps Einar down to the ground. Then I crawl back through the hole and down the pile of ice with Gunnar's assistance.

Gram is sitting with her back against the wall of the tunnel, her gun clutched in one hand. She looks up at the three of us. "You found him. Wonderful."

"We also found Ragnar and Benjamín. They're both dead," Gunnar says quickly. "Ragnar was killed by an arrow, so we know the Riftwatchers are here. And my brother says the doorway has been opened."

Einar sizes up Gram with calculating eyes. "Who's this?"

Gunnar tightens his grip on the chain binding his brother's wrists. "Someone is going to need to stay here and guard him while we continue on. Ingrid, I thought that perhaps you—"

"Sure, I can do that." Gram brandishes the handgun.

"If he tries to run, shoot him." Gunnar turns his brother around and looks him in the eye. "This is Ingrid. She's Grandfather's friend. She's also very good with a gun, and her bullets are lethal so I wouldn't test her."

Einar mumbles something under his breath and reluctantly lowers himself to the wet ground opposite Gram. He leans his back against the wall, his eyes focused on her, on the gun in her hands.

"Will that chain really keep him from manifesting?" I ask.

"Yes," Gunnar says. "At least from manifesting fully."

Einar turns his attention to me, his eyes once again looking silver in the dim light. "They're both keeping secrets. You should ask about—"

"Stop talking." Without warning, Gunnar slams Einar across the face with his elbow. Einar's head snaps sharply on his neck, his body falling over to the side.

"Gunnar!" I've never seen him lash out like that. Even in the tunnel when his life was in danger, he was still calm and collected. I reach out and lean Einar's body back against the wall. He's unconscious but still breathing.

"Sorry. I shouldn't let him get to me."

I glance from Gunnar to Gram. "What did he mean? What kind of secrets?"

"Ignore him, Rory," Gunnar says tersely. "He's just trying to get into your head."

"You can't trust him," Gram adds. "Even if he's a decent person underneath, right now he's...affected."

"We just told you the truth back at the campsite, remember?" Gunnar adds.

I do remember, but if Einar can read my mind, he can read Gram and Gunnar's minds too.

"Search his pockets," Gunnar tells me. "See if he has the pentacompass."

Einar's words replay in my brain as I go through his jacket and pants pockets. He's got the usual stuff in them—a crumpled tissue, a set of keys, his cell phone—but no bloody rocks that point the way to eternal damnation. "He doesn't have it," I say.

"Benjamín didn't either. Annika or Lars must have it. We have to find them."

"How are we going to do that?"

"We're going to have to find the doorway. Luckily, I brought along a spare." Gunnar pulls a dark rock from a small zippered compartment in his backpack.

"You had another pentacompass this whole time?" I grit my teeth. "Why didn't we use it instead of spending so much time looking for tracks?"

"It doesn't work unless you add demon blood to it."

Gunnar removes the St. Benedict necklace and unscrews the pendant—which I now see is a tiny vial—from the chain. "I got some blood from Benjamín when I was looking through his pockets." He tilts the vial and lets a few drops of blood drip onto the second pentacompass. As the blood comes in contact with the stone, it sizzles and smokes. Gunnar's eyes meet mine. "Still trying to decide if you believe?"

"What's happening?" I ask, my eyes transfixed by the stone. I'm trying to come up with a scientific explanation, but my brain is failing me.

"When demon blood hits a demon artifact, it becomes activated." Gunnar flattens his palm and the stone spins around wildly, eventually pointing farther down the dark tunnel. "Time to go," he says.

"Gram, are you sure you'll be okay?" I look worriedly from Einar to my grandmother. "How's your ankle?"

"The ibuprofen is already kicking in," she says. "I'll be fine. I'll keep an eye on him and you two take care of the rest."

"Keep an eye out for the others—Annika and Lars," Gunnar says. "And the Riftwatchers. It's possible they'll find you before we find them."

"I'll do whatever needs to be done," Gram says.

My stomach knots at the thought of leaving my grandmother in imminent danger, but then I remember how calm and adept she was when we stopped at the twisted bridge. She's a great shot and she's able to make quick decisions. Even injured, she's probably more capable than I am.

"Just a minute," I tell Gunnar. I pull the pink lunch box out of my pack and undo the clasps. I find a folded silver blanket and wrap it around Gram's shoulders. Then I take two of the hand warmers out of the bundle and slip them loose into my backpack in case Gunnar and I need them.

I give Gram the rest of the bundle. "Just in case either of you get too cold. We'll be back as soon as we can. Be careful, okay?" I swallow back a lump in my throat. "I don't want to lose you."

Gram reaches out for my hand. "I'm not going anywhere. Be strong and hurry back."

"We will," I promise.

∼

Gunnar and I clamber over the ice pile again and continue toward the doorway. "I hope Einar behaves himself," I say.

"Me too." Gunnar looks over at me. "She's strong, you know? Your grandmother."

"Yeah," I say softly, still wondering what kind of secrets the two of them are keeping from me.

"How are you?" he asks. "That was a hard hit you took back there."

I had almost forgotten about the blow to my chest. My adrenaline must have kicked in during that fight. "It hurts, now that you mention it. But I'll live. Thanks to this helmet." Then I blurt out, "What's it like knowing your twin brother is possessed by a demon? Does it make you think differently about him?"

Gunnar shakes his head. "No. His decision to take the demon back makes sense to me. He went from feeling isolated and unloved with special powers to just feeling isolated and unloved."

In front of us, a puff of steam filters through a crack in the wall. The smell of sulfur permeates the air.

"You can still trust him knowing that he's possessed?"

"I have trouble trusting most people," Gunnar says. "I still love him though. He's still my brother."

"I guess that's the thing I'm having trouble with. He could've killed us, Gunnar. And then he made you so angry that you bashed him across the face. What if he's not still your brother? Isn't there ever a time when a human and a demon get so tangled up there's no…separating them anymore?"

"I don't know." Gunnar's jaw tightens. "But I know he's still Einar. The part where he made me angry—that was 100 percent my brother. We've always known how to get under each other's skin. I overreacted by hitting him. I'm sorry you had to see that." Before I can respond, he points up ahead. "Look."

The beam of his headlamp illuminates walls of rippling rock—the entrance to the lava tubes.

28

As we hurry forward I look around in wonder. I expected the walls to be slick like volcanic glass; instead, they're rough and ridged, a dusty gray color with bands of red and iridescent purple woven throughout.

Removing one of my gloves, I run my fingers over the texture. "I can't believe lava made these. I was imagining having to crawl through some tiny tube like you'd find on a children's playground. This is bigger than the ice caves."

"Some of the passages will probably be small, but this one demonstrates how powerful the previous eruptions were."

The tube we're walking in ends abruptly in a cavern with several other tubes leading out from it, like spokes on a wheel. Gunnar holds the pentacompass out before him. It twitches on his palm before turning to point at a spot between two of the lava tubes. We spend a moment quickly evaluating each of the openings.

One is slightly larger than the other, with uneven ground and clusters of rocks that we'll have to scramble over. The other is smoother, but barely high enough for me to walk in without hunching over. There are no indications which way Black as Death might have gone.

"What do you think?" Gunnar arches an eyebrow.

My gut wants to take the first path, but I'm pretty sure that's just because of my claustrophobia. I don't want my personal weakness to mess up this job.

"This one." I point at the tighter tunnel.

Gunnar ducks low to enter the tunnel. I follow, the water rifle bouncing against my back with each step. The smell of sulfur stings my nasal passages. Sure enough, the tunnel shrinks as we continue and soon both of us end up crawling on our hands and knees.

"Do you hear that?" Gunnar pauses and cranes his neck to look over his shoulder at me.

I close my eyes to prevent being blinded by his headlamp. "Hear what?"

"There's a bubbling sound. I think it—"

A huge blast of steam pours from a hidden crack. Gunnar pushes my body back with both hands to keep me from being burned. My head takes yet another bump as I land flat on my back. We end up in a heap on the tunnel floor. Gunnar's chest is smashed against my face. His heart is beating rapidly.

"Are you okay?" I ask.

He doesn't answer at first, but gently untangles his legs from mine and rises to his knees. Pulling off one glove, he feels the skin of his face.

"I think so. But that steam could have blinded me." He reaches down and pulls me to a seated position. "Are *you* okay?"

"Yeah. Thanks for pushing me out of the way."

"To be honest, I'll be glad when we're out of here and we can stop saving each other."

"Seriously." I look down at my gloved hand, still clutched in Gunnar's bare fingers. "But until then, I'm really glad you're with me."

"Same." He squeezes my hand.

Another blast of steam spews from the crack in the wall. We're far enough back to enjoy the warmth without having to worry about getting burned.

I swallow back a yawn and let my eyes fall shut. "Feels good."

He snorts. "Yeah, this would be a nice moment if it weren't for literally everything else happening."

"True that." I roll my neck in a slow circle in a futile attempt to get rid of some tension.

"We'd better try the other tube so we don't get our faces burned off." He starts crawling back the way we came and I follow him, relieved when I'm able to rise back to a standing position.

Gunnar grabs my arm before I duck into the opening of the next tube. "Wait," he says, his expression deadly serious. "There's something I should probably tell you before we make it all the way to the doorway."

"Okay," I say slowly. *What now?*

"There's more to the story that Ingrid shared," he starts. "She held back, I think, because she was worried about you. There are some things it's never easy to hear, but it's especially hard to process them when you're already under a great deal of stress."

Gunnar sounds exactly like my grandmother, who constantly praises my resilience but goes out of her way to protect me from everything I'm supposed to be able to handle.

"I'm not a delicate flower," I protest. "I don't know why you guys think you have to keep secrets from me for my own benefit, but I wish you'd knock it off."

"I know. So here goes." Gunnar sucks in a sharp breath.

I wait expectantly. Just as he's about to speak, he turns his head sharply.

"You're really building up the suspense here," I say.

He lifts a finger to his lips. "I heard something."

"I don't hear any—" My words fall away as a blast of light hits me in the face.

A broad-shouldered man dressed all in black emerges from one of the other lava tubes. I realize all Gunnar has for a weapon is the demon blade. I flail for the rifle, but I'm too slow. The man lifts a crossbow, the arrow pointed directly at Gunnar's chest.

29

The man whistles sharply, and two other shadowy figures emerge from the same tube—a man and a woman. They're also holding crossbows. "Place your weapons on the ground," the man tells us. "I don't want to hurt you, but I will if you make this difficult."

Gunnar lays the curved knife down on the ground. "Riftwatchers, yes? You shot me in Skeiðarársandur."

"I don't know what you're talking about," the man says, lowering his bow as he reaches for Gunnar's demon slasher. "I am a Riftwatcher, yes, but I didn't shoot anyone. My name is Ulric. I'm here to guard the doorway."

"Well, someone shot me with an iron-tipped arrow from a crossbow," Gunnar says.

Ignoring him, Ulric gestures at me. "Put the gun down."

I slowly place the rifle on the ground. The woman picks it up and ejects the magazine. "Iron casings." She shakes one of the bullets. "With holy water."

"What does a demon want with holy water and a demon slasher?" Ulric takes the rifle from the woman's outstretched hand. He loops it over his shoulder.

"I'm not a demon," Gunnar says. "You're thinking of my brother. We're twins."

"I heard you took your brother's demon after he almost got arrested," Ulric says.

Gunnar shakes his head. "We both know better than to try something like that."

I study his face carefully. Taking Einar's demon because he thought he could handle it better sounds like something Gunnar would do. His eyes aren't silvery like Einar's were, but maybe that only happens when a demon is partially manifested. Maybe Einar's demon came from the open doorway. Maybe both brothers are possessed now.

"Why should we believe you?" Ulric asks.

Sighing, Gunnar pulls off his left glove. "I don't care if you believe me or not, but go ahead and test my blood with the pentacompass if you feel the need."

Ulric makes a small incision in Gunnar's palm with the demon slasher, and Gunnar holds his hand over the pentacompass. A drop of blood falls to the rock. There's no sizzling, no smoking. He squeezes out a couple more drops. Still, the pentacompass displays no reaction.

"Satisfied?" Gunnar asks. "We're on the same side here. Aurora and I were on the way to seal the doorway before you stopped us."

"So it's been unsealed?" the woman asks.

"I don't know for certain. I killed a man named Benjamín," Gunnar says. "He was partially manifested, so it seems likely that the door has been opened."

"Ulric, we need to finish executing our plan," the woman urges, gripping her weapon.

"What plan?" Gunnar asks.

"Never mind," Ulric says. He turns to the other Riftwatchers. "You two finish...doing what needs to be done. I'll go with these two and help seal the door."

The other Riftwatchers disappear into the darkness.

"Where are they going?" I ask, worried about what will happen if they run into Einar and Gram.

"They're going to search for any escaped demons," Ulric says.

"Well, they can't just go around shooting everyone," Gunnar says. "Aurora's grandmother is injured and is waiting for us back in the ice caves."

"We'll detain people only until we can be sure they are not possessed, after which they shall be free to go."

"So why didn't you do that at Leyndarmálsstaður?" Gunnar asked bitterly. "Instead of murdering an entire village."

"I assure you I had nothing to do with that," Ulric says.

Gunnar doesn't respond, but I can tell by the tightness of his jaw that the Riftwatcher's words didn't help matters.

"Let's move." Ulric nudges us toward the lava tube.

"If Rory and I are going first, at least give us back our weapons," Gunnar says. "We have no idea how many demons we might run into."

Ulric hands the demon slasher to Gunnar and the rifle back to me. We make our way across the rocky terrain, doing our best to keep our weapons wielded with one hand while using the other hand for climbing and balance.

I jam my gloves into my pockets and unzip the collar of my jacket. It's probably twenty degrees warmer here than it was on the surface. "Good thing I dressed in layers," I say.

"There are a lot of geothermal vents in this area." Gunnar points at a tiny trickle of water that's running along the left side of the tunnel. "Careful where you step. I bet that's hot."

I glance back at Ulric. The Riftwatcher is lagging slightly behind Gunnar and me. At first I assume it's just because he's out of shape, but then I realize he appears to be favoring his left leg. I wonder if he took a spill in these tunnels like Gram did.

The lava tube narrows so that we have to walk in single file. Gunnar is ahead of me. I'm in the middle and Ulric brings up the rear. The tube twists sharply to the right. When we round the corner, Gunnar pulls me close to him and grabs the rifle from my hands.

"What are—?" I ask, startled.

"Shh." He shakes his head, then lifts the rifle. As Ulric rounds the sharp turn, Gunnar points the weapon at him. Before he can retract the string on his bow, Gunnar shoots Ulric point-blank in the face. Ulric stumbles backward, dropping his crossbow. I grab it.

"You said we were on the same side," Ulric moans. "Why would you shoot—"

Before he can finish his question, Gunnar hits him hard in the head with the butt of the rifle. Ulric crumples to the ground.

My eyes widen. "I wasn't exactly enjoying his company, but why—"

"He might not have had anything to do with my parents' deaths, but he's definitely the one who shot me," Gunnar says. "You don't see a lot of crossbows in Iceland, and I remember the way the shooter favored his left leg as he ran back to the car."

"Looks like I'm not the only one who's observant," I say. "I was so freaked out I didn't even notice that. What should we do with him?"

"Leave him here," Gunnar says. "His friends will come looking for him. We need to keep moving. It's almost midnight. If by some chance Benjamín was already possessed and the band hasn't opened the doorway, they'll be getting ready to do so at any moment."

"Do you think my grandmother is safe?"

"Yes," Gunnar says. "Ingrid has a weapon and the means to stay warm. Einar is under control. Even if the other Riftwatchers find her, she's not possessed. They might kidnap or kill my brother, but they'd gain nothing from hurting your grandmother."

"She'd be a witness to a crime," I point out.

"An injured, elderly woman pulled out of a freezing cave and talking about demons and demon hunters? No one would take her seriously and the Riftwatchers know that. They're ruthless when it comes to their agenda, but they're not bloodthirsty." He gives me a reassuring look. "And from what I know of Ingrid, she's tough, she's resourceful, and she's a crack shot. If anyone is going to be okay today, it's her."

He's right. I need to stop worrying about Gram and start worrying about everybody else. I'm still not sure I believe in demons, but I can't deny what I've seen with my own eyes. I believe in something, and if there's a door that can be opened to let a lot more of that something out into the world, I want to be sure it stays closed.

Gunnar and I follow the pentacompass through several more lava tubes, stopping just long enough to place a cave marker each time we change directions. He scrambles up a small hill of boulders to duck into a new passage and I am close behind him. Suddenly the pentacompass starts spinning in circles.

"We're here," Gunnar breathes.

He swears under his breath as he tilts his light toward the center of the chamber. A large crack, thin at the edges but three feet across in the middle, runs through it. The faintest hint of gray smoke curls in the air above the crevasse.

"My brother was telling the truth," he says. "They've already opened the doorway."

30

I step forward to examine the chasm in the ground. It looks like every other crack and fissure we've seen over the past day. I try to imagine a cloud of supernatural monsters seeping out of it. "This is the doorway?"

"Yes," Gunnar says.

"It's not very majestic."

"Were you expecting an actual door?" His voice is tinged with sarcasm, or maybe that's frustration, because we're too late.

"Maybe," I admit. "Something like a big metal plate in the wall adorned with serpents and tongues of fire. It's possible I watch too many movies."

"Evil often disguises itself as mundane," he says. "The more elaborate or majestic something is, the more people take notice."

"So now what do we do?" I shine my light directly at the doorway. All I see is darkness receding into forever. I wonder what would happen if I slipped and fell into the chasm.

Or jumped.

"We have to reseal it," Gunnar says grimly. He removes the medallion from around his neck and uncaps it. "The blood of a demon can magically seal the doorway."

He walks along the middle of the chamber, stopping every few feet to let a drop of blood fall into the chasm. Smoke curls upward from the darkness. I trace its path with my light, taking in a ceiling of sharp stalactites above our heads. The ground shifts gently under my feet as the opening begins to seal together, leaving only a jagged crack. When Gunnar reaches the widest part of the opening, he bows his head and speaks quietly under his breath. I'm not sure if he's praying or if he's doing an incantation or something that is part of sealing the doorway, but I'm suddenly hit with a sense of foreboding.

"We should probably hurry," I say.

"I've just got to finish the rest," he says. "A few more drops should do it."

The ground rumbles sharply as a droplet of blood falls from his vial.

My head snaps from right to left as I quickly scan the dark chamber with my headlamp. "Is this shaking due to the door being closed?"

"No, it's a little earthquake or something," Gunnar tells me, his attention still focused on the doorway. *Drip.* "Don't worry. The volcano is not going to erupt."

"Okay, but an earthquake still sounds bad."

Drip. The ground rumbles a second time. A giant stalactite from above Gunnar's head breaks off and plummets down toward him. I see it happening, almost in slow motion. I leap forward to prevent him from being impaled. As I push him to the ground, the stalactite lands behind us, fracturing into jagged shrapnel. Gunnar ends up on his hands and knees, the vial with Benjamín's blood slipping from his fingers. It falls to the floor of the cave, and dark red liquid dribbles out of it.

"Oh my God. I'm so sorry." I flail for the St. Benedict medallion. "I didn't mean to make you drop it." I press the metal circle back into Gunnar's hand.

He lifts himself back to his feet without answering. He looks warily up at the ceiling before making his way back to the chasm in the floor. He tips the tiny vial. "I don't have any more blood."

"So now what?" I ask. "Do we have to go all the way back to Einar?"

Gunnar shakes his head. He pulls the demon slasher from his pocket. "I can get more blood, but you're not going to like it."

You're not going to like it? A fist tightens around my heart. So my suspicions were correct. Gunnar is possessed, just like his brother. Somehow, he must have tricked Ulric and the others. He lifts his head and his soft blue eyes study me with trepidation. It's seems impossible. He's too kind to be housing a demon.

"What I wanted to tell you before Ulric found us is that my brother was right about me keeping secrets. I owe you an apology. This isn't the right time or place for this, but there are no other options."

I lean slightly away from him. Swallowing hard, I say, "It's okay. I've been wondering if maybe that was the secret that your brother kept mentioning—that you're possessed too. I think part of me has known ever since that night at the restaurant in Vík. I just didn't want to believe it."

Confusion flickers across Gunnar's face. He cocks his head for a moment, a shock of blond hair falling in front of his left eye. And then his features relax. He tucks the lock of hair behind his ear. "I'm sorry, Rory, but you don't understand," he says. "I'm not possessed, you are. You've been possessed your entire life."

31

My brain screeches to a halt, temporarily rejecting reality as I attempt to process his words. *I'm possessed? No, that's not possible. I must've heard him wrong.*

I am still in a fog as he approaches me. I watch him as if I were a third person witnessing the scene. He reaches for my left hand. "I only need a little bit."

My brain finally catches up and I yank my hand back from the curved blade. "Wait a minute. What did you say?"

"I'm not possessed, Rory. You are."

"No." I shake my head. "There's no way. I would know if I were *possessed.*"

"I understand why you might think that, but—"

I cut him off. "No one walks around with a demon in them all oblivious. Especially not for years!"

Gunnar doesn't respond to this. He just waits. Waits for it to sink in that this is exactly how it was for his brother.

But that's Einar, I think frantically, and everyone said he had a troubled childhood. My childhood was normal. *Except for the part where you got kicked out of multiple schools for being reckless. And the part where you took every dare, no matter how foolish, and then couldn't explain later why you did it. And the part where you never made any real friends.*

Okay, fine. But none of that makes me a *demon.* I think back to Gunnar's words from last night. *Not all demons are evil. They're chaotic and self-serving, but some of them are just impulsive…*

"No." I shake my head violently. "I don't believe you. You're trying to trick me." I'm not sure if I'm talking to Gunnar or the voice inside my head.

"Why would I do that?"

"Because you're the possessed one, not me."

Gunnar holds out his hand, the cut clearly visible, to remind me that his blood didn't react with the pentacompass.

"But what about this?" I point to my iron bracelet. "Gram said a demon couldn't get to me if I wore it."

"The iron band works to keep a demon inside someone, just as it does to keep it out. And it keeps the demon from fully manifesting, from taking over."

"Why would my gram want to keep a demon *inside me*?"

"Because the alternative is an exorcism that could kill you."

"Like it killed my mother," I say softly.

"And inside you, the entity can be controlled. If it decides to leave, who knows who it would choose to inhabit, what it would do?" Gunnar snaps his fingers. "The tea she gives you. That also helps. It's got special protective herbs in it."

My gut twists violently as a montage of images plays in my brain: tea parties when I was a small child, tea with dinner, Gram bringing me a cup before bed each night to help "calm anxiety and encourage deep sleep." Gram and I have been drinking her special tea together for as long as I can remember and I never even questioned it. Is it possible Gunnar is right?

He hands me the demon slasher. "We don't have time to argue. Do it yourself if you don't believe me."

"Fine." I take the dagger from his hand. It's heavier than I expected. I have to adjust my grip on it to control the blade. I turn the sharp edge toward my palm. Wincing, I cut into my flesh. A line of red forms on my hand. It's blood. Completely non-demon, normal human blood.

And then Gunnar holds the pentacompass beneath my palm. A single drop of blood falls. When it makes contact with the stone, the blood sizzles and smoke curls upward.

"No," I say softly, shaking my head. "This can't be."

But the words feel hollow, even to me. I can't deny what I just saw with my own eyes.

Gunnar removes the demon slasher from my shaking fingers. "Look, Rory, I know you have a lot of questions, but right now we need to seal the door and get out of here... while we still can."

I nod dumbly, still in shock. Part of me remains outside of my body, watching this scene as if it's a movie instead of my life. "How do I do it?"

"Just envision the ground sealing together in your mind and let your blood drip into the crevasse. Three more drops should do it."

"It's that simple?"

"Demon blood is powerful, especially in certain hands."

In my hands. In my *possessed* hands. I follow Gunnar's instructions. Smoke rises from the crevasse, and a coldness rushes through my body. Voices chant in my head in a language I've never heard before.

Another wave of revulsion moves through me. I think of Einar manipulating me into kissing him, of Benjamín lowering his head and charging at Gunnar. I think of every demon I've read about. Tricking people, lying...killing. There's something unholy in me that's been there since I was a baby. *Demons are parasites...* Who knows how entwined we are, whether my demon has integrated itself into my brain and vital organs? Who knows whether I can still be saved?

No wonder I've spent my entire life feeling like an ostracized freak. I'll demand an exorcism the moment we return to civilization. My mother wasn't afraid. I won't be afraid either.

"Rory?" Gunnar's voice cuts through the reverie. "Are you all right?"

I realize that the chanting has stopped; the curls of smoke are fading away.

"Let's go," I say wearily.

"You're not going anywhere." A pale girl with a curtain of long black hair stands in the opening to the chamber.

32

I recognize the girl immediately—it's Annika Lee. She's wearing fashionable snowboarding pants and a puffy, down-filled jacket that hugs her slender frame. She cocks her head to the side as she considers Gunnar and me. Her eyes glow silver in the dim light.

Lars appears in the doorway behind Annika. He strokes his braided beard.

Annika strides into the center of the chamber, frowning as she considers the sealed doorway. I reach for the water rifle slung around my back and she shakes her head. "I wouldn't do that." Her eyes lock onto mine as her body starts to shimmer.

My fingers bend backward at an unnatural angle. Pain floods through my hands. Screaming, I fall to my knees. The pain radiates upward, into my arms, into my chest. My breath whistles in my throat as I curl into the fetal position. "Stop," I beg.

Gunnar lunges forward, brandishing the demon slasher.

Annika looks away and the pain stops. "Do you know how hard we worked to get here so we could open the doorway?" She clucks her tongue, as if Gunnar and I were unruly children who just destroyed a jigsaw puzzle she'd spent hours completing. "Why would you close it?"

"You know why," I tell her, gingerly wiggling my fingers to see if anything is broken.

"Because some *human* told you that big bad demons would escape out into the land? All we want is to be free, like everyone else. Isn't that right, Lars?"

"That's correct," Lars confirms in a gravelly voice.

"What gives you the right to trap us underground like vermin?" Annika strides toward me, a confident smile on her face. Her eyes flick briefly to Gunnar as she bends down and helps me back to my feet. "And certainly you can't trust anything *he's* told you. He's not on your side. He can't be. He isn't one of us."

"She isn't one of—" Gunnar abruptly lifts a hand to his throat, making a gagging sound.

"What's that you were saying?" Annika asks playfully. "I didn't quite hear you."

"What are you doing to him?" I cry. "Let him go."

"I'll let him go, as soon as he lets that go." Annika points at the demon slasher Gunnar is still clutching in one hand.

Gunnar drops the blade and Annika releases him. He crumples to the ground in a heap.

"Gunnar!" I start toward him.

"Oh, he's fine," Annika sneers. "Mortal bodies aren't *that* weak." She holds out her right hand and the demon slasher floats through the air and lands gently in her palm.

Gunnar's eyelids flutter open. He massages his throat with one hand. "Rory, run," he groans.

Annika turns her attention back to me. "She doesn't need to run. We're not going to hurt her. Why would we do that?"

"Because I'm not one of you," I say firmly.

"You will be." Annika tosses her black hair. "I can feel the presence within you. Take that bracelet off and experience your power."

"No," I say. "I'm not handing control of myself over to some demon."

"It's not *handing over* control," Annika replies scornfully. "It's sharing control. It's synergy. You'll both be stronger. Aren't you even a little curious?"

"About how it would feel to be a monster? No, thanks."

"Monster. So dramatic. Do I look like a monster to you?" Annika twirls in a circle. "It's more like being a superhero."

"Don't listen to her," Gunnar begs.

"Definitely don't listen to me. Listen to *yourself*. This is who you are."

I shake my head. "I get to choose who I am."

"Is that so?" She arches an eyebrow. "And you don't even want to explore your power? You know, all possessed entities have special powers. Mine is telekinesis. People tend to think of that as being able to move things with your mind, but I can also stop things with my mind." She smiles sweetly at Gunnar. "Like a heartbeat."

He grabs at his chest. "What are you—?" He sinks to his knees, then falls to the ground, his face reddening.

"After thirty seconds, the tissue will start to die," Annika says. "After a minute, the pain will be so bad that he'll pass out."

"Stop!" I lunge for her, both of my fists striking her in the stomach.

Lars makes a hissing sound as he steps forward, his skin starting to shimmer.

"It's fine," Annika says to him. The blows glance off her as if she's made of solid stone. As I prepare to strike her again, she smiles serenely. "Take your bracelet off, and I'll let your frail human pet live…for now."

Gunnar's face has gone from red to blue. He's still standing, but his eyes are closed. "Fine, whatever," I say, my voice cracking.

I fumble with the clasp of the MedicAlert bracelet. It takes me a few seconds to unfasten the chain. As the iron falls away from my skin, a wave of warmth rushes through me.

I gasp softly. It's not just warmth I feel, but a strength coursing through my limbs. Holding out a hand, I see that I'm also glowing with silver light. "Now let Gunnar go," I say, tucking the bracelet into my jacket pocket.

Annika rolls her eyes, then flicks her wrist as if she were

throwing something into the garbage. Gunnar's body lifts off the ground and slams into the back wall of the chamber.

I rush toward him, pressing a hand to his chest. He groans but doesn't open his eyes. His heart beats faintly beneath my fingertips.

Lars steps between Annika and me, his forearms still emitting a silvery glow. His body seems to have grown in size. He watches me intently.

"It's fine," Annika tells Lars. "And the human is fine," she tells me. "Now let yourself feel it. Feel what the world has been denying you."

I don't want to let myself feel it, but I'm afraid if I put my bracelet back on that Annika might kill Gunnar. I take a few deep breaths and pretend to embrace the power flowing through me. *Think of what we could do together*, a little voice whispers.

That is exactly what I don't want to think about it, but of course, as soon as I try to block those thoughts out they multiply. My skin glows brighter. Some part of me is desperate to know what my power is. I feel lighter, faster, as if the boundary between my body and the environment were blurry. "I feel like I could fly," I murmur.

"I don't know about flying, but you can probably jump high." Lars squats down low and then lifts his body up into the air, almost banging into one of the stalactites hanging from the ceiling of the cave.

I bend my knees and rocket my body upward, my hands raised above my head. I don't get as high as Lars, but I'm definitely clocking more hang time than I did as a human.

As a human. What am I doing?

"There has to be a catch." I direct my attention inward, trying to connect with the demon that's supposedly been possessing me my whole life.

"Not everything that feels good has a catch," Annika replies. "Come with us, Rory. We need to find the others."

"Ragnar and Benjamín are dead."

She maintains a neutral expression, but some of the light fades from her eyes. "How?"

"Ragnar was dead when we found him and Gunnar killed Benjamín in self-defense." My gaze moves to Gunnar, who is still lying motionless on the ground. His skin is returning to a normal color. "You promised you'd let him live," I add.

"What about Einar?"

"Einar is still alive. We left him back in the ice caves."

Annika's expression softens slightly. "I'm glad to hear that. I've grown rather fond of him over the past few months. You will take us to him, but first we must reopen the doorway." She pulls the demon slasher from her pocket and cuts her palm. She walks the length of the doorway, drizzling her blood along the crack. She closes her eyes for a moment. The ground splits open again, faint gray smoke rising up from the chasm.

Suddenly, Gunnar leaps up from the ground and lunges for Annika. His body slams into her and the curved blade falls from her grasp.

"Get the knife, Rory!" he hollers.

I look toward the demon slasher but something holds me back. Gunnar reaches out with his right hand, seizing the hilt of the dagger. He lashes out at Annika, puncturing the front of her winter jacket, but missing her heart.

She shrieks—an angry, inhuman sound.

Lars leaps for Gunnar, but Annika gets there before him, sharp claws, bursting through the fingers of her gloves. She knocks the blade out of Gunnar's grasp, striking him hard across the abdomen.

Gunnar slumps to the ground again, blood seeping from jagged slashes in his coat.

"You liar!" I scream at Annika. "You promised you'd let him live."

"He attacked me," she yells back, silver eyes flashing fury.

Lars grabs me under my arms, pulling my body back from Annika.

Annika cocks her head to the side. "Let her go," she tells Lars. "She isn't going to hurt me."

Oh no? I curl my right hand into a fist. The second Lars releases me, I strike Annika hard in the face, wincing as my flesh connects with the sharp edge of her nose ring.

She laughs. "I know you can do better than that."

"Go on," Lars chimes in. "I love a good girl fight."

My lips twist as my teeth sharpen within my mouth. My hands curl slightly, my fingernails growing and transforming into silvery claws. "That's it," Annika hisses. "Give in, embrace it." She pushes me with both hands and I stumble backward, catching myself just before landing on the seat of my ski pants. Crouching low, I prepare for her next attack. Now that my demon has manifested, Annika either can't attack me with her magical powers or she doesn't want to.

"It feels good, doesn't it? It feels…right." She leaps high into the air and lands on me.

Both of us end up on the ground. We trade punches. Blood seeps from my nose, but it doesn't even really hurt. I still feel more alive than I ever have before.

But then I catch a glimpse of Gunnar out of the corner of my eye. A pool of blood has formed beneath him. His eyes are closed. There is no way he is going to survive. For all I know, he's already dead. A series of images flash across my mind: meeting him at the airport, arguing about the sweater, him opening the door to his guesthouse room in Vík, him teasing me from the warm water of the geothermal pool, him offering to show me around town when this is all over. For a few days I felt connected to someone other than Gram, and now that connection has been severed. What good is feeling alive if you're all alone?

"You didn't need to kill him," I lash out, intending to slap Annika across the face.

She catches my wrist with one hand. Her lips twitch, as if she's finding this whole situation amusing. "You said he killed Benjamín, right? If you want to stay alive, you learn not to take unnecessary chances. You'll understand eventually."

"No, I won't." I grab her hair and drag her back to her feet. "I'll never understand being a monster. I'm sending you back to hell where you belong, so you can't hurt anyone else." I pull her toward the crevasse.

And then something weird happens.

Annika starts to separate into two forms—I'm pulling a smoky-gray shadow toward the doorway to hell, but her physical body hasn't moved. Ignoring the human part of her, I direct my attention to the hazy outline. "I'm sending you back to hell," I say again. I reach out with my other hand and grab the figure, digging my claws into its back. My hand tingles and burns as the demon struggles against my grip.

I expect the presence inside me to say something, to tell me to keep going or to stop, but there's only silence. This is my choice.

"Let her go!" Lars growls. The look on his face is pure hatred, but he's keeping his distance.

He's afraid of me.

"What're you doing?" Annika asks. "What's happening to me?"

I'm not even sure, but I think I might be performing an exorcism. With the hazy form still gripped in my hands, I step up to the doorway and throw it downward with all my might. Lars cries out in what sounds like pain. As he lunges for me, I scoop the demon slasher off the cavern floor, turning just in time to bury the blade between his ribs. I attempt to grab him as I did with Annika, but he jumps out of reach. Pulling the glistening black blade from his wound, he holds it out between us. "This isn't over," he says, his breath labored. Then, with the dagger still clutched in his hand, he disappears back into the lava tubes.

I bite into my hand and reopen the wound on my palm. Quickly I bleed into the full length of the crevasse as I will the doorway to close again. The ground rumbles beneath me as the crack seals.

Annika's body lies motionless next to the doorway. Turning away from her, I hurry to Gunnar's side. I can't feel a pulse, but his skin is warm to the touch. I pull up his fleece and the T-shirt underneath, exposing three jagged wounds, all of which are bleeding profusely.

I fumble in my backpack for the pink lunch box. The bleeding kit consists of a combat tourniquet, some liquid Band-Aid, and a sheet of wound dressing with clotting agents woven into the fabric. It's meant for moderate lacerations and scalp wounds. There's no way it's going to fix Gunnar— the dressing isn't even big enough to cover his injuries. But maybe if I combine it with my newfound powers...

Leaning over, I whisper in his ear. "You said my blood was magic. Can it help you?" I press my bleeding hand to the wounds on Gunnar's torso before covering them with the dressing.

And then I pray.

33

I don't even know who I'm praying to—if I'm possessed, does that mean I have to pray to Satan? Will God still help me if I want to do the right thing?

Sending my pleas out to the universe in general, I apply firm pressure against Gunnar's skin, visualizing the jagged wounds, the blood clotting, the edges coming back together. I don't know if it's working or if it's all in my head, but strength seems to flow from my body.

Bending low, I rest the side of my face against Gunnar's face, the angle of his cheekbone firm beneath my skin. Even in death he is beautiful, his eyelashes feathered together, his lips a pale pink.

"I'm so sorry," I say. "This is my fault."

Gunnar's eyelashes flutter. I pull back, almost certain I imagined it. I lift one hand from his wounds and rest my bloodstained fingertips against his throat, slowly tracing them down the side of his neck in search of a pulse.

His eyelashes flutter again. This time I know I didn't imagine it.

"Gunnar?" I say.

"Rory," he chokes out, his eyes still closed. "Is she gone?"

It takes me a second to realize he means Annika. I scan the chamber. She's sitting on the ground with her back against the wall, staring off into space. She's probably in shock.

"It's safe," I say, not ready to explain what happened when I sent Annika's demon back to hell. Is that my power? Am I some sort of species-traitor exorcist? "Are you...okay? I thought you were dead."

"Me too." His eyes flick open and his soft blue gaze washes over me. "Whatever you're doing, I think it's helping."

"That's good, except I have no idea what I'm doing." My voice cracks. I swallow back a lump in my throat.

Gunnar lifts his head from the floor of the chamber, tilting his neck just far enough so he can see my hands pressed against his midsection. "Let me see."

I lift the dressing. The jagged red gashes have closed up to the point where he's no longer bleeding.

"Incredible," he says.

"I did that?" I can't believe it either. "I grabbed the dressing from our bleeding kit, but I never thought it could—"

"Because it can't," he says. "You did that. With the help of your blood."

I gently adjust Gunnar's T-shirt and fleece so his wounds are covered. "Rest for a few minutes. I need to check on Annika."

His eyes widen in alarm. "I thought you said—"

"It's okay. She's…normal now."

"How? Is it in me?"

I shake my head. "No, somehow I pulled the demon out of her and tossed it back through the doorway."

"The doorway." Gunnar rolls onto his side. "Did she open it again?"

"She did, but I resealed it."

"Wow. You got a lot accomplished while I was dying."

"It's one of the few good qualities of Americans," I say. "We tend to be workaholics."

Gunnar laughs weakly and then clutches his midsection. "Hurts to laugh."

"I'll try to be less funny." I squeeze one of his gloved hands. "Now, seriously. Just rest for a few. I'll be right back."

"Be careful," Gunnar mutters.

As I cross the damp ground to Annika's side, something shiny glimmers in the light of my headlamp. My bracelet! It must have fallen out of my pocket. I loop it back around my wrist and fasten the clasp.

Annika's chest is rising and falling with slow, steady breaths. "Wake up," I say, shaking her gently.

Her eyes open. "What happened?" she asked. "I feel so... weak."

"You're not weak," I say. "You're back to normal. Unpossessed."

Her eyes narrow at me. "What if I didn't want to be unpossessed?"

"I guess you're out of luck. But you've got to get up so we can get moving, assuming you still want to be *alive*."

Grumbling, Annika allows me to help her back to her feet. She goes to her backpack and rummages around until she finds a canteen. Unsnapping the lid, she takes a long drink. "What about him?" she asks, gesturing toward Gunnar.

"He's going to be okay." I return to Gunnar's side. "Can you walk?"

He uncurls his legs and lifts himself to a seated position, one gloved hand wiping bits of down stuffing from his midsection. His fingers toy with the gouges in the front of his coat. "I still can't believe..."

"Me neither," I say. I reach down to pull him to his feet. "But right now we need to get back to Einar and Gram."

Gunnar is unsteady, but he manages to stand with my help. He rests one hand on my waist. "I thought I was going to die without ever getting to do this." He brushes his lips against mine. "I'm glad I met you, Aurora Quinn. And not just because you saved my life."

I kiss him back. For about ten seconds the world belongs to us.

34

We find Einar and Gram in the same place we left them, just on the far side of the pile of ice chunks. Gram looks wan and cold, but she's still got the gun clutched in both hands. Next to her Einar has his eyes closed.

"He's been out for most of the time you've been gone," she says.

Annika bends down and strokes the side of Einar's face. His eyelids flicker and he groans softly, but he doesn't fully wake.

"Did you find the pentacompass?" Gram asks.

"I totally forgot about that in all the chaos." I turn to Annika. "Do you have it?"

"Are you talking about the Hellfinder? That piece of rock with blood smeared on it?"

"That is exactly what I'm talking about."

Annika turns away from Einar long enough to dig through her backpack. She wrinkles up her nose as she hands over the pentacompass. "The past few days are kind of a blur," she says. "I can't believe we followed that thing all the way out here."

I give Gram the pentacompass. "I also found out some other interesting things. About me."

"I see," Gram says. "Then I imagine you have questions."

"I do, but they can wait. How's your ankle?"

Suddenly the ground shakes. A rumbling sound drowns out her reply. Bits of rock and ice fall from above our heads.

"More earthquakes?" I ask Gunnar.

"I don't know. That felt different," he says. "We need to keep moving. Ingrid, can you walk at all?"

"I'll do my best," Gram says, letting me help her back to her feet. She leans heavily on her ice axe.

Gunnar bends down and shakes Einar, who snarls in response. "You need to get up and walk with us, Einar. None of us is in any shape to carry you."

"What if I refuse?" Einar says, without opening his eyes.

Gunnar sighs. "Then I guess I drag you."

"Why not just let me die?"

"Because you're my brother, and I love you."

"And I love you too," Annika says, bending down to Einar's level.

His eyelids blink open. "I thought you were dead."

"I'm right here," she says.

He reaches out to touch her face. "But you're different."

"Yes, but that doesn't mean *we're* different." She smiles. "At least not to me."

"Really?" Einar's voice is full of skepticism.

"Really," she says. "Come on. We can talk more once we get to safety."

"All right." Slowly, Einar gets to his feet. "Where's Lars?"

"I don't know," I say. "I stabbed him but he escaped... with the demon slasher. He could be anywhere."

"We don't have time to look for him," Gunnar says.

"Do you think other demons escaped?" I ask.

"Yes," Gunnar says grimly. "They'll show themselves eventually. We can't see them until they take a human host, and even then only certain people can see them."

People like me. My certainty about wanting an exorcism wavers. The thought of a demon inside me makes me sick, but if Gram can teach me to control it, and if I can use its power for good, maybe I shouldn't be so quick to rid myself of it. After all, Gunnar is alive because of my magical blood.

Because of my demon.

"I could walk more easily if you untied my wrists," Einar says.

"The chain stays on," Gunnar says. "We take no chances."

Einar sighs. "So little trust."

"Maybe you don't remember it, but you attacked us," Gunnar reminds him. "Trust will have to be earned."

"You sound so much like Grandfather," Einar sneers.

"Einar." Annika speaks to him softly in Icelandic and he falls quiet.

We continue toward the chamber where we'd left our rope and climbing gear, but before we get halfway there a series of explosions shakes the entire tunnel. A stalactite breaks off and shatters right in front of my boots. I look up at the ceiling of the cave, imagining the stalactites crashing down, impaling us as if we were trapped in an iron maiden.

"The Riftwatchers are setting off explosives," Gunnar says. "They must have found the doorway resealed and decided to blow up the entire network of caves in case any demons escaped."

My breath sticks in my chest. If we don't all get out of here soon, we could end up trapped underground forever.

35

We retrace our steps through the passageways, Gram and me leading the way. She's using her ice axe as a cane and moving more quickly than I expected, but I can tell by her expression that she's in a lot of pain. She declines to use me for support, but I stick close to her anyway.

The explosions have caused the tunnels to warm, which has caused melting. Icy water sloshes around our ankles, slowing our progress and snaking its way beneath the layers of our protective gear. Ahead of me, Gram stumbles. She flails her arms and almost ends up going down face first into the freezing water.

I grab her by the back of the coat to help her regain her balance. "Are you okay?"

Her skin looks ghost-white in the glare of my headlamp. "The water got into my boots and I've lost all feeling in my feet," she says. "I'm just trying to keep moving, but it's difficult."

"Hold on to me," I say. "We can fall down together."

I expect her to refuse the offer, but she reaches out for my gloved hand. I wrap my fingers around hers and the two of us continue to lead the way.

Behind us, Annika sounds like she's struggling. "How much farther?" she asks between labored breaths.

"We're almost there," I say, trying to keep everyone's spirits up even though I know the chamber with our climbing gear is at least twenty minutes away.

Another blast echoes through the tunnels. I turn to look behind me. "Why aren't they blowing everything at once?" I ask Gunnar.

"Probably because they're still in the tunnels," he replies. "Either that or they don't want to create a major event on the surface where people might realize what they've done."

"Why would the Riftwatchers still be in the tunnels?" I ask.

"Hunting demons," he says. "They don't just sacrifice other people's lives to keep evil from escaping out into the world. They give their own lives too, if it comes to that."

"That's messed up."

"Some would say devout," he replies.

It hits me that "hunting demons" now includes Einar and me. I glance furtively around again, praying that we make it back to the surface alive.

When we finally reach the cavern with our rope, I nearly fall to my knees in relief.

"I'm going first," Gunnar says. "I can climb the rope and then hoist the rest of you out one at a time."

"Okay," I say. "I'll go last, just in case anyone has trouble."

Gunnar shimmies quickly up the rope and then lowers his harness back down. Gram goes next, then Annika, then Einar. Finally, I slide the nylon harness around my legs and waist. Gunnar pulls me back to the surface.

I exhale deeply as I step back onto the glacier. It's colder above ground, especially now that it's nighttime, and my breath makes a cloud of fog in front of my face. Gunnar and Gram are huddled together, speaking softly, while Annika rolls up our rope. Einar is standing alone, gazing forlornly into the distance. His body trembles slightly.

I walk across the snow. "I have some hand warmers if you're cold," I say.

He turns to me, and I see that his eyes are wet with tears. "I'm not cold. I just can't believe my friends are dead." He looks away. "Ragnar and Benjamín were two of the only people who accepted me the way I am."

Annika comes up behind us. "I'm still here," she says. "And I accept you."

Einar's shoulders slump in defeat. I'm not sure if he doesn't believe her words or her acceptance isn't enough for him.

"Your brother accepts you too," I say.

Einar looks over at his brother, who is removing the anchors he screwed into the ice yesterday. "No, he doesn't."

"He does," I say. "We talked about it. And I obviously accept you since we're in the same position."

Annika touches Einar gently on the back, between his bound hands. "I'm going to see if your brother needs help."

We watch her leave. Einar studies me quietly for a few moments. "When did you realize it?"

"Gunnar told me a couple of hours ago."

"That must have been quite a shock."

"It was. It still is. It's going to take me a while to wrap my brain around it."

Einar looks down at the ground. "I'm sorry about earlier. When I got close to your group, I could read your thoughts about my brother. I wanted to hurt him, to get back at him. When I realized you were possessed, I thought if I could bring out your demon I could take you away from him—bring you over to our side." He blinks hard. "But what I did was...very wrong."

"Rage makes us do reckless things," I say softly.

Einar nods but doesn't reply.

Gunnar, Gram, and Annika join us. "How do you feel about hiking over there and setting up camp for the night?" Gunnar points to the nearest mountain. "We'd have some shelter from the wind."

"I can't believe you want to camp out here," Annika grumbles. "I just want to get home."

"I know, but it's not safe to hike in the dark," Gunnar says. "And Ingrid can't possibly walk all the way back on her ankle.

I was thinking tomorrow I could hike in until I can pick up a signal and call for a rescue."

"What about the Riftwatchers?" I ask.

"We'd have to take turns keeping watch," he says. "We've still got better weapons than they do."

"Are you including Rory and me when you speak of weapons?" Einar asks quietly.

"Well, I hope it doesn't come to that." Gunnar looks from his brother to me. "But, yes, I suppose I am."

"Camping it is then," Annika says. "Let's get a move on."

Gunnar looks up at the sky. "At least it's not snowing."

"Bite your tongue," Gram says.

The five of us head toward the mountain. Annika and Einar fall in on either side of Gram. Gunnar and I end up walking next to each other a bit behind the rest of the group.

"How are you doing?" I ask him.

"I don't know, to be honest. I'm glad my brother is still alive, but I'm worried about the consequences of the doorway being opened, even for just a couple hours. Who knows how many demons might have poured out into the wilderness?"

"But you said they can't hurt anyone unless they find bodies to possess."

"Right, but they don't need bodies to move. If any of them escaped the tunnels, they could make their way into the surrounding farms and villages and possess people there. And no one would know it."

"I would know, right?"

"Correct, but it's not like you can hang out in Iceland and hunt demons."

"Gram and I can work from anywhere," I say. "I don't necessarily *have* to leave."

"Yes, you do," Gunnar says. "You're not a Riftwatcher. You have a life somewhere else that you deserve to go back to."

"I know. But everything is different now."

"It doesn't have to be." His eyes lock with mine. "Rory, you spent almost eighteen years possessed without it ever really affecting you. Exorcism or not, you can choose to continue that."

I look over at him. "It sounds like you *want* me to leave."

Gunnar shakes his head. "That's not it. I just—"

"You just what?"

"Everyone leaves eventually," he says. "Maybe it'd be easier on both of us if we just skipped to that part."

His shoulders slump as he looks away. I want to comfort him and remind him I know what it's like to be left behind— abandoned. But I'm still so confused about his feelings for me.

"I have a question," I say.

"Yes?"

"How long have you known I was a demon?"

Gunnar exhales deeply. "You're not a demon. You're possessed. But to answer your question, Grandfather told me shortly before you and Ingrid arrived."

"So you knew this whole time and you still pretended to want to be my friend, to show me around town—"

"All of that is true," Gunnar says softly. "No pretending."

"How can you want to be close to me knowing what I am?"

"Being possessed doesn't define you. It's not who you are," Gunnar says. "It's just one of—" His words fall away abruptly. He lifts a hand up to his eyes and squints into the distance. "Do you see that light?"

I follow his gaze. Sure enough, there's a round white light moving in our direction. As it grows closer, I realize it's mounted on the front of a sled.

A dogsled.

ercury and Saturn come loping into view. It's Nasrin and her team! She's got eight dogs this time instead of six.

"How did she know we needed help?" I ask.

Gunnar shakes his head. "No idea."

Nasrin slows the team as she approaches. The dogs come to a full stop and she hops off the back of the sled. Immediately Mercury and Saturn and the two dogs behind them collapse to their bellies. One of the dogs closest to the sled starts barking. It's Salmon. I smile and give him a little wave.

"Need a ride?" Nasrin lifts her goggles up onto her forehead. Her eyes take in the disheveled appearance of our group and widen slightly when she realizes Einar has his wrists bound. "You seem to have picked up a couple of members, but I can fit all of you on if you don't mind a tight squeeze."

"You're a lifesaver," I say. "How did you know we were still out here?"

"It's a long story. I'll explain once we're somewhere safe."

"Is it safe for the dogs to run at night?" I ask.

"It's not ideal," she says. "But they've done this path so many times they know where the safe places are. I can take two in front, two in back, and someone can stand back here with me."

I glance at Gunnar. "I can stand in the back. That way you can...stay close to the others."

"Okay."

We pack our belongings into the cargo hold. Gunnar takes a seat next to Gram behind Einar and Annika. I step gingerly onto the back runner of the sled next to Nasrin.

"It's just like surfing," she says. "But easier, since you have something to hold on to."

"What if I've never surfed?"

"Then just hold on tight."

Nasrin calls out to the dogs and they take off running. In front of me, everyone is quiet. I think we're all just relieved we don't have to walk all the way back to civilization.

I keep my knees slightly bent and my grip tight around the back of the sled. The wind blows my hair back from my face. I see why Nasrin compared it to surfing—the icy ground is flying beneath my feet. I feel powerful and alive.

Suddenly there's a series of huge cracking sounds behind me, like gunshots. More explosions from the Riftwatchers? I turn my head sharply. "What was that?"

"Avalanche," Nasrin yells. "But I think we're far enough ahead of it."

"You *think*?" Jeez, this girl has ice in her veins.

"Don't panic." She leans hard, turns the sled sharply.

Another series of blasts shatters across the sky. This time when I look back, I see the snow plummeting from high in the mountains, just to the left of us. Nasrin hollers at the dogs. They bark. We speed up and continue to veer right.

There's a new noise now, a dull roaring sound, like radio static turned all the way up. It's snow, I realize. Rolling mountains of snow, coming for us, threatening to swallow us up. I force myself to stare straight ahead.

Annika turns around and the fear in her eyes almost does me in. Her lips contort into a scream, but I don't hear it over the roaring snow. Next to me, Nasrin is crouched low, her muscles coiled tight. She looks determined. She looks confident. And then, just when I think everything is going to be fine, I am ripped from the back of the sled and my entire world goes white.

37

The force of the avalanche tosses my body around like a ragdoll in a hurricane. My neck twists one way, my legs another. I try to lift my arms, to propel myself along and keep my head about the surface, but it's futile. All I can do is wait.

And hope.

What flashes before my eyes isn't my parents or grandparents. It's the townspeople of Leyndarmálsstaður. Did they see the wall of snow before it swallowed up their houses? Did they know they were about to die?

Suddenly my body stops moving. I am still surrounded by whiteness. I burrow my arms up (or is it down?) toward my face and push the snow away from my nose and mouth, creating a tiny airspace for myself while I figure out what to do next.

"Gram!" I yell. "Gunnar?" My chest feels tight. I have no idea if the avalanche took the entire dogsled or not. I start to hyperventilate as I imagine my grandmother trapped like me.

Stop. I take in a breath and count to four before exhaling slowly. Then I think logically about my predicament. All I can do is try to reach for the surface and hope some part of my body shows through. But which way is the surface?

Gathering saliva in my mouth, I use my tongue to push it out onto my face, which is gross, but a good strategy to figure out which way is up. My spit dribbles toward my left eye, which means when the snow stopped moving it left me almost completely upside-down.

There's no way for me to reorient my body—the snow is packed tight against me. I kick hard with my right foot, praying that my crampon or the toe of my boot might find air. I don't feel any change in my surroundings so I try my left foot.

"Gram," I call again. "Nasrin?" My voice sounds muffled, as if I'm underwater. Pressure builds in my head. I replay the last few seconds before I fell off the sled in my mind. Nasrin was steering at a hard angle. She seemed confident we could escape the avalanche. Probably everyone else is okay. Probably they're looking for me. All I have to do is survive.

My chest aches beneath my layers of clothing, but this time I don't think it's panic. I think it's because I'm starting to use up the oxygen in the little cave I carved around my face. That means I'm breathing mostly carbon dioxide.

My fingers are still bracing the snow away from my mouth, but I'm afraid to enlarge the space. I could mess up and the snow might collapse and suffocate me. *All you have to do is survive.* If only it were that easy.

I fight the urge to cry. I don't have enough air for that. I count the passing seconds in my head. Thirty... sixty... ninety. My head is pounding now. I don't know if it's from being inverted or from lack of oxygen. If this is how it ends for me, at least I've seen a lot of the world. I've had adventures other people only dream about. I've felt love from my grandparents and Macy, affection from Gunnar. If I die today, I'm glad I helped him rescue his brother. A single tear runs from my eye toward my forehead. I blink hard, my eyelashes frozen over with snow.

Don't give up. The voice inside me is soft, but firm.

Holy crap. I almost forgot I was possessed by a demon. *Can you help?*

Maybe...

I can just barely reach my bracelet with my left hand. I pull hard, breaking the slender chain. A current of warmth courses through my veins. I muster all my strength and kick upward with both feet. I channel the power within me. I envision myself breaking through the snow. Escaping. Sur-

viving. The heat inside me intensifies. I can't see my skin, but
I know instinctively that it's glowing. Claws explode through
the fabric of my gloves. My teeth sharpen again, their edges
pressing against my gums. I concentrate everything I feel—
the energy, the power, the determination—into my arms and
hands. Then I punch outward with my fists. The snow gives
way slightly. The tiny cave around my face expands, and I feel
a trickle of water against my cheek. The heat of my body is
melting the snow! I keep punching out from my face, my
neck, my chest. Soon there's a hole big enough for me to
twist my body around so I'm positioned upright.

The pressure in my head dissipates. I inhale deeply and
then punch upward with both fists, my claws slicing their way
through the melting snow. In a few seconds, I break through
the surface. "Gram!" I scream.

"Rory!" Her voice carries across the glacier. I swallow
back a sob. *Thank you*, I tell the demon. *Thank you so much.*

Hands are pawing at the snow now. People are yelling,
but I can't make out any words. Within a couple of minutes,
my head and neck are free. I suck in a deep breath of air. My
claws have disappeared and the glow of my skin has faded.
Nasrin and Gunnar are kneeling in the snow. Gunnar pulls
me from my snowy prison and lays me flat. Stars glitter above
my head. My whole body shudders with sobs.

"Oh my God, Rory." He blinks back tears. "I'm so glad
you were close to the surface."

I don't tell him that I wasn't, that I pounded my way out
of the snow with the help of a demon.

"You should rest for a few minutes," Nasrin says softly. "I
will prepare the dogs."

I turn my attention back to Gunnar. "Gram," I choke out.
"Where is—"

"Right here." Gram's head peeps over Gunnar's shoulder.
I cry even harder. "I thought I was going to die."

Gram sniffles. "Not me. I knew we'd dig out this entire

mountainside if we had to, and that you'd find a way to stay alive until we found you."

Gunnar brushes snow from my face. "We were using the ice axes to probe the snow. I didn't think we would ever find you." His voice cracks. "But then I heard you scream for your grandmother."

I use my hands to lift my body to a seated position. "Everyone else is okay?"

"Yeah. We banked hard to try to get out of the path, but you got clipped by the very corner."

"I lost my bracelet," I say. "Do you happen to have another iron chain I could wear?"

"Yes," Gunnar says, unzipping a small pocket in his backpack. "I can't believe you didn't lose your helmet in all that."

"Hey," Annika says, her brow furrowing. "We should probably get moving. It looks like—"

"Just a second," Gunnar says.

"All right, but—" Annika's words fall away as the ground all around us starts to shake. She points behind us.

We all turn to look. The sky above Huldulogafell has gone a hazy gray. Plumes of smoke and steam are rising from cracks in the surface.

"I don't believe it," Gunnar says. "The volcano is going to erupt."

38

Gunnar tosses me a slender iron chain and I loop it around my neck. Gram helps me back to my feet and all of us head for the sled. This time I sit next to Gram, and Gunnar stands with Nasrin on the back of the sled. She hollers to the dogs and they take off running.

I look back at Nasrin. She's crouched low, her mouth hollering out commands to the dogs, who somehow find an extra reserve and run even faster. Gunnar is also bent low, mimicking Nasrin's form. I wonder if I looked as cool as he looks riding the back of the sled. *What are you even thinking? Of course you did.* I smile to myself. I definitely did.

Until I fell off, anyway.

Behind them, Huldulogafell continues to vent clouds of steam and ash.

"We should be safe now," Gram says loudly. "We're far enough away."

Nodding, I turn back around to check our progress. Up ahead I see the gray-brown of the trail leading back to the parking lot.

Nasrin slows the sled to a stop at the edge of the glacier. "Is everyone all right?"

Einar and Annika bob their heads. Gunnar says he's fine. Gram mumbles something about quite enough adventure for one week. I couldn't agree more.

"Will the people who live nearby be okay?" I ask.

"The lava probably won't reach any of the homes or guesthouses," Gunnar says. "If by some chance it did, people would have plenty of time to evacuate."

The dogs pick their way down the edge of the glacier and back onto the ground.

"We need to stop here for a minute while I change the runners back over to the wheels," Nasrin says. "Would one of you give my dogs some water?"

I start to volunteer, but Gram holds me by the wrist. "I think you should sit here and relax." She brushes some snow from my hair.

"We can give the dogs water." Annika hops off the sled and Einar follows her. Gunnar turns to help Nasrin with the sled.

"How are you holding up?" Gram asks. "I can't imagine what you just went through."

"It hasn't hit me yet," I say. "I heard what sounded like explosions before the snow fell. Do you think the Riftwatchers caused the avalanches?"

"I don't know. If so, they probably just wanted to bury any demons who might have escaped the tunnels."

"But they could have killed us."

Just then there's a rumbling noise in the distance, followed by what sounds like thunder. Chunks of white snow explode upward into the air as the volcano erupts. Jets of bright orange magma light up the dark sky.

"That's...impressive," Annika says.

"Oh, there's no way the volcano will erupt," I say, glaring at Gunnar. "Am I allowed to say 'I told you so'?"

He laughs. "You're allowed to say it more than once. Honestly, I don't understand it. I checked the daily reading for the past several weeks and there's been absolutely no indication of an increase in pressure that would be required for an eruption."

"Maybe it's me," I say. "I'm kind of bad luck like that."

Gunnar ruffles my hair. "You definitely seem a little accident prone."

"You have no idea," Gram says.

"Hey." I poke her in the arm before turning back to Gunnar. "Says the guy who fell through the ice yesterday."

Gunnar smiles. "I forgot about that. Seems like it happened in another lifetime."

"If you two will excuse me, I'm going to say a quick hello to my favorite sled dogs." Gram slides out of her seat and heads for the dogs at the front of the sled.

"It has definitely been an action-packed week," I say. "You really think the people who live nearby are safe?"

"The lava won't make it more than a couple of kilometers at most. The ashfall isn't the best for crops, but luckily no one is growing anything right now." He pauses. "We might have some mild flooding to deal with and the airport might have some smoke delays, but that's about it."

"I can't believe I just saw a volcano erupt," I say. "That was almost as cool as the dogsled ride."

"Almost, eh?" Gunnar grins, brushing a lock of half-frozen hair back from my face. His expression turns serious. "I'm really glad you didn't die today."

"Likewise," I say, giving Gunnar a quick hug.

39

The sky has grown hazy with smoke. Bits of ash float through the air. I'm still trying to wrap my head around how close I came to dying in an avalanche. Closing my eyes, I think about the members of Black as Death who died in the ice caves. Benjamín and Ragnar weren't themselves when they attacked us. If I had known about my powers then, maybe I could have saved them. Perhaps my powers could have saved Lars too. He surely died in the explosions, the avalanches, or the eruption.

Nasrin takes us back to the dog farm and lets us off in front of the building. She unlocks the door to the small lobby with the sledding souvenirs and memorabilia. "Give me a few minutes to deal with the dogs and I'll be back. We can provide you dry clothing and throw your wet items in the laundry for you. And you're welcome to use our facilities to clean up. We have plenty of towels."

"I could really use a shower," Einar says.

"Yes, you could," Annika agrees.

He bumps her playfully with his shoulder as they duck into the building together. It's nice to see that the two of them are able to joke around. I'm guessing they're both going to be traumatized after the adrenaline wears off and they have to deal with the reality of losing three of their friends.

I exhale deeply, embracing the warmth of the lobby, relieved to be back indoors. I can't believe we were in the tunnels for less than a day. I feel like I lived an entire lifetime with Gunnar and Gram.

Nasrin reappears from the back. "You are welcome to spend the night. We're not open for business tomorrow so we can lay out some blankets here."

"Nasrin, thank you so much," Gram says. "Your hospitality is overwhelming. I definitely wasn't looking forward to a six-hour drive in the dark, not after everything we've been through today."

"It is our pleasure," she says. "If someone would like to follow me, I can show you where the shower is located."

Einar turns to Gunnar. "It would be easier to take a shower if I had use of my arms."

Gunnar nods. He pulls his brother aside, removes the chain, and circles it around Einar's neck, speaking quietly into his ear for a few moments. Einar's demeanor has changed since Annika joined our group. I hope we can trust him.

Einar follows Nasrin, who reappears in a few moments with an armful of warm clothing. We take turns ducking inside the small customer bathroom to change. I'm a little dismayed when I peel off the wool sweater Gunnar gave me and see the mud caked into the fibers and a rip in one sleeve. That must have happened when I was fighting Annika. My fingers find the tag in the neck: the washing instructions are in Icelandic, but I'm almost positive you're not supposed to machine-wash wool.

Keeping the sweater separate from the rest of my dirty clothes, I splash warm water on my face and change into a pair of black leggings and a bright blue fleece. Then I find Gunnar stretched out on a blanket next to the glass front window. He's pulled his hair back into a tight bun, making his cheekbones look even more pronounced than usual. He's watching a news clip about the volcano on his phone. Outside the window, ash flutters down like tiny flakes of snow.

I settle next to him. "So what's the word on the eruption? Is it expected to be bad?"

"Scientists are stymied. The university and the local news are both sending teams out via helicopter. We should know more tomorrow." He checks the time. "Make that later today."

Nasrin reappears from the back of the house in a pair of track pants and a long-sleeved shirt. She's carrying a tray with a tea kettle, several mugs, and a basket of bread and cheese. "We figured you might be hungry. Sorry it's not the fanciest meal."

My stomach growls on cue. "It's amazing," I say. "Thank you so much."

"You're welcome." Nasrin smiles as she scoops up all of the wet clothing that we've piled on the floor. She returns to the back of the house.

My eyes flick around the room. It's weird going through something so momentous with people you barely know. The past couple of days have changed me, bonded me not just to Gunnar, but to Einar and Annika as well. In a way, escaping death with someone automatically makes you family.

Gram ducks out of the bathroom and hobbles across the floor. "Is that warm bread I smell?"

"It is," I say. "And some piping hot tea. How's your ankle?"

"It hurts," she admits. "I'll get it checked out first thing when we're back to Reykjavík. Hopefully it's just a sprain."

We eat in silence. The bread is simple but delicious. I'm devouring piece after piece like it's been days since I had a hot meal. Annika, I notice, isn't eating. A single tear rolls down her cheek.

"Are you all right?" I ask.

She looks past me, toward the big front window. "It's all starting to hit me."

Gram reaches out and pats her on the hand. "I'm very sorry for your loss."

"Thank you," Annika replies quietly. When Einar ducks back through the door, wet hair hanging around his shoulders, she hops up from her seat. "Shower time," she says with false brightness.

"It's up the stairs and to the left," Einar tells her. He pours himself a cup of tea.

"How are you feeling?" Gunnar asks him, his expression carefully neutral.

Einar shakes his wet hair back from his face. "You mean am I going to kill everyone in their sleep?"

"I mean, are you in control? Or do I need to rebind you?"

"I'm in control," Einar says, swallowing hard. "I don't want anyone else to get hurt, brother. Some of the things I said and did down in the caves... I was just angry."

Gunnar gives his brother a soft look. "I know you were."

Annika and Einar lay out blankets on the other side of the lobby. They talk softly to each other. Annika reaches up to brush a lock of Einar's hair back from his face. Her fingertips linger on his jawbone and he leans in and brushes his lips against hers. She doesn't seem at all concerned that he's possessed by a demon.

"What are you staring at?" Gunnar asks.

"Sorry." I look away. "I guess I was just wondering if that could work."

"What? Him possessed and her not possessed?"

"Yeah."

"Anything can work if both parties want it bad enough, don't you think?"

I smile. "Who knew you were such an idealist?"

"I don't think of it as idealism." Gunnar rubs at his chin. "I think of it as free will. If you care about someone, you find a way to be with them, even if it isn't in exactly the way you hoped it would be."

"That makes sense. It's similar to how Macy and I are friends even though we live in different countries."

"How did you meet her?" Gunnar asks. "Online?"

"No. She lives in Seattle during the summer, which is where Gram and I live when we're not traveling. I actually met her on a train."

"You struck up a conversation with a stranger on a train?"

"No. There was a homeless guy in our car and the police were harassing him. I told them to leave him alone, offered to pay for his ticket. She said something to me later about how she'd been too afraid to speak up, that she was glad I was there."

Gunnar smiles. "I can absolutely see you doing that."

"It didn't help," I say with a shrug. "They still kicked him off."

"All right, but you made a friend. And it probably helped the man to see that someone was willing to stick up for him."

"Maybe," I say. "And the cops let me give him a few dollars at least, so there's that. Wow, do you always find a way to see the positive in situations?"

"Not always. I just try to recognize that most things are complicated, and there are usually more possibilities than we think."

Gram returns from the shower, her gray hair hanging in wet ringlets across her shoulders. "Your turn, Rory."

I turn to Gunnar. "If you're asleep when I get back, do you want me to wake you?"

"I think I might just wait until we get home," he says. "I'm tired."

"Okay." I give him a smile and then grab my things and head for the back of the house. I bring the wool sweater with me, intending to at least rinse off some of the dirt in the shower.

The room adjacent to the backyard has a washing machine and tubs full of equipment. A wooden doghouse sits in the corner. Bending low, I see there's a single dog sleeping inside of it—probably the pregnant mother.

A narrow staircase leads up to a second floor. I tiptoe up the stairs quietly, just in case Nasrin and Taslima are sleeping. I turn left, looking for the bathroom.

The first door I try opens into what looks like a bedroom.

It's small and neat, containing a single bed, a wardrobe, and a small desk. The walls are bare except for a couple of framed pictures of the dogs.

In a picture I recognize a younger Nasrin standing next to an older man in the sled she took us out on. A team of six dogs stands at attention; one, I think, might be Mercury. The other picture is Nasrin and Taslima kneeling down next to a litter of puppies. Both women look so proud.

Beneath the frames is a bookshelf. My eyes are drawn to the spines. I scan the titles, wondering what sort of stories Nasrin enjoys. There's a mix of classics and paperback mysteries, some in English, some in what I presume is Arabic. I'm about to turn away when my eyes land on a brown leather-bound book that looks familiar. My hands shake as I remove the book from the shelf. There's no title. Just a stylized letter R overlaid on a telescope.

40

I suck in a sharp breath. If Nasrin is a Riftwatcher, it explains how she knew we were heading back from the glacier. She'd either been in direct contact with Ulric and the others or they got a message out to their headquarters who had, in turn, notified her.

I push the book back into its slot and duck out of the room. I turn toward the stairs, intending to head back to the front lobby and inform Gram and Gunnar about my findings. At that moment, a door farther down the hall opens and Nasrin ducks out.

"Rory, hi," she says. "Are you next for the shower? The bathroom is down here. Sorry, I was just brushing my teeth and washing my face."

I freeze for a moment, unsure of what to say. If I don't take a shower now, it might look suspicious. But for all I know, the Riftwatchers are on their way here. Gunnar said they had other people like me who identified demons. What if they come here and discover Einar and me?

"You're familiar with the Icelandic water, right? The way the geothermal heat—"

I nod quickly. "The sulfur smell, yeah."

"You can just run the cold tap for a few seconds to get glacial water to brush your teeth," she says. "I'm going to sleep, but please wake me if anyone needs anything."

"Okay." I plaster a smile on my face. "Thanks again."

Nasrin strolls down the hallway and disappears into the room where I'd left the Riftwatcher manual. I don't know why someone like her would work for them, but at least if she's settling in for the night, that means a group of Riftwatchers aren't going to descend upon us before morning.

I hop into the shower and try to enjoy the warm water coursing down over my skin, but I can't. I feel too vulnerable. After a few minutes I hop out, get dressed, and head back downstairs.

I tiptoe around the sleeping bodies. "Gunnar," I whisper. He opens his eyes. "Yes?"

"I found something upstairs. A Riftwatcher manual just like the one you had. In Nasrin's bedroom."

He sits up in the dark. "If she's a Riftwatcher, you and my brother aren't safe here. We need to leave."

"I'll wake up the others," I whisper, "if you want to start packing the SUV."

Gunnar produces a key ring from the pocket of his jacket and heads out the front door to the gravel parking lot where our vehicle is parked.

I lean over and shake my grandmother's shoulder gently. "Gram. Gram, wake up."

She blinks hard, her eyes heavy with confusion. "What is it, Rory? Are you all right?"

"Nasrin is a Riftwatcher," I say. "Gunnar thinks it's safer if—"

"We leave." Gram sits up, fully awake.

I wake Einar and Annika next. They're both exhausted and confused but neither protests the decision to leave. They slide on their damp boots and start carrying their belongings outside.

We've got everything packed and are ready to head out when I remember I left my wool sweater in the bathroom upstairs. I curse under my breath. I should leave it. I could buy another one. Gunnar would probably even buy me another one. But I don't want another one. I want that one.

"One second," I tell Gunnar. "I left something upstairs."

"We can replace whatever..." he whispers, his words fading as I duck through the back of the house. I creep back up the stairs. The entire hallway is dark. No problem. I grab the sweater from where I left it on the bathroom sink and tiptoe back to the stairs.

I descend carefully so as not to trip. *Almost there.* As I rush toward the door that leads back to the lobby, I run into a tub of dog food. The lid pops off and clatters across the floor.

The pregnant dog immediately starts barking. She pokes her head out of the doghouse and growls at me. "Good dog," I say, tossing a handful of kibble in her direction.

I hurry back through the lobby, but I'm too late. Before I can reach the door, a hand clamps down on my shoulder.

41

I spin around. It's Nasrin.

"Oh, hey." I try to play it cool. "Sorry, I didn't mean to wake the dog."

"Why are you leaving now?" she asks. "It's after two o'clock."

"I know, we were all just having trouble falling asleep and we decided we might as well head back."

"I see." She cocks her head to the side slightly. She's not buying my story.

I glance through the big picture window. Gunnar is getting out of the driver's seat and heading this way. "Okay, if you must know, I went into your room by accident. I saw your Riftwatcher manual."

"So?"

"So I asked how you knew we needed help out on the glacier, and you said something about explaining later, only you never did. But let me guess—"

"Yes, the Riftwatchers told me your group was still out on the glacier and that I should try to find you."

"But why?" I ask.

"Because they didn't want you to die."

"They shot Gunnar with an arrow."

Nasrin stiffens. "I don't know anything about that," she says. "But I'm sure they weren't trying to kill him."

"Oh, well, in that case," I say, my voice heavy with sarcasm. "Did they tell you to give us food and a place to stay tonight?"

"Yes, but—"

"Are they coming here?"

Nasrin looks away. "The elders don't inform me of their every move. It's possible they might want to speak to your group about what happened in the caverns."

"Nasrin, I don't trust them, and I don't understand how you can either."

Gunnar pokes his head in the door. He shakes his head in disbelief when he sees me holding the sweater. "Is everything all right here?"

"Yeah," I say. "Just explaining why we're leaving."

"We're grateful for your hospitality," Gunnar says. "And for what you did for all of us out on the glacier. But we're not staying to be interrogated by Riftwatchers."

Nasrin shifts her weight from one foot to the other. "I know their methods can be controversial, but the Riftwatchers just want to keep everyone safe."

"How can you say that with a straight face?" I say with exasperation. "They nearly just killed all of us, including you and your dogs."

Nasrin looks at me with a puzzled expression. "What do you mean?"

"The avalanches. I heard explosions. They blasted the mountain and the tunnels. We could have all died."

She shakes her head. "No, Rory. That sound you heard was the natural sound of snow breaking off from a mountainside. The Riftwatchers didn't cause the avalanches. They did set off some charges in the tunnels, but they wouldn't have set up an avalanche without telling me."

"So I'm just supposed to accept that it happened naturally?"

"I don't know. It's possible the tunnel explosions or the volcanic activity triggered the avalanches," she says. "But the Riftwatchers would never hurt me on purpose."

"How can you be so convinced of that?"

"Well, for one because my father has been a Riftwatcher since before I was born. He's back in Syria, still monitoring a doorway there. The Riftwatchers helped my mom and me escape the war."

"Don't you think if they cared about your family they would have helped all of you come here?" I ask.

"It's not that simple," Nasrin says. "My father hopes to join us someday, but someone has to stay close to the door, and he is better equipped to live safely in Damascus than most people."

"I'm glad the Riftwatchers have helped your family," Gunnar interjects. "But they killed my parents. I don't blame you for joining up, but just remember that they don't do anything without an agenda. Watch your back."

With that, Gunnar grabs my hand and pulls me out the front door.

I turn to look back over my shoulder to see if Nasrin is going to follow us outside, if she's going to try and stop us from leaving, but all she does is stand in the window and watch as we drive away.

Back in Reykjavík Henning is asleep, but one of the servants is up early to receive us. He offers to prepare a light breakfast, but none of us is hungry. Gunnar gives me a hug goodnight and wishes me Merry Christmas before he and Einar head upstairs to their bedrooms. Annika, Gram, and I settle into guest bedrooms, with Gram and me sharing a bed again.

I can't sleep though, so a little after nine a.m., I sneak out of the room and down to the kitchen. I flip on a tiny light over the stove and root around until I find a tea kettle and some sachets of green tea. I can't help but think about how my grandmother fed me special herbal tea for years to keep the demon inside of me from gaining too much power.

Can you hear me? I think, as I fill the kettle with cold water and ignite one of the burners.

If my demon can hear me, it doesn't feel like talking. I wonder if I have any other special powers beyond the ability to pull demons out of people's bodies. Well, that and increased speed and strength, not to mention the magical blood that saved Gunnar's life.

I perch on the edge of a high-backed wooden chair. What kind of life could I have with those abilities? I let my mind wander. A barrage of images floods my brain, visions of a Rory Quinn who is strong and powerful, a girl who is well liked, popular even. A girl who fixes problems instead of creating them.

There's a soft creak from the direction of the stairs. Gunnar appears in the doorway. He's wearing plaid pajama pants and a black T-shirt. His hair hangs down over his shoulders. "Can't sleep?"

I shake my head. "I've got a lot on my mind."

"Anything in particular?"

"Everyone who died," I lie. That's what I should be focused on anyway, not cataloguing my newfound superpowers and thinking about how they might make people like me.

"You can't blame yourself—you know that, right?"

"Can't I?" The kettle whistles softly. I fill my cup with boiling water and then return to my seat at the table. "If I had known I had the power to banish demons, I could have saved Benjamín. Maybe Lars too."

Gunnar grabs a second cup and tea bag from the cupboard. "Yes, but if your grandmother had told you what you were, would you have really embraced your various powers?" He fills his cup from the kettle. "Or would you have demanded an exorcism right then and there?"

I drop my chin. Gunnar is right. The only reason I know what I can do is because fighting Annika one-on-one gave me the time and opportunity to explore my abilities. When Benjamín charged us, we had only seconds to react.

"You didn't kill anyone, all right?" Gunnar continues.

"The Riftwatchers killed Ragnar, and I killed Benjamín. And who knows what happened to Lars. If he got trapped in the tunnels, that means the Riftwatchers killed him too."

"I would've killed Annika, though. I was going to throw her body into the chasm."

"And if you had, it would have been out of necessity, not malice."

I take a long drink of tea. The liquid burns my throat. "I just wish things had turned out differently."

"I know." Gunnar reaches out and laces his fingers through mine. "But they died the moment they opened the doorway and demons possessed them. There's no way we could have safely captured, bound, and transported all of them back to civilization, especially not when the Riftwatchers were trying to trap them in the tunnels."

"I still can't believe they caused another avalanche," I say darkly.

"After thinking about it, I'm inclined to agree with Nasrin. I don't think the Riftwatchers caused the avalanche this time."

"You think it was the volcano?" I trace the rim of my teacup with one finger.

"It definitely could've been triggered by geothermal or tectonic activity." Gunnar sips his tea slowly. "Or it could have been Lars."

"Lars?"

"On the way back to Reykjavík, while you were asleep, Annika told us Lars was possessed by a destruction demon, that he caused cave-ins in some of the tunnels. He's probably the reason we had to climb over that pile of ice."

"Is it possible he caused the volcano to erupt too?"

"Anything is possible," Gunnar says. "Scientists still have no explanation for the sudden eruption, and I've heard stories of some incredibly powerful demons."

"God, that's terrifying," I say. "If Lars could do that,

imagine what else he could do. Do you think he's still alive?"

"There's no way to know for sure." Gunnar squeezes my hand. "I just don't want you to feel responsible for anything that happened. What we did is not the same as what the Rift-watchers did to the village of Leyndarmálsstaður, and to my parents."

"How is it that easy for you?" I ask. "You eviscerated a guy. A guy with friends and family. Is that really not weighing on you at all?"

"It is," Gunnar says. "It hurts if I dwell on it. But if I hadn't killed him, I'd be dead. Probably you and your grandmother too." He drops my hand. "The world is dark and ugly, Rory. And that means sometimes you have to do dark and ugly things to survive, and to protect the people you care about."

42

The next day Henning insists on having a private physician come out to the house in the afternoon to examine each of us.

Aside from a huge bruise on my chest where Einar hit me with his slingshot and every muscle in my body aching, I feel mostly recovered, so I volunteer to let everyone else go before me. My grandmother goes first. I text Macy while I wait for the doctor to finish with Gram.

> **Me:** Merry Christmas! Sorry I'm late.
> **Macy:** No worries, I figured you were out of range.
> **Me:** You can say that again. You would not believe the places I've been. I almost died!
> **Macy:** Whaaaat?
> **Me:** I'm not even exaggerating. I got caught in an avalanche!
> **Macy:** OMG! Are you okay?
> **Me:** I'm fine, but I'm going to see a doctor today, just to be sure.
> **Macy:** And Gunnar? He's fine too?
> **Me:** As fine as ever ;)
> **Macy:** LOL, I knew it! You're getting married, aren't you?
> **Me:** No, but I can say definitively that he's nice…and a good kisser.
> **Macy:** Woooow! Well, I don't have anything THAT exciting to report, but I might have met a girl. She's Japanese. She works at one of the stores on base.
> **Me:** Ooh, what's her name?
> **Macy:** Sakura. She's 19.
> **Me:** Pictures??

Macy sends me a link to an Instagram account. The first

picture is a girl barefoot on a beach. She's twirling with her arms out, the bottom of her sunflower-print T-shirt-dress billowing out around her long legs. She's wearing casual makeup and has her hair in two wispy pigtails.

Me: OMG, adorable. Does your dad know?
Macy: I'm not sure he's ready for that.. I might tell him, if it goes anywhere ;)
Me: Well, I hope it does!
Macy: Me too. And back at you, heh.
Me: Oh, speaking of pictures…

I attached the selfie that Gunnar took of the two of us on the dogsled. Her response is almost instantaneous.

Macy: !!!
Macy: You were not kidding about the cheekbones.
Me: I know, right?
Macy: He looks almost too pretty to be real, like maybe he was grown in a lab.
Me: Ha. He definitely has a lot of…positive features.
Macy: Heh. I bet he does.
Me: I can't believe I like a guy with better hair than me.
Macy: And me! Hey if you're nice, maybe he'll share some haircare tips.
Me: LOL

The door to the bedroom we're using as an exam room opens and Gram slips out into the hallway.

I tuck my phone back in my pocket. "How are you?" I ask.

"The doctor thinks my ankle is sprained, not broken. She said to stay off it for the next few days. If the swelling doesn't resolve, I'll need to go get an X-ray. Otherwise, clean bill of health."

"I'm glad you're okay."

"Me too." She pats me on the shoulder and then limps toward the stairway at the end of the hall.

Gunnar goes next. I head downstairs to wait for him. I

worry about what the doctor is going to say when she sees the long scratches on his torso. How much has Henning told her about our mission? Can we trust her?

Gram is in the spacious kitchen, leaning against the counter across from the stove. "Tea?" she asks somewhat nervously. Normally she'd pour me a cup without asking.

"Sure." I want to make sure to keep my demon in control until I decide what I'm going to do about it. "But I can get it. You should probably be sitting, right?"

"I suppose you're right." She hobbles across the room and lowers herself gingerly into a chair at the big wooden table. "I hope I'm not too much of a burden to everyone over the next few days."

"Highly unlikely," I say, bringing us two cups of hot tea.

Someone has placed a platter of rye bread in the center of the table. Gram sets a slice on a napkin and begins to break it into pieces. "I suppose there's a lot we need to talk about," she begins.

I laugh under my breath. "Probably an understatement."

She sips her tea. "I'll do my best to answer all your questions. No more keeping secrets, I promise."

I start to remind her that I'm not a child, that I can handle the whole truth, but then Gunnar strolls into the room, his eyes tired, his blond hair pulled back in a low ponytail.

"Hey. How'd it go?" I ask.

"Not bad."

"What did the doctor say about your—"

"The horrible scratches I got from a dog?"

"Yeah, those."

"She asked me how long ago it happened, and I had no idea what to tell her so I just went with 'about a week' and she said they were healing up nicely." He makes a face. "The same cannot be said for my shoulder, however, which she said looked infected, and that I should have a course of IV antibiotics."

"Fun."

"I get to spend the next couple days in the hospital." Gunnar grabs an apple from a bowl on the counter and polishes it with the hem of his T-shirt. "Which is unfortunate, because I was hoping to show you around the city like I promised." He pours himself a cup of tea.

"I can take a rain check," I say, my cheeks reddening slightly as I remember our flirty conversations.

"It's good to hear you're all right." Gram looks from Gunnar to me. "I'm going to go take a bath. Rory, I hope the two of us can chat more later."

"Definitely," I say.

Gunnar slides into the chair across from me. "How are you?"

"Oh, I haven't gone yet. I think your brother and I are last to—"

"I don't mean physically. I mean...with everything else."

"I'm still processing. I'm not sure what I'm going to do." I glance around the room, my eyes landing on the window. Soft feathery snowflakes are falling from the sky. They've painted a thin layer of white on the grass. It reminds me of a few days ago, looking out on the street from our apartment in Paris. How can so many things change in less than a week?

"You mean about whether you're going to get an exorcism?"

"Right." I turn my gaze back to Gunnar. "God, it sounds so messed up when you say it like that."

"It is messed up. But *you're* not messed up. Just the situation." Gunnar blows gently on his tea. "I'm here if you ever want to talk. And I won't judge you or tell you what to do. I told my brother the same thing."

"At first I was 100 percent sure I wanted the exorcism," I say. "I think it was the shock, and feeling like whatever is inside me is the reason I've gone through life feeling like no one likes me."

"And now?" Gunnar says gently.

"Now I wonder if maybe you're right. It's possible I've felt that way because of what happened with my dad. I know it's not his fault, but maybe some part of me decided early on that if my own father didn't even want to be around me, what chance would I have with strangers? I alternated between being closed off and trying too hard, until eventually I just gave up."

Gunnar sips his tea. "What happens to us as children can have a huge effect, especially if we don't acknowledge it and address it."

"I'm still not sure how you made it past my walls."

"Oh, I think there are still a few left for me to climb," he says with a smile. "But never underestimate the power of ridiculous hotness."

I snicker. "It's all such a blur. I can't believe my grandmother kept such huge secrets for so many years."

"Have you two talked about everything yet?"

"Not yet." I sip my tea. "Part of me is angry, but part of me knows that if she'd made different choices, things might not have turned out the way they did…and I might never have met you." I blush again.

Gunnar smiles. "I feel like we still would have met somehow."

I arch an eyebrow. "Really? Why?"

"I don't know. I just think I'm supposed to know you." He clears his throat. "You don't feel the same way?"

"I do," I admit. "But I've been blaming it on hormones."

"You are the least romantic person I have ever met." Gunnar's grin widens. "And for some reason I like that."

I laugh. "My tutor, Alannah, once told me that the secret to a good relationship was finding someone who saw your flaws as endearing instead of annoying."

Gunnar reaches out and ruffles my hair gently. "Smart woman, your tutor."

43

Gram and I have a long talk later that night. "You have to know how much I hated lying to you," she says. "But I promised your mother I would keep you safe, and this felt like the best way."

I cross my arms. "Letting me live with a demon inside me for seventeen years—without ever telling me—felt like the best way?"

"Yes." She looks gravely at me. "I didn't know how you would respond, and I knew an exorcism could kill you." Her expression softens. "Sometimes there are no easy answers. When all of your options are bad, you just pick the best of the worst and deal with it."

It's similar to what Gunnar said. But maybe there *are* other options now—me. I pulled that demon out of Annika with surprisingly little difficulty. And Annika is still alive.

Perhaps I'm the easy answer, at least when it comes to certain things.

"Is that why you've been pushing me to think about college? Because you thought once I knew the truth, I wouldn't want to be around you anymore?"

"Yes and no. I knew there was a chance you might hate me for the things I did...and didn't do. But also, since your granddad died, we've done almost everything together. I wanted to encourage you to establish new friendships and support networks. I think that's best for you no matter what happens with us."

"I could never hate you," I say. "I just need you to recognize that I'm not a little kid anymore."

"You're right. You're absolutely right." Gram folds her hands in her lap. "Henning said he'd be willing to attempt an exorcism if it was what you wanted. No pressure to decide," she adds quickly.

"About that," I say. "At first all I could think of was having the demon ripped out of my body as quickly as possible. I didn't care if it was painful. I didn't care if it was going to be violent. I didn't even care about the fact that I might die."

"And?" Gram listens intently.

"I don't know. It saved me in the avalanche—that's for sure. But even before that, it helped me in the tunnels. I thought it'd be like this evil force trying to get me to do things that I didn't want to do—things that hurt other people. But instead I felt safe and strong. Is that crazy? Is that some sort of demon mind-meld trick it's playing on me?"

"I don't think it's crazy," Gram says. "From what I know about demons, they're almost completely focused on their own survival. If you had died in the avalanche, your demon would've died too."

"That makes sense," I acknowledge.

Gram sips her tea. "Is it true you separated Annika from her demon in the chamber with the doorway? When you were sleeping on the ride back to Reykjavik, she tried to explain to the rest of us what had happened."

"I did," I say. "I yanked her toward the doorway and said I was going to send her back to hell. And then she started to split into two forms. One of them was human. The other was more of a smoky shadow. I grabbed on to the hazy figure and threw it down into the crevasse and then sealed up the door."

"I have heard of demons who are able to exorcise other demons. Banishers. It's extremely rare. Usually..." Gram trails off.

"Usually what?" I push her.

"Does Nasrin know about this ability?"

"Not unless one of the others said something. Why?"

"Usually demons with the power to banish other demons are hunted down. The Riftwatchers would want to control you so they could use your power to their gain. And other demons would want to destroy you so you can't use your power against them."

"Lovely."

Gram leans in close to me. "If you want my advice, you should rid yourself of the demon. It's your only chance at a normal life. You're young and strong. You would survive the exorcism."

I shake my head. "I've never had a normal life, Gram, and I'm okay with that. But I've always felt like something was missing, and maybe this is what it is—this realization of who I am and what I can do."

"What are you saying?"

"I'm still thinking everything over. But maybe this not-normal life is the one I'm meant to lead."

"Well, I'm here for you if you have more questions," she says. "And I'll support any decision you make."

"Thanks."

"I know Gunnar is going to be in the hospital for a couple of days. I was wondering whether you might want to invite him to come to Paris for New Year's Eve."

"Definitely. Could we invite Einar too?"

"Einar and Annika are traveling to Sweden tomorrow. She wants to go spend some time with her parents and also take care of some of the issues with the band."

"Oh my God," I say. "I completely forgot about the band. Poor Annika. Telling all of the Black as Death fans that three-fourths of the band has died is going to be a nightmare."

"Yes," Gram says. "On the bright side, the new album is selling extremely well. Hopefully the fans will be supportive of her."

I admire Gram's ability to find a silver lining to almost

everything, but my heart goes out to Annika for having to deal with a bunch of legal and professional stuff while she's grieving.

"As far as Paris, we could invite Henning though, if you're okay with that," Gram says.

"Sure," I say. "You two were pretty close, huh?"

"Indeed. I wouldn't have trusted just anyone with your mom."

A pang of sadness moves through me. My mom gave her life for love.

Later I come across Henning parked in front of the television set, focused on a news report about the volcanic eruption. I hover in the back of the room, watching from a distance. The scientific community is still mystified, but so far there have been no reports of casualties.

"I feel as if I should apologize to you," Henning says, without looking away from the screen. "But also that seems wholly inadequate."

"Apologize for—?"

"For not being able to save your mother."

I take a seat on the sofa. "I might not agree with some of the choices you've made, but when it comes to my mom, I know you did your best."

He turns his wheelchair to face me. "I'm glad to hear that. For what it's worth, I am deeply sorry."

"Thank you," I say. And then, "I just wish no one had died."

He nods gravely. "I was partially responsible for several deaths when I was working with the Riftwatchers. Even when you can convince yourself you did what you could in the moment, it's easy to second-guess yourself later, wonder whether you could have saved someone if you'd made a different choice."

"How did you not go crazy from guilt?"

"Well, I had Gunnar and Einar to look after, so that helped. But I suppose the main advice I can give you is to say I focused on the people I *could* save, and I never forgot the ones who were lost." He looks past me for a moment, his expression growing tense. "I still remember every face, every name."

"Do you think I'm making a mistake staying possessed?"

His lips slant upward. "I allowed myself to become possessed and stayed that way for years, so I'm probably the wrong person to ask. The real question is do *you* think you're making a mistake?"

"I feel strangely okay with it. Maybe dark power is only dangerous if you have a dark soul to match."

Henning studies me carefully. "It takes strength to wield a great deal of power and yet not abuse it."

"I'm not sure if I'm strong, but I am definitely afraid of what I might be capable of, so there's that," I say.

"I believe you are strong," he says.

"Do you think the Riftwatchers made it out of the tunnels?"

"Yes," Henning says. "They're very good at what they do."

"Will the group come after Einar?"

"Possibly, if they know he's possessed again. They might also come after you. I would watch your back."

"My back is literally getting on a plane in a couple of days," I say.

"I don't just mean here in Iceland. If the Riftwatchers learn what you can do, they'll come after you. They'll chase you all across the world, and they won't stop until they find you."

Epilogue

I am still thinking about Henning's words a couple days later as I walk through Keflavík airport with Gram, Gunnar, and Henning. My eyes flick around the terminal, from the woman sitting cross-legged on the tile floor charging her phone to the gray-haired man reading a book in the security line. The man's eyes meet mine for a nanosecond and then he returns to his novel. The girl holds her phone up as if she's taking a selfie, but what if she's really taking a picture of me? Are the Riftwatchers everywhere?

A man in a housekeeping uniform smiles at us as he rolls by with a mop bucket. I turn around to give him a long look, but he keeps moving, his eyes focused ahead of him. Perhaps people's gazes are simply drawn to Henning's wheelchair, or to Gunnar, with that perfect bone structure of his.

"Rory? Are you all right?" Gram asks.

"A little on edge," I admit.

"You'll feel better once we get back to our cozy flat." Gram squeezes my arm.

I relax a bit once we find our gate. This area is crowded, and no one is paying us any attention.

Gunnar taps at his phone and shows me the screen. "Have you seen this?"

It's a heavy metal website. I skim the first few paragraphs of the article. Black as Death's new album has already hit the top of the charts. News of their deaths spread quickly, and some fans are speculating it's another publicity stunt, while others are positive that the band found the doorway to hell and went down inside to explore. Either way, everyone wants their newest songs.

"Cool," I say. "I'm glad at least that their families will be well taken care of."

Gunnar's phone buzzes and he switches to his messages. "Einar says Annika has spoken to everyone's family. Ragnar's parents were adamant about retrieving his body, but she told them there was a collapse in the tunnels, and due to the recent eruption, no one could safely get back there anytime soon."

"And the other families? How are they managing?"

"Well, not great, as you might imagine, but they're not threatening to mount a search party to find the boys or anything. Annika was close to all of their families and they trust her."

"That's good," I say. "I'm really glad she's doing okay."

"Thanks to you," Gunnar says. "As aggressive as she was, I don't think we would have been able to bring her back with us possessed."

I think about the demon inside me. I don't think I could become as brutal and merciless as Annika was in the chamber with the doorway. At least I hope not.

The gate attendant instructs people who need extra time to board to get in line. Gunnar is going to board early with Henning. Gram and I wait in the second group.

After boarding the plane, I settle into my window seat and do my standard safety checks. Then I lean my head against the window. A few minutes later I drift off to sleep.

When I wake up the pilot is announcing our descent into Paris, the city of light. Finally our adventure in Iceland is officially over.

On New Year's Eve, the four of us bundle up into our heaviest winter gear and take a rented car to the Eiffel Tower. Blankets cover the frozen grass. Families and couples huddle on them, many clutching cups of coffee and other warm beverages.

As it nears midnight Gunnar hops up from our blanket.

"Do you want to go for a walk?"

"Sure." I let him pull me to my feet.

The two of us stroll around to the front of the tower and head down Avenue Pierre Loti. We veer off onto a side path before we reach the Champs de Mars fountain. The moon is high and full, illuminating the frost-coated tree branches above our heads.

"Exploring Paris has been fun, but I still hope to show you Reykjavik someday." Gunnar wraps his arms around my lower back. "I know you would love the city."

The top of my head fits under his chin. I rest my cheek against his puffy quilted jacket. "I guess I'll have to come back," I say playfully. "When it's warm."

He laughs. "It's never warm."

"Well, in that case, forget it." I punch him playfully in the chest. "Nah, I can take it. Besides, I've still got my special Icelandic sweater to keep me warm, assuming I can figure out how to clean it."

"Handwash it," he says. "Cold water. Be gentle with the soiled fibers. Lay it flat to dry."

"Sounds like a lot of work."

"The best things are." Gunnar kisses me on the top of the head.

"I guess I should say thank you for that sweater. You were right."

"I know I was." He grins. "Clearly you *love* it since you risked getting caught by Riftwatchers to go back for it."

"Temporary insanity," I reply. It's still not something I would pick out for myself, but Gunnar selected it for me. He gave it to me. It's become sort of a talisman, like as long as I possess it, the two of us will be connected in some way.

"If you come in the summer, it'll be a *little* warmer. You'll still need a jacket, but no hat and gloves. And we can have twenty hours of daylight."

"That's a long date," I say.

"Date, eh?"

I lower my voice. "Did you change your mind about taking me on a date?" I ask. "The possessed girl? Who may or may not lose control and kill you?"

"I don't think you'd kill me." Gunnar winks. "I am intrigued by this notion of you losing control, however."

I frown. "Sometimes I worry that I have no control at all. What if the things I think I want are actually the things my demon wants? Did your brother ever talk about that?"

"Not really," Gunnar says. "Not to me anyway. With Einar, it wasn't the possession, but the knowledge of Henning keeping everything a secret for so long that seemed to affect him the most. He was always introverted, but he really pulled away from both of us once he learned the truth."

"I mean, all those times I got in trouble at school—maybe it wasn't me." I gnaw on my bottom lip. "Maybe it was a freaking agent of Satan controlling me like a puppet master."

"But the things you told me didn't seem like bad things. It's good that you protested American foreign policy in a country that was forever damaged by it. And almost all people our age have tried alcohol. You just ended up getting caught."

"Right, but you said not all demons are evil. Some are just mischievous or seeking new experiences or whatever." I sigh. "I guess I just wonder if I'd be a different person if I had gotten an exorcism."

"Maybe, but your grandmother spent a lot of time making sure you stayed in control. It can be tempting now that you know the truth to rationalize decisions that didn't end well as not being yours, but we all make questionable or impulsive choices sometimes. And sometimes we make good choices that turn out badly. I think if you've always felt in control, then you've always been in control."

"I have," I say. "For the most part anyway."

"Also, for what it's worth, I like the person you are now,"

Gunnar says. "I like that you do what feels right in the moment, consequences be damned."

I laugh bitterly. "Well, you're the only one who likes that."

"I'm being serious," Gunnar says. "You're worrying about whether being possessed somehow altered who you really are, but have you thought about how sharing a body with you for seventeen years might have also changed your demon?"

"Well now, that's something I hadn't considered." I laugh lightly. Perhaps my demon and I have learned from each other, found a way to coexist peacefully. *So now what?*

Behind us, voices start to chant. I realize they're counting down from ten in French. Gunnar and I turn toward the Eiffel Tower just in time to see the fireworks begin to explode above it.

I squeeze his hand as the brilliant sparks of color light up the sky. He turns to me and brushes my hair back from my face. "Can I kiss you?"

My heart beats wildly in my chest. "I can't believe you're going to be one of those guys who asks first," I tease.

"You mean polite and unassuming?" His lips curl upward. "The kind of guy who cares about consent and wants our first kiss to be perfect?"

"Okay, when you put it like that…" I lift my chin so our lips meet, soft, and then harder. My body relaxes into his. The moment feels warm and safe, as if we've kissed a thousand times before.

He wraps his arms around my waist and pulls me tight against him. "Is this improper enough for you?" he asks, his mouth trailing hot kisses across my neck.

"Getting there," I murmur. My entire body floods with heat as I pull his lips back to mine. When we break apart a few seconds later, I have to hold on to his arm for balance. "You know, technically this is our second kiss. You kissed me next to the doorway to hell."

"Oh, right," he says. "But that one only counts half."

"Half? Why?" I narrow my eyes at him.

"Because we both thought we were going to die. People do rash and impulsive things in life-threatening situations. When I think back, that day almost doesn't feel real to me anymore."

"That's too bad," I say. "Because you told me you were glad that you met me."

"Well, that part is 100 percent true."

"I'm glad I met you too."

We head back to where we left Gram and Henning. Gunnar's phone buzzes in his pocket. "Probably Einar wishing us Happy New Year," he says. He swipes at the screen and his smile fades.

"What is it?" I ask.

Gunnar shows me a news story from a Reykjavík newspaper. The headline reads: *Four People Missing after Eruption.* I scan the first few lines. A newlywed couple and a mother and daughter, ages ranging from eleven to thirty-four, have all vanished from the Hoffell area.

"Riftwatchers?" I ask.

"Yes. At least they didn't destroy a whole town this time."

"Do you think they killed them?"

"Killed or captured."

Before I have time to process this information, an alert pops up on the screen. There's been a huge earthquake in Reykjavík and three more volcanoes have erupted in the past couple of hours. Scientists continue to be mystified as to what's causing the chaos.

I look up into Gunnar's blue eyes. "Lars," I say softly. It has to be him. Nothing else makes sense. He's still alive, and he's powerful enough to kill thousands of people, unless someone stops him. But who or what is strong enough to stop a demon capable of causing earthquakes and volcanic eruptions?

We are, the voice inside me says.

Are we? I still don't know the full scope of my powers. I don't know if I'm strong enough to stand up to Lars.

But I know I have to try.

BOOK CLUB QUESTIONS

1. The author has stated in interviews that unlike most book ideas that either start with plot or characters, *Hellfinder* started with the setting. She visited Iceland multiple times and loved it so much she was determined to set a book there, spending years considering various ideas before the storyline came together in her head. What is one place where you have been (local, national, or international) that you love so much you'd like to share it with other people? What is it that makes this place so special to you?

2. Early in the book, the main character Rory reflects on how after her grandfather died, at first she and her grandmother stayed in Sydney because they thought they'd feel closer to him, but it didn't work. Have you ever tried to hold onto something or someone you lost by keeping things the same? How did it work out for you?

3. Rory is uncomfortable at times because other characters in the book believe in supernatural things. Do you have close friends or family members with viewpoints you can't understand? How do you navigate these relationships when your belief systems collide?

4. At one point in the book, Rory admits that when she was younger she probably tried too hard to make new friends and that it backfired on her. Have you ever tried too hard at something? Discuss.

5. Some of the characters go from trying to kill Rory to basically being on her side by the end of the book. Do you believe in "good people" and "bad people" or do you think

we're all just people who behave in "good" and "bad" ways, depending on internal and external factors affecting us at the time? Why do you think as you do?

6. Have you ever participated in any of the activities Rory, Gram, and Gunnar do in *Hellfinder*? What's the most exciting thing you've ever done?

7. Gram spends much of the book keeping big secrets from Rory. How do you think it felt for her to hold back that critical information for so long? How do you feel when friends or family ask you to keep secrets?

8. Rory has a difficult decision to make near the end of the book. Do you think she makes the right choice? Why or why not?

ACKNOWLEDGMENTS

As always, a huge and heartfelt thank you to my readers. I know this book is different from everything else I've written and I hope you enjoyed Rory's journey.

I am forever grateful to Jaynie Royal, Pan Van Dyk, and the entire team at Regal House for giving this story a chance to live outside of my imagination. C.B. Royal, your brilliant cover captures the high-energy storyline and majesty of Iceland in ways I never imagined.

The following friends, readers, blurbers, and industry geniuses have supported me in general and/or this book specifically: Vilborg María Ísleifsdóttir, Christina Ahn Hickey, María Pilar Albarran Ruíz, Sarah Reis, Marcy Beller Paul, Philip Siegel, Tina Connolly, Victoria Scott, Kristi Helvig, Jude Atwood, Laura Scalzo, Jennifer Laughran, Jessica Spotswood, the Regal House Summer 2023 author group, the YA Valentines, and the Apocalpysies. Solidarity forever!

Speaking of solidarity, my mother, brother, and sister continue to support me in this writing endeavor, regardless of how things are going. Thank you for always believing in me, even when I struggle to believe in myself.

Finally, I want to thank the people of Iceland. I've been fortunate enough to visit three times, and everyone has been welcoming and kind. From tour bus drivers who explained Icelandic culture, to random strangers who explained World Cup soccer (er, football), to Air BNB hosts who knocked on the door to tell my friend and me the Northern Lights were out over Reykjavík (a rarity, indeed!), all of my memories of your amazing country are filled with joy and wonder. I hope I am fortunate enough to make more memories of Iceland in the future.